FATAL DIVISIONS

Also by Claire Booth

A Sheriff Hank Worth mystery

THE BRANSON BEAUTY
ANOTHER MAN'S GROUND
A DEADLY TURN *

* available from Severn House

FATAL DIVISIONS

Claire Booth

This first world edition published 2020
in Great Britain and 2021 in the USA by
SEVERN HOUSE PUBLISHERS LTD of
Eardley House, 4 Uxbridge Street, London W8 7SY.
Trade paperback edition first published
in Great Britain and the USA 2021 by
SEVERN HOUSE PUBLISHERS LTD.

British Library Cataloguing in Publication Data
A CIP catalogue record for this title is available from the British Library.

ISBN-13: 978-0-7278-8997-3 (cased)
ISBN-13: 978-1-78029-719-4 (trade paper)
ISBN-13: 978-1-4483-0440-0 (e-book)

All Severn House titles are printed on acid-free paper.

Severn House Publishers support the Forest Stewardship Council™ [FSC™],
the leading international forest certification organisation.
All our titles that are printed on FSC certified paper carry the FSC logo.

MIX
Paper from
responsible sources
FSC® C013056

Typeset by Palimpsest Book Production Ltd.,
Falkirk, Stirlingshire, Scotland.
Printed and bound in Great Britain by
TJ International, Padstow, Cornwall.

For
Shannon,
Lori and Fred, Kindra and David,
Paul, Akira, and Evan

ONE

Maggie was concerned. It was that worried mouth downturn she'd been doing a lot lately when she looked at him.

'Look, I'm fine. Seriously. I'm going to work, I'm mowing the lawn, I'm even taking Maribel to Girl Scouts. I'm living a normal life. Everything's normal.'

Hank smiled at his wife. A forced mouth upturn he'd been doing a lot lately when he looked at everybody. Maggie sighed.

'You are not OK. You've been in a funk ever since you all figured out who killed that guy in the apartment. And since . . . well, the car crash.'

Hank's smile dissolved. He couldn't keep it going. As long as he didn't think about the crash that killed six teenagers last month, he was OK. That was why he was throwing himself into work. And chauffeuring a bunch of five-year-old girls around. Nothing took your mind off things like a group of giggling Daisy Girl Scouts in the backseat.

Maggie grabbed his hands and pulled him down on the couch next to her. The house was actually quiet. The kids were in bed, and Maggie's dad was downstairs in his basement en suite. Maybe Hank could make some noise and wake one of them up. Then they'd no longer be alone and wouldn't have to have this conversation she seemed so determined to start.

She said a few things and saw he wasn't listening. That led to her letting go of his hands and standing up. He was relieved, but a little surprised she gave up that easily.

'Fine,' she said. 'Will you be here tomorrow afternoon? One of the kindergarten moms is dropping Maribel off since I'll be mid-shift at the hospital, and someone needs to be here when she gets home.'

'Where's your dad going to be?'

Maggie shrugged. 'I don't know. Kiwanis, maybe?'

'OK,' he said. 'I'll tell them I'm working from home for the afternoon.'

'Good. Now I'm going to bed.' She turned and started down the hallway. He watched her go, which he realized was the last thing he wanted.

'Can I come with you?'

She turned back to look at him, confused.

'What kind of question is that? Of course you can. Where else would you sleep— oh . . . you're not talking about sleep, are you?'

He stood up. She held out her hand, and this time there was no reluctance when he took it. He kissed her right there in the hallway and prayed that everyone stayed asleep.

The next day, Hank left the office at noon, lugging his laptop and a large stack of performance evaluations. It actually was work better suited to doing at home, where he could spread everything out without fear that a deputy would walk in and see his buddy's personnel file. Plus, he was looking forward to having lunch with Maribel and hearing about her day at kindergarten. Her latest thing was the politics of recess. They appeared to be just as convoluted and ruthless as the politics in Branson. She seemed to be traversing them a lot better than he was, though.

He got home and fixed two peanut butter and raspberry jam sandwiches, cutting the crusts off hers and dropping them into the dog's bowl. Guapo, whose finely tuned ears always caught that sound, came tearing down the hall from Benny's room, scrabbled across the kitchen linoleum, and emptied his dish in two seconds. Then he sat on Hank's foot and waited for a pat on the head.

'You're supposed to be in your crate,' Hank said as he leaned down to scratch behind Guapo's ears. As always, the left one stood straight up and the right one flopped over like a limp piece of flannel. 'Who forgot to put you in there this morning? And what horrible things have you done with your freedom?'

He removed his foot from underneath the mutt's sizable rump and poured out two glasses of milk. Lunch was all set when the doorbell rang – that would be Maribel and the carpool mom.

He opened the door to find a six-foot-two barrel-chested man instead.

'Hello, Hank.'

'Father Tony?'

The priest gave him a beatific smile and stepped over the threshold, which forced Hank to shift to the side. He stepped forward again and peered outside. There was no sign of his daughter or a kid carpool anywhere on the street. He closed the door on the chilly November air and turned to face his guest. What would the etiquette be in this situation? Could one be blunt with a man of the cloth? He decided to try it.

'What are you doing here?'

'I'm here just to say hi, maybe chat a little.'

Everything clicked into place.

'Maribel isn't coming home right now, is she?'

Father Tony had the grace to look sheepish. 'No. She is at a friend's house for the afternoon. We just needed a reason to get you home.'

'"We"? You mean, you and my wife?'

'Yes,' Tony said calmly. 'She thought it might be good for us to talk, and she knew it would be impossible to get you to come down to the church.'

'So you ambush me?'

Tony grinned. 'I prefer to think of it as meeting my parishioners where they are at. And we did not figure you would want me showing up at the sheriff's station.'

Thank God he hadn't done that. It wasn't that Hank didn't like Tony. He did, a lot. The priest was kind and generous as well as eminently sensible, which was one of Hank's favorite qualities. And the guy was exhibiting it now, Hank had to admit. It was sensible to corner him here at home. Shrewd, even. Hank gave in to it, and invited Tony into the living room.

'Actually,' Tony said, unslinging a soft cooler from his shoulder that Hank hadn't noticed he was carrying, 'I brought a little something for lunch.'

He pulled on the zipper and the smell of chile relleno escaped. Yep – shrewd. And crafty. Approaching Machiavellian. And also an excellent cook. Hank led him into the kitchen. They pushed aside the peanut butter sandwiches and dished up the stuffed and fried peppers. They ate in silence for a minute or two, and then Tony asked how the kids were doing. Hank smiled to himself. Exactly as he would play it if he were the one doing the interrogating. Get the person comfortable. Talk about non-threatening topics. Pretend to be interested in a three-year-old's bedtime antics.

He took another chile and chided himself. This wasn't an interrogation. It wasn't like Maggie had called the Gestapo on him. Tony was a concerned friend. He dug into his second helping and let Tony lead the conversation. The priest took another helping too, and apologized for the excess of cheese.

'I cannot help it. I always add more than I should.'

Hank, who thought that there was no such thing as too much cheese, could only shake his head in protest. His mouth was full.

'Ah, you forgive me my weakness for cheese?'

Now Hank was nodding.

'That is kind of you to do so.' Tony took a bite. 'I guess it is always easier to forgive others than to forgive yourself.'

And there it was. Hank had to smile. It was very well done. He took another bite to give himself time to think.

'Too much cheese really only hurts yourself,' he said slowly. 'You're not harming others with your actions.'

'What about you?' Tony said, pointing at Hank's almost clean plate. 'I'm harming you, right?'

Hank sighed. The priest's counseling net had tightened to the point of no escape. 'I'm eating this of my own free will.'

'Yes. That is correct.' Tony put down his fork and leaned forward. 'And those teenagers, they also chose to eat the cheese. They chose to drive down that road. They chose not to follow your directions to go home.'

'They wouldn't have had a choice if I'd followed them.' That was what people didn't understand. He'd abandoned them. He pulled them over, gave them just a lousy little warning, and allowed them to drive off. If he'd followed them to make sure they went home, they wouldn't have died. He was responsible.

Tony looked at him like he knew exactly what he was thinking. So the priest decided to drop the light-handed food metaphor and whack him with a figurative cudgel instead.

'You need to come to some kind of acceptance. Of what happened, and your role in it. There are different ways to do that. You could consider that it was God's will, which is of course what I would recommend. You could think that without the crash, that murder would probably not have been solved – and where's the justice in that? You could appreciate that the investigation brought your young deputy back to you. Sam, right? He has gotten better, his spirits have lifted. These are important things. You need to acknowledge them.'

Hank made a few noncommittal sounds that he hoped would end the conversation. But Tony's bludgeoning wasn't done.

'So I think that perhaps you need to take a break. Go do something enjoyable, where you have space to breathe. Do you like fishing? Camping?'

Hank started to shake his head, but then stopped himself. It wasn't a bad suggestion. In fact, everything Tony said was completely reasonable. He told the priest he would try. Tony beamed, and rewarded him with a story about the last parish fundraiser – spilled lemonade, a flimsy aluminum dish of red spaghetti sauce, and Mrs Ragnelli's slippery high heels. Apparently, her dry-cleaning bill was the highest ever charged down at the Speedy Son Cleaners.

'Now she's trying to figure out who spilled the lemonade so she can get reimbursed.' Tony grinned and rose to his feet. 'I will meet with her tonight to try and calm her down. I just hope she does not wave the bill in my face again.'

Hank stood as well. 'Now that does make me feel better – that I'm not the most difficult thing you have to do today.'

Tony chuckled as Hank walked him to the door. He was halfway down the walk when Duncan's car pulled into the driveway. Benny popped out and raced into the house. Duncan followed much more slowly. He said hello to Father Tony and shambled up to Hank on the doorstep.

'You better be all fixed by now. That took forever.'

His father-in-law was incapable of sugar-coating anything.

'So this was a coordinated campaign?' Hank asked. 'You were in on it, too?'

'Maggie gave me my marching orders – keep Benny away while the priest guy was here. Make you think it was some playdate that was already planned.' He stretched. 'We've been sitting in the car down the street for a half hour waiting for him to leave.'

Hank peered out at the Camry in the driveway. 'Why is Aunt Fin still in the car?'

'She's got no kid stamina. She can walk five miles no problem, but she can't survive two hours at a McDonald's PlayPlace with a three-year-old.'

Hank didn't blame her. That was the seventh circle of hell. Even experienced parents were exhausted by it. Dunc's sister never had kids, so it was all new to her and probably ten times as torturous. He watched her climb slowly out of the car and drag herself toward the house.

'I am seventy-eight years old, my boy, and I could have happily gone to my grave without experiencing that place.'

Hank helped her up the steps. 'I appreciate you guys doing that.'

She reached up and patted his cheek.

'It's the least I could do, dear. You all have let me stay here longer than I have any right to ask for. I'm the one to be thanking you.'

A thought slowly hatched as Hank watched her walk into the house. He alone knew the real reason Fin drove down from her home in Columbia two weeks ago. And it wasn't because she wanted quality time with Duncan. She'd asked for Hank's help. Giving it to her might solve more than just her problem. It might satisfy Father Tony, too.

Sheila thought she hadn't heard correctly. It sounded like he said he was going to take some time off. She patted at her hair, which was pinned up in its customary way, and waited for him to continue.

'Are you going to say anything?' Hank asked. He was standing in front of her desk, hands jammed in the pockets of his jeans.

'You're really going on vacation?' she said.

'Not vacation, really. I'm just taking a few days off. I thought I'd go up to Columbia and visit my old college roommate. He still lives there.'

That sounded like a vacation to her. Hallelujah. The man

needed to get his bearings back. He'd been driving her crazy ever since the car crash. Moping around, startling at every little sound, not doing much work, and generally being a real pain in the ass.

'I think that's a great idea,' she said. Possibly with a little too much enthusiasm, because a wry smile appeared on his face.

'Yeah, that was Maggie's tone, too, when I told her,' he said. He turned and studied the big white board where she, as chief deputy, was responsible for posting the shift schedule. 'It doesn't look like anyone else is off, so it shouldn't leave you shorthanded or anything.'

Sheila nodded. 'Yeah, Doug Gabler got back from his camping trip yesterday, so we're fully staffed.'

'Great. So, ah, as far as outstanding issues – there's the house burglary up north off of Highway Sixty-five, the bozos who keep drag racing out near Taneyville, and the . . .' He trailed off and looked at her. 'You know all this. I guess I should just be asking if there's anything you need from me before I go.'

Sheila couldn't think of a single thing. She should come up with something. It would make him feel better.

'Can I go ahead with the new jail deputy rotation?' she asked.

He looked surprised that she'd even asked. And truthfully, she wouldn't have bothered to, under normal circumstances. If he were here working, she would just have done it unilaterally, maybe giving him an update halfway through the process – if she felt like it. That was how their relationship worked, and they both knew it.

'Uh, yeah, that's fine. Go ahead,' he said. He gave her a nod that was more firm and confident than she'd seen in a while. He went into his office for a minute and emerged with some paperwork and a travel coffee mug. 'Call me if anything comes up. I can come right back and—'

Her compassion only went so far. She stood up and made shooing motions with her hands, but her voice was kind. 'Get on with you. Out. Have a good time, relax, relive your college exploits. Whatever. Just get.'

He gave her a smile she couldn't quite decipher. Amusement, with a little bit of gratitude? He paused on his way out the door.

'And with the jail thing, just watch your back with you-know-who. I don't want you hassled because of me.'

She gave him a wave as he left, and then sat down to work on the staffing schedule. She didn't anticipate mere hassling. She expected people to flat out choose sides. And she was looking forward to it.

TWO

H ank was all set with Jerry. His college roommate had been delighted by his call.

'Dude, of course you can stay here. As long as you need to. Guest bedroom's all yours. We'll go paint the town. I'll show you all the new places.'

Jerry had no kids, two divorces, three cars, and the disapproval of every one of his friends' wives. Hank loved him. And he loved Columbia. He was actually looking forward to this. It was a good feeling. He pulled a duffel bag out of the closet, but before he started packing he needed to find Aunt Fin.

She was just finishing a game of Candy Land in the living room. The kids were getting ready to start another one when Dunc yelled out from the kitchen that he was ready to walk the dog. Fin usually went with him. Hank caught her eye and gave her a discreet head shake.

'I'm going to pass tonight, Duncan,' she called.

She waited until she heard the door slam, then stood up and told the kids she needed to take a break from the game. She turned on a Maggie-approved cartoon program and followed Hank into the kitchen, sitting down with a concerned look on her face. She knew he would only want to talk about one thing, and he didn't want others overhearing.

'Fin, I want to apologize in advance for this. I might be putting you in an awkward position, and that's certainly not my goal.'

He explained that he'd basically been ordered to leave town, by both his wife and his priest. So he was going up to Columbia.

His good friend lived there, which made it a perfectly under-standable destination choice. But seeing Jerry wasn't his real reason for going.

Fin leaned forward. Anticipation and dread made her face flush all the way to the roots of her snow white hair. Hank reached across the table and grabbed her hand. He didn't need her having a heart attack.

'I'm going to look into it – into your problem,' he said. 'This is the perfect opportunity to poke around without anyone thinking it's strange for me to be up there. Who knows? I could find your husband's secretary, and everything will be fine.'

'But you need a break. After . . . all that with the crash. That's the point of you leaving. That you won't be doing police work. I just told you because I thought you might know what *I* should do. I didn't mean that *you* should do something.'

She really was a very nice lady.

'I know that.' He gave her hand a squeeze. 'But this would work out pretty well. It would give me the opportunity to see what's going on. The only thing is, we need to come up with a reason to explain why you're not coming with me. Why you're still staying here in Branson.'

Comprehension dawned. 'Oh. Because under normal circum-stances, I'd probably go, too. I see. I mean, how long do I need to be visiting my brother?'

Hank nodded. They just needed an excuse to account for why she was continuing to stay here, he said. She studied the pumpkin-motif tablecloth for a moment.

'No.' She raised her head and looked him dead in the eye. 'I am a grown woman, and I should go home.'

That wasn't what he meant at all. He spent fifteen minutes trying to talk her out of it.

'Fin, please,' he finally said. 'You're scared. Please let me figure out what's going on before you go back.'

'No. I married Lew and I can't cower down here anymore. If he's responsible for Tina being missing or hurt, I'm going to have to face it – face him – eventually. It might as well be now.'

'What's now?'

They both jumped a good foot out of their chairs. They hadn't heard Duncan come in. He rolled his eyes and let Guapo off the leash. Before Hank could stop her, Fin was on her feet.

'I'm going home. Now. Well, tomorrow. That's what we were talking about. It's a good opportunity. I can give Hank a ride.'

Wait, what? How would he get home if she drove him up there? And, more importantly, how would he survive three hours in a 2008 Buick LaCrosse with ride-the-brakes Aunt Fin? She gave them both a firm nod and went off to pack. The two men stared at each other. Dunc shrugged.

'She blows in, she blows out. No warning either way. Same as Mary Poppins, only old and crabby.'

'Like you're so young and cheerful,' said Hank.

Dunc barked a laugh. Then he wagged a finger at Hank. 'I'm still sure that she came down here to get away from Lew because she thinks he's having an affair. She's just too embarrassed to say anything to me about it. So you be nice and don't upset her any more than she already is.'

Hank said he would try. And he meant it, although not in the way Dunc wanted. He was going to try his damnedest to show Fin that her worries were unfounded. All he had to do was prove that Lew hadn't killed anybody.

Sam Karnes got there first thing in the morning. It was his third trip out to the split-level with the added-on garage on a little street just off Highway 65 as it headed north toward Springfield. Two days ago, the first call had come in. Folks came home to find their house burglarized. He took the report, Alice Randall took pictures and dusted for prints around the broken window, and they assured the couple they'd investigate and each drove off in their department vehicles. Yesterday, the lady called back with a list of additional items that were missing. That wasn't all that unusual. But she'd done it again last night. So here he was, pulling into the gravel driveway in his squad car, the sun barely up. The garage door was open, and both the woman and her husband stood inside. The cruiser crunched to a stop on the rocks, and Sam climbed out. He didn't get three steps before the lady was at him, flapping a sheet of paper.

'Here's the more I was talking about,' she said. 'They've cleaned us out, that's what.'

The garage looked pretty darn full to Sam. He walked toward it.

'Mrs Balefski, ma'am, we went through all of this when I took the report two days ago. We looked through your garage. Just like we went through the house.'

She kept waving the paper at him.

'Look, kid,' she said. 'Just because you're inexperienced don't mean that we got to suffer. You got to add this stuff to your report. The insurance – they're telling me that I can't file a claim till it's all reported to the cops.'

Sam took the paper, which had the wonderful effect of getting Mrs Balefski to take a step back. He ignored her dig at his appearance – it wasn't his fault he looked younger than his twenty-six years – and scanned the list, which ran the full front and back of the sheet. He picked an item at random.

'OK, show me where the cordless drill was stored.'

'What?'

'Where did you keep the drill? And the power washer?'

Mrs Balefski looked at her husband, who was leaning against a garage support post and eating a piece of toast. He finished it before turning and picking his way through the junk into the back of the tilted building. Sam followed, less sure-footed in the mess and more than a little suspicious of the construction. He doubted the county building department had signed off on it. Or even knew about it. They got to a back-tool bench, and Mr Balefski pointed at a jumble of wires in the middle.

'They were on top of there.'

Everything else Sam asked to see was the same. It had all been kept on top of other messes, surfaces that didn't keep an imprint or a dusty outline that would lend credence to their claims. He decided to make them go through the whole list – he hadn't been planning to, but after five or six questionable locations, he figured he was going to make them work for it. He took photos of everything and scribbled in his notebook. They started to look a little worried.

They should. Sam was now beginning to doubt the antique family silverware they told him about yesterday as they'd showed him the empty box under their bed. They, of course, hadn't had a receipt.

He got to the end of the list and saw the last item.

'A car?' he said before he could stop himself. 'You didn't notice a car was missing?'

Mr Balefski straightened up, said yes in a pretty indignant way, and stomped out the main garage door and around to the back. While the side of the building was clear and paved with gravel, the area behind it was full of household junk and untamed weeds. No part of it could be seen from the house.

'There weren't nothing back here important, so we didn't think to look closer,' the man said.

'Except a car.' Sam looked at the semi-clear rectangle where it must have been parked and tried not to roll his eyes.

Mr Balefski glared at him and jabbed a finger at a bunched-up tarp. 'That was covering it, and from out there' – he waved toward the front of the garage – 'I could see the edge of it and thought the damn car was still back here.'

Sam would have been a lot more inclined to give this guy the benefit of the doubt if the rest of the 'stolen' list had seemed more plausible. He readied his pen and asked for the details. A 2002 Honda Civic, blue, two-door, dent in the passenger side.

'You have the VIN?'

'It's on the damn car.'

OK. That was enough. He knew people didn't tend to grant him a lot of respect because of his age, and because of looking kind of tall and gawky. But Hank had flat out told him. Being treated like a youngster was one thing. Being disrespected was something else. And that had to be dealt with firmly, fairly, and fast.

'Mr Balefski. I'm talking about whether you wrote down the VIN somewhere safe. Like a responsible vehicle owner.' Sam readied his notebook and pointed his pen at the guy. 'I'm going to ask you the same question about the license plate. Which could be on the damn car, too. But if you don't have it written down, then we're done here. Am I making myself clear?'

They stared at each other for what felt to Sam like an excruciatingly long and awkward time. Maybe he shouldn't have said that last bit. Finally, the guy stomped back out front to his wife. She hurried into the house and came out with another sheet of paper with a Missouri license plate number. They bought it second-hand and never wrote down the VIN, she mumbled. Sam took it, folded it into his notebook with their itemized list and walked back to his car without saying another word. The woman trotted after him. The guy didn't.

'Would it be important to know if the keys were in the car?' she whispered to Sam. He turned toward her and she shooed him back in his original direction. 'I might've left 'em in there. Cuz I can't find 'em in the house.'

Now Sam did roll his eyes. She gave him a dirty look and stepped away as her husband approached.

'Uh, so this stuff's going to get added to the report, right?' she said a little too loudly. 'So we can tell the insurance company?'

Sam told her how to request a copy of the official report once it was done and drove off before they could think of anything else they were 'missing'. He waited until he was out of sight of the property before he pulled over and ran the plates on the cruiser's computer. It did come back to a 2002 Civic belonging to the Balefskis. He let out an exasperated sigh and entered it as stolen. He couldn't add a 'skeptical' notation to the computer database, but the narrative attached to his police report would sure mention it.

THREE

Hank and Fin wanted to be on the road by eight. He was disappointed with how blasé the kids were about him going away. They were more upset that Fin was leaving. Maggie and Dunc, on the other hand, tried to hide their relief. It hadn't been easy having another adult in the house for so long.

He loaded Fin's bags in her cavernous trunk. And then approached her carefully.

'It's still a little dark out. I'm happy to drive.'

'Oh,' she said, clearly surprised at the offer. 'I don't . . . well, I usually do my own driving.'

Hank had experienced it once. He really didn't want to again.

He shot a look at Maggie and Dunc, who were on the porch in their bathrobes. Maggie gave it a try. 'It'll give you a chance to do some more knitting.' That was good. She even unleashed her persuasive take-your-medicine doctor voice.

Fin didn't look swayed. Dunc waved her over. 'Come here, Finella,' he told his sister. He put his arm around her shoulder and led her out on to the front lawn. Thirty seconds of talk and she came back over, got her knitting out of the trunk, gave Hank the keys, and settled herself in the passenger seat. He was too surprised even to say thank you. Instead, he walked back to the porch to give Maggie one last kiss. Then he shot Dunc a quizzical look.

'I told her you're still in a funk, and it'd probably make you feel better if you could drive,' Dunc whispered. 'You know, make you feel like you were doing something right for a change.' Maggie groaned. Dunc shrugged. 'Well, it worked, didn't it?'

And that was the important thing. Hank would take any kind of character assassination if it meant escaping Fin's brake-heavy driving. He slapped Dunc on the back and got in the Buick. As they pulled away, the kids finally deigned to notice, popping out of the front door and waving madly.

They headed up Highway 65 at a leisurely pace. Which was all the car was suited for. It was big and low, and the soft suspension made it feel like they were floating along. The steering needed the barest touch. He fiddled with the seat adjustment until he was comfortable, and they rode in easy silence through Springfield and east on the interstate until the exit for the city of Lebanon. From here on out, it was mostly a connection of little-frequented roads through rural Missouri. Luckily, Fin was amenable to having breakfast at the Steak 'n Shake first. He had a couple of breakfast tacos and Fin ordered a stack of pancakes. They both got milkshakes for the road.

Hank waited until they were out of Lebanon and sailing north on Highway 5. It was a big improvement over the two-lane danger that he and Maggie used to drive in college when they came down to see her family in Branson. Now it had stretches of passing lanes and wide center dividers. He remarked on it and Fin told him to wait and see the wonderful stretch of US

54 from Lake of the Ozarks up toward Jeff City. It was now a full-on divided highway. Just heavenly, she said.

'We'll definitely get there faster than I expected,' Hank said. He took a sip of chocolate shake and looked over at her. 'So I guess we should start talking about Tina.'

Fin poked at her shake with the straw. Hank could practically hear the internal conversation she was having.

'You're worried,' he said. 'I think I know you well enough to say that you don't get that way if there isn't cause. So you're not going to tell me that you're probably overreacting, or that I should forget it. You're going to tell me what you know, and you're going to let me take it from there. And if it really is nothing, then we'll find that out, and no one will be the wiser. OK?'

She swished her melting drink around and then looked at him with blue eyes amazingly like her brother's. 'OK.'

Hank turned his gaze back to the road. She didn't need him constantly looking over as she tried to collect her thoughts. They drove another few miles before she began to speak.

Tina had been hired about a year ago. Maude had retired, and Lew needed a new secretary. Although nowadays, apparently, they're called administrative assistants. So the ad was placed, online and in other such tech-y places, and Tina Hardy applied. She was in her mid-forties, which was certainly younger than anybody in the office, except the young men who did the driving and truck-loading. When Hank asked for more of a description Fin figured she was probably about five foot six, with glasses and dark blonde hair that was shoulder length and carefully highlighted. She seemed to fit in well. She was into a few things that the other ladies weren't, like working out and foreign films, but she was nice and had participated in the office Secret Santa, which was a big plus. She knew what she was doing as far as the job went. She was good at all those business software programs – even designing a couple of ads that Lew used to promote the company.

Of course, Closeout Castle was already a local institution, so the ads just needed to herald new arrivals and reinforce the treasure hunt aspect of the chain's stores. 'How Low Can Lew Go?' is what he'd ask folks in the commercials. Customers could find everything from high-end small appliances for eighty percent off to novelty pencils for a nickel each. And the selection was constantly changing. People would come from all over the state to Columbia, conveniently situated right in the middle. Until lately. People weren't willing to drive anymore. They wanted it shipped to them. They wanted to do it all on their computers. Point-and-click, point-and-click. These days, Lew said that phrase like it was a profanity.

But back to Tina. They were happy with her job performance – her and Lew and Marco Cortello, the company's financial officer. She included herself in that list because ever since she married Lew twenty years ago, they kept her in the loop on things. Until about six months ago. Then it gradually started to change. She didn't even notice it at first. As she looked back on it now, though, she could see that Lew had slowly stopped discussing things with her.

He certainly didn't say anything about Tina taking the day off. Fin only found out because she called the office looking for Lew. Hank tried to pin her down on a date, but she couldn't remember exactly. Maybe three weeks ago? She was positive Marco answered the phone and said Tina had the day off. Fin didn't think anything of it. And she didn't think anything of it when Lew came home that night with bloody knuckles and torn pants, because he said he'd helped unload a truck and took a tumble against the concrete loading dock. She only started to think something when Tina's day off turned into several. And then became an official vacation. Which got extended when her out-of-town mother fell ill.

'I called up human resources. I wanted to get her mother's address so I could send flowers. We take care of our own at the Castle. I knew the men wouldn't think of it, though, so I figured I'd just handle it. But they had no address and no idea when she was coming back. They said Lew was just keeping them updated. Only Lew.'

Hank had been nodding along with Fin's story, not hearing anything too worrying. Until that last bit. Lew was the only person in contact with this woman? And her reasons for missing work kept shifting? He asked Fin to write down the name of the HR person she had spoken with.

'Oh, there's only one. Doreen. There used to be two, but

then all the payroll got automated or some such, and now it's just Doreen.' She placed her melted shake in a cupholder and rummaged through her knitting bag for paper. She wrote down Doreen's information and the number for Marco the finance guy. She added Lew's typical daily schedule, and slid the paper in the side pocket of Hank's duffel bag in the backseat.

They spent the rest of the drive talking about the kids, and her knitting, and Duncan's exploits as a child. She slowly relaxed, until they pulled into the neighborhood a little bit west of the university campus. Then she fell quiet and started to fidget. They pulled up in front of a solid two-story squarish home, all brick with white shutters and a shiny black front door. It swung open and out bounded Lew, arms wide in welcome.

Her spreadsheet was so lovely. Shifts and hourly rates and total hours per pay period. And no overtime at all. Which meant a balanced budget, for the first time since Sheila had been in charge of staffing. When she started with it, Darrell Gibbons had been the sheriff and he never cared. That old snakecharmer could talk the county commission into any extra funds he needed, so they were always able to make ends meet. But Hank . . . Hank was a different story. The commissioners hated him. He was not the good ol' boy they'd expected. He didn't play nice with the local power players. He was incapable of keeping his mouth shut when he thought someone was doing something wrong. And his arrival had coincided with a spike in the county murder rate, which was both expensive for staffing and bad publicity.

She smiled. Hank's arrival also had meant her promotion to chief deputy and a level of autonomy she never expected to have as one of the only African-American deputies in south-western Missouri and definitely the only one in Branson County. Sure, she had to bail his tender-hearted, white-boy ass out every once in a while, but that was a small price to pay for a rank she never thought the system would let her achieve.

She hit print and watched her spreadsheet roll out of the machine. Then she started on the white board, changing shifts to correspond with her new system. She was pulling a chair over so she could reach the headings at the very top when Sammy walked in.

'Geez, Sheila, you could fall. I'll do it for you.'

She climbed up on it and looked down at him.

'I'm just fine, thank you. Plus, I don't like your handwriting. It would ugly up my board.'

He laughed and held the chair steady, despite her trying to swat him away. She finished and hopped down. Sam put the chair back in the corner.

'Is the Chief in yet?' he said. 'I need to talk to him about this burglary case.'

'Oh, he's gone. He went on vacation.' The phrase came out before she thought about it. She paused. 'That's not exactly accurate. He . . . he's taking a break. He went up to Columbia for a few days, to visit a friend or something. I think Maggie laid down the law. Told him to get a change of scenery and come back in a better frame of mind. I think he was driving her crazy.'

Sam eyed her. 'I don't think his wife was the only one.'

Sheila chuckled. Her young Sammy was becoming more astute every day. She gave him a nod and pointed at the white board.

'I'm going to send out an email – because I do know that nobody ever looks at my board – and let everyone know there's a new schedule. We're going to try to be . . . more efficient.' That was a good word. She'd use that in her memo to the department. 'Efficient staffing' was a much better spin than 'axing your overtime'.

The only change to his week, she told Sam, was a change on Wednesday from investigation follow-up to patrol duty. He said that was no big deal and stepped over to peruse the actual board, much to her delight.

'Oh, I see. My switch is because otherwise Bill Ramsdell would be the patrol shift as overtime. Just like here, and over here,' he said, immediately spotting the different squares on the board where she'd taken extra shifts away from people. He let out a low whistle as he realized the extent of what she'd done. 'People are going to be ticked off. Super ticked off. Are you sure about this?'

She nodded. 'Yeah. We've got no choice. We are so far over budget, the next option is going to be laying people off. I'm hoping this will save us enough money that we won't have to do that. It's not even like we're cutting anybody's salary. We're just not doing overtime anymore.'

Sam scratched behind his ear, which she knew meant he was having a serious think on things. She waited.

'You need to say that – in your email. That you're trying to avoid layoffs. Don't say "saving money". People hate that.'

See? Astute.

Sam examined the board again. His eyes widened.

'What'd you do with the jail schedule? It's not on here.'

Too astute.

'That . . . um . . . that's going to be its own thing from now on. Partly because a lot of the patrol guys were using it to rack up overtime,' she said. 'So I'm just going to separate it out.'

He raised an eyebrow. 'Partly?'

Good heavens. He was picking up on everything. Before long, he'd be ferreting out all of her plans. Time to change the subject.

'You mentioned that home burglary?'

He lit up and whipped out his notebook. He took her through the investigation so far, including his suspicions about the Balefskis' honesty.

'You think they staged it?' Sheila asked.

'No,' he said. 'I think there really was a burglary, especially with the car missing. I think they're just stretching the list of what actually got taken – trying to get more cash out of the insurance company.'

'Well, luckily, that's the insurance investigator's problem, not ours. Finish up the report, and those two can start dealing with that company instead of us.'

'Could I look into the missing car, though? Try to run it down? I've got the rest of today before I have to report for patrol tomorrow.' He gestured at the board and grinned at her.

With that smile, how could she say no? She agreed and told him to get himself gone before she found a clerical job for him to do. He loped out of the office on those huge feet and she turned back to her computer. She pulled up her second spreadsheet and got to work.

FOUR

Lew Lancaster, his thinning silver hair immaculately styled with some kind of miracle pomade and his navy blazer perfectly pressed, showed Hank into the front room. A man in his late fifties rose from the couch to greet them. He introduced himself as Marco Cortello. The financial officer Fin mentioned, Hank thought, stealing a glance at his aunt-in-law. He shook the man's hand while having an internal laugh at Duncan's expense. This six-footer with the lean physique of a tennis player, the smile of George Clooney, and the baritone of Johnny Cash was much more likely to be having an affair with Tina Hardy than the octogenarian Mark-down Lew was. Which was a thought worth pondering some.

'How long you been working with Lew here?' Hank asked.

'Almost twenty years,' he said, his glamour-shot smile wavering a little. 'It's getting hard to believe.'

'Wasn't that just when you were starting to expand, Lew? How many employees did you even have back then?'

'Oh, a few. Maybe five or six.'

'And now,' Hank said, 'just look. All the stores, and then your main office. How many folks you got there now?'

'Four,' Marco said. 'And then the warehouse guys. And us two, of course.'

'How'd the two of you find each other in the first place?'

'Oh, he's better at numbers than I am,' Lew said. 'Can't sell anything worth a damn, but he's great with the financials.'

The two men looked as if each was daring the other to contradict that statement. Interesting.

'Well, we were just finishing up,' Lew said, holding the front door open.

A frown flashed across Marco's face before he suppressed it. He gave Fin a kiss on the cheek and took his leave. Lew turned to Hank and offered up orange juice, coffee, and pastries. Hank took the last two and said sure, he'd love a tour. Because this wasn't an obligatory visit with a random in-law – this was reconnaissance.

They started outside, with Lew showing off work they'd had done around the place, including the backyard gazebo and then around front to see the enlarged picture window.

'It was nice to meet Marco,' Hank said as they strolled across the lawn. 'Do he and his family live here in Columbia?'

'Oh, he doesn't have kids. His wife is a professor at the University of Missouri in St Louis, so they have a place here and a place there and go back and forth.'

Marco was getting more interesting by the minute, but he couldn't think of any more questions that wouldn't start to arouse Lew's suspicions. As they walked back inside, Hank decided that to effectively search the inside, he would become very interested in closets. What with the growing kids and all, they were always trying to maximize storage space, he explained as he poked through the coat closet in the foyer. Did Lew happen to have any ideas? Of course Lew did.

The next ten minutes were spent on the science of organization, with Lew talking and Hank rummaging around. He had to admit the closet under the stairs was a dazzle of shelving and neatness. The pantry was next. Then the study, which was the only messy room Hank had seen. He tried to take in as much as possible before Lew shooed him out.

'This is only for work. No space or organization issues here.' He closed the door firmly and practically pushed Hank back toward the living room. He went willingly, because ol' Lew had provided the perfect segue.

'So business is good?'

He thought he felt Lew tense, but by the time he turned to look, the older man had an easy grin on his face.

'You bet. Expanding, even. We're in the planning stages for store number five. Got to make sure all the numbers pencil out, though, before we pull the trigger.'

Hank started a follow-up question, but Lew had already turned toward the kitchen. Hank could see the muscles in his stooped shoulders tighten and his hands ball into fists. Stress, or just old age? He followed, and they found Fin attaching artwork to the front of the fridge. Hank recognized the bold stylings of a certain three-year-old and the slightly more refined brush strokes of a kindergartener.

'Benny and Maribel let me take some,' Fin said, with the first true smile he'd seen from her all day. She pointed at several in particular. 'We made these paintings together.'

He hadn't realized Fin spent so much time with the kids during her visit. He reached out and gave her hand a grateful squeeze. Lew, on the other hand, looked at the fridge like she'd just covered it with rock concert handbills from the local Blue Note nightclub. Hank was just about to defend his kids' talent when the doorbell rang.

'That,' he said, 'should be my friend Jerry.'

Doubt was not something Sheila bothered with. She didn't have time for it, and it usually wasn't necessary. She was generally right about things, and in the rare instance that she wasn't, she fixed it and that was that. So this was a new feeling. She knew she was taking the correct course of action, but had she timed it wrong?

The jail staff had always been allowed to trade shifts and reschedule themselves any way they wanted. It was one of the only perks of a shit job. But it had to stop. Letting patrol officers sub in to cover jail slots meant they had to be paid overtime, as did jail officers trading amongst themselves if the work crossed over into a different pay period.

So now there was a set-in-stone schedule, and any changes would have to be approved by her or Hank. It was exceedingly sensible and fiscally necessary. She had explained this in her memo and was in the middle of explaining it in person to the jail staff – all ten of whom were giving her stone-cold death stares – when the doubt started to creep in. Should she have waited until Hank got back? She hadn't thought she needed cover, but looking at the more than just hostile expressions on these men's faces, maybe she did. And it pissed her off. She was the one who made this department work. She should be able to command the kind of authority necessary to do this. But she wasn't a man and she wasn't white. And Hank was.

'I don't see why you got to change things. They're fine the way they are. You don't even know what you're doing.' That was Berkins. Three hundred pounds of fat and attitude. He'd been jail forever and thought he was God's gift to both correctional facilities and humanity in general. The other officers called him Bubba. The frequent flyer inmates called him Fat Bastard. Sheila just wanted him to retire.

'Nobody's taking a pay cut,' she said again.

'Hell, yes we are,' said Stevenson, who Sheila was pretty sure had paid for his shiny new pickup with just his massive overtime earnings. 'We got the way we do things. We switch when we want to. That's the deal.'

'And how we gonna cover when somebody's sick? Huh?' said Bubba, who called in sick all the time.

'That'll be figured out by me or Sheriff Worth. You guys won't have to worry about it anymore.'

That prompted a barrage of invective from most of them that came damn close to insubordination. She let them go on for a moment and then closed her file folder with a snap. They shut up. Thank God. She surveyed the room and decided to dismiss the ones who were currently on shift. That would split up the group, make it harder for them to feed on one another's anger – or even worse, to start plotting something.

Those men filed out of the room. She thanked the rest of them for coming in and made sure to state clearly that they'd get paid for their time. She watched them go out the other door to the parking lot and then walked back to the administration building.

Only two people said nothing during the meeting, which caught Sheila's attention for two very different reasons. Sheila wasn't surprised Molly March hadn't spoken up at all. She was brand new, young, and seemed to alternate between shy and terrified. She was also the only woman on the jail staff. Like about half of them, she hoped to work her way up to patrol. She was currently on the swing shift, so Sheila rarely saw her. She needed to change that. Check in with the kid more often. Make sure she was doing OK. She made herself a note to look up her contact information.

The other person she wasn't going to contact at all. Gerald Tucker had just sat there and stared at her through the entire meeting, arms crossed and eyes unblinking. On a personal level, she wasn't concerned about him. She knew he didn't give two shits about her, except that she was a proxy for the sheriff. Because he had it out for Hank, like no one she'd ever seen.

Tucker had been a long-time patrol deputy until Hank demoted him to the jail. The asshole had left his guard duty post at the wrecked *Branson Beauty* showboat and the thing blew up. Hank was positive Tucker deliberately caused the explosion, and Tucker knew it. He'd run against Hank in the last election and almost won. If he had, the good ol' boys' network would have come roaring back, and it'd be Sheila working in the jail right now.

So a quiet Tucker was a thoughtful Tucker – and that was a dangerous Tucker. He had powerful allies. He could hatch a revolt quietly. She'd thought it would be easier to quell one without Hank around but now she wasn't so sure. She'd need to keep a close eye on him. She pushed open the door to her office and sat down to think.

FIVE

Hank introduced Fin and Lew to his college roommate.

'This is Jerry Heinrich. We met in the dorms and then got our own apartment off Nifong Boulevard.'

Jerry was still as lean and lively as he'd been when they graduated. He crackled with energy as he stepped into the house and shook hands all around.

'And you're the lovely Maggie's aunt?' he asked Fin. 'How wonderful to finally meet you. Any McCleary family member is an honor to know. This guy' – he gave Hank a light punch in the arm – 'is lucky to have nabbed himself one.'

Hank winked at Fin. 'Even if I did get Dunc as part of the deal,' he said. Fin cackled with delight and gave Hank a big hug.

He whispered quickly in her ear and then grabbed his duffel bag off the front step. He turned toward the driveway and stopped. 'Really, Jer? Are you kidding me?'

'Had it six months. Traded in the Corvette.' He spread out his arms with a flourish. 'You like it?'

That was an enormously stupid question. 'It' was an Acura NSX sports car. And it was beautiful. A low-slung, turbocharged, God-knew-how-many-horsepower, six-figure-price-tag master-piece. It was to his minivan as a cheetah was to a hippopotamus. Hank folded himself down into the supercar's passenger seat as Jerry loped around the front and swung behind the wheel with a practiced fluidity. 'Buckle up, man. We're taking the long way home.'

An hour later, they pulled up to Jerry's house, which was technically only five miles away from Fin's place. It was in a much newer part of Columbia, with big stone-fronted houses that had high ceilings and tiny backyards and HOAs. Jerry had moved here after the most recent divorce.

'Yeah, Denver was great – I mean really great – but it was her town, you know? So I wanted to come back to someplace that was mine. And my IT can operate from wherever.'

That was certainly true. Jerry owned an information tech-nology company that provided support services to restaurants and retail. It had started in the basement of a rental he had with his first wife. It began so slowly, Hank and Maggie would bring them over crock-pots full of food so they wouldn't starve. He finally landed a big client and celebrated by buying a boat instead of paying off the credit cards. He said it was fine and the debt could wait. She said it wasn't, and walked out. That had been the end of marriage number one.

But his boundless faith in the concept hadn't been misplaced. He knew what he was doing, and now it was a multi-million-dollar company. Hank had hoped that his spending hadn't increased along with his success, but based on what he was sitting in, that was not the case. Jerry hit a button and the garage door rolled up.

Definitely not the case.

Two of the spots in the garage were taken by a BMW coupe and an old VW bug with only three wheels that Hank hoped Jerry was restoring. He turned to his friend.

'You said I'd be able to borrow your crappy little commuter car.'

'Yeah,' Jerry said. 'That's it.'

He pointed at the BMW.

'You commute in the BMW?'

'No. I commute in this.' He pointed at what they were sitting in. 'But dude, you know me. You didn't think I'd have, like, a Prius sitting around, did you?'

Hank started laughing, and a weight he'd carried long enough that it had become a perpetual ache started to lift off his chest.

'No, I guess not,' he said. 'So what's with the Bimmer, then? Is that for when you actually need trunk space?'

Jerry chuckled as he let them into the house. 'Nah. That was Cindy's. She wanted the Denver house, so as part of the settlement, I got the car. I don't drive it.'

There was an edge to that last bit. Hank eyed him. Maybe this latest breakup had hit his friend harder than he was admitting. It was good he came to visit. For both of them.

They were getting dressed for work when Tyrone stopped and pointed at his wife.

'I almost forgot,' he said. 'I wanted to tell you about something. Out in your area.'

Sheila smiled at him as she buckled her duty belt. 'What's up?'

'Out on Nighthawk Lane off Buena Vista. It's Rodney's route. He said yesterday that one of his customers hasn't been collecting his mail. The box is packed full, and he hasn't seen any activity at the house.'

'How old is the resident?' Sheila asked.

'It sounded like he was older.'

'We'll definitely do a welfare check. Send me his address when you get in.'

With a flourish, he pulled a paper out of the pocket of his mail carrier pants. 'All ready for you, baby.'

She raised an impressed eyebrow. 'Very nice. I'll get Sammy on it first thing. Tell Rodney thanks.'

'Oh, hell no. He'll go off thinking he should start reporting every twitch his residents make. Or be calling himself a reserve deputy or something. No. Rodney doesn't need encouragement.'

She laughed and leaned in for her hug. It was their morning

ritual, and she looked forward to every time he wrapped his arms around her. With the overtime uproar that awaited her at the office, this was definitely going to be the best part of her day.

Clyde Timmons. Nighthawk Lane. Not a bad way to start a patrol shift. Sam grabbed a latte at the new coffee place in downtown Branson and pointed the squad car north. He covered the five and a half miles pretty quickly and parked right next to the mailbox, which was fair about to burst with letters. The nice mailman had rubber-banded the door to the rest of the box to keep it from hanging open, but it still bulged out. He could see the White River Valley Electric bill on top.

He walked up the gravel path to the little frame house. It was square with a wrap-around porch that was in pretty good shape, sagging only on the corners. He stepped up, pulled open the glass storm door and rapped authoritatively on the wood one. No response. He tried twice more before he let the storm door swing shut with a squeak. He walked around, peering in windows. When he got to the kitchen, he saw a plate of what looked like fried chicken and congealed collard greens on the table. Not your typical breakfast food.

He went around the house trying to peek in windows, but all the blinds were drawn tight. Banging on the back door met with the same silence. He scratched at his ear for a moment and then headed decisively back to the front. Based on the totality of the circumstances, he felt it reasonable to fear for the old guy's safety. At least, that was what he was going to tell Sheila. The gentleman could have slipped in the shower and broken a hip. Or had a heart attack. Not much else should keep a man away from a dinner of fried chicken like that.

He knelt down so he was at eye level with the front doorknob. This was excellent. He hadn't yet had a chance to use his lock-picking skills in real life. He'd been practicing a lot – broadening his skill set, Hank called it – but this was the first time he would do it officially. He rubbed his suddenly sweaty hands on his pants and got the little tools out of his belt. It took him less than five minutes, which wasn't great but not terrible, either.

Sam twisted the unlocked knob and pushed the door open, announcing that he was with the sheriff's department. All he got in return was a waft of cold air that was stale and ripe at the same time. Which didn't bode well for Mr Timmons. He stepped into the little front room, the wood floor creaking under his feet. There was a recliner across from a small TV, and an end table with a half-full glass of something sitting on a paper towel coaster. Sam took a few more steps and was able to see into the kitchen, with the meal on the table. One lonely fly buzzed above the drumsticks. He turned. The smell wasn't coming from there.

The first bedroom was obviously for guests. A double bed with a dark wood headboard, neatly made, with one of those bumpy chenille bedspreads like his grandmother had. No personal items at all. The bathroom was next. He yanked back the shower curtain and found only a build-up of soap scum. There was just one door left, at the end of the hallway. It had to be another bedroom. Sam readied his radio to report an old guy dead in bed and pushed open the door.

His hand fell to his side as the door clunked into the blood-spattered wall. A man lay crossways across the floor, one leg bent up against the bed frame and the other underneath it. His arms were flung up, but they'd given no protection. His face was beaten and blood matted the thin hair on the back of his head. The bed covers were crumpled, like he'd fallen there before he hit the floor. The nightstand lamp lay on the carpet, next to the body. The contents of the closet spilled out every-where. Slivers of light worked their way through the closed window blinds, catching little motes of dust stirred up by Sam's movement.

He turned as carefully as he could and stepped back out into the hallway. Mr Timmons stared up at him with the eye that hadn't been beaten shut. The only sound was Sam's breathing. He reached for his radio, then decided a direct call would be better. He pulled out his phone and was about to punch the Chief's number when he remembered. He dialed Sheila instead. Then he walked outside and sat down on the porch step, wondering why this poor man had gone from serving up an ordinary dinner to getting attacked in his own bedroom.

SIX

Sheila hung up the phone and slumped back in her chair. A homicide. This certainly hadn't been part of her plan for the time that Hank was gone. Sam had sounded remarkably composed. Still, she needed to get out there. With resources. She called the crime scene techs and Larry over at EMS and then headed out.

She hoped that she'd get there and find it was all an over-reaction. A natural death, where the guy just collapsed on the floor. Then she scolded herself. Sam deserved more credit than that. He hadn't even been pretty sure. He'd been absolutely positive. And when she got there, she saw why.

'Jesus.' It was hard to tell whether the guy had been ambushed or whether there'd been a fight. Either way, he'd certainly gotten the worst of it.

'Are you sure it's Timmons?' she asked Sam. He had hung back in the narrow hallway to allow her an unimpeded view.

'Basically. What's left of his face matches his DL photo. So do his height and weight. I think he's a veteran, so his prints should be on file somewhere for us to compare with the body.'

She nodded. Her Sammy was doing good. She snapped her nitrile gloves absentmindedly as she looked things over.

'And nothing else's been messed with? Just this room?'

'Near as I can tell. I haven't gone through stuff. I wanted to wait for Alice and Kurt. But definitely nothing's been ransacked or anything.'

A heavy tread came toward them, and they both turned around. Kurt Gatz and his equipment took up the width of the hall. They all did a shuffle, with Sheila and Sam stepping into the bathroom so Kurt could get by. He trundled the rest of the way down the hall and they heard a long, slow sigh. Sam rubbed vigorously at the back of his head and looked intently at the bathroom tile. Maybe he wasn't doing as well as she thought.

She started to say something when Alice popped into view. Like
Kurt, she also had her camera.

'Quite a switch from a car theft, isn't it, Sam?' she said. He
smiled weakly. She hadn't seen the bedroom yet.

Sheila snapped her gloves again.

'Why don't you start in the other rooms? Then we can get
to going through things while Kurt works in the bedroom. I
think there's only space for one of you in there, anyway.'

Alice nodded and headed back toward the front room. Sheila
pointed.

'You, too. Go set up a perimeter along the back of the
property.'

'I did. While I was waiting for you,' he said.

She thought for a moment. 'Then start on the neighbors. This
here in the house will keep. Get talking to them before they all
start gossiping together and mixing up their facts.'

He gave her a look she couldn't figure out and followed Alice
down the hall. Sheila turned back and stood on the threshold
as Kurt, his little white protective booties rubbing on the floor,
squeezed himself into a corner and started photographing. He
finished with the section by the door, and Sheila stepped inside,
her own booties making the same noise. Had the killer come
into the room this way as well? One of the two windows was
sealed shut around a window air conditioner. The other
was covered by aluminum blinds that looked bent with use, not
with forced entry. She'd check that, obviously, but couldn't get
over there until the body was moved.

She knelt down. Now up close she could see that one hand
was scraped and would probably be bruised if he'd lived long
enough for that process to take place. She touched his left arm,
which was flung awkwardly up over his face. The forearm felt
broken. Dear God. She leaned farther to get a better look at the
back of his head, but couldn't see much without moving him.
She didn't want to do that yet.

'Holler when you're finished,' she told Kurt, and walked back
out. She heard a rig pull up. She stepped outside to find an
ambulance parked on the street and lanky Larry Alcoate ducking
under the tape. He grinned at her.

'You requested my services, ma'am?' Larry was always good

for a joke and was about to start with one until he took a closer look at Sheila's expression. 'This is more than a suspicious death, isn't it?'

'I hadn't seen the scene yet when I called you,' she said. 'It's definitely a homicide. It's going to be a while before you can move him.'

'OK. I'll move the rig out of the way, then.'

He pulled down the street and the spot was immediately filled by a pair of squad cars. About damn time. She walked out to meet them, taking care not to step on the gravel driveway in case there were tire tracks.

'Orvan, I need you to monitor the front here. Nobody gets in. Hoch, go find Sam and help with the neighborhood canvassing.'

Neither man moved. Their white-boy faces stared back at her impassively. Finally, Hoch spoke. 'That'll take longer than an hour. That's all I got left on my shift. Then I'm leaving.'

Shit. She turned to Derek Orvan. 'You're on days, right?'

He nodded. That meant he had hours left on his shift. She sent him out to help Sam and put Hoch on guard duty. For the hour. There was no way she was authorizing overtime for him. Although she knew she'd have to grant it to somebody eventually. There weren't enough deputies to run this, as well as cover the county patrol. She called the man who was slated to patrol the far eastern reaches of the county and told him to report here instead. He could relieve Hoch.

That ruddy bastard had heard her conversation and was smirking as he stood against the crime scene tape. Fine. As long as he went home without extra wages in his pocket. She put her phone away and took a look around. Neighbors were starting to congregate at the crime scene tape. Not many, but then it was a pretty sparsely populated street. Lots of maybe an acre, left to their natural wooded state. No manicured lawns in sight. She made a wide circle of the house, noting a boot tread in the dirt that had to be Sammy's. There were no other footprints. Then she climbed to the porch and followed it around. All of the windows were locked and dusty. The one to the kitchen had a smudged sill. She tapped on the glass to get Alice's attention. The tech looked up from photographing the dining table and nodded as Sheila pointed to the spot.

Hopefully the inside would tell them more. Sheila stepped into the little living room. It was clear that Timmons lived alone. And it appeared he didn't get many guests either. There was just the recliner, which was comfortably broken in with an afghan thrown over the back and a pillow stuffed just so along the side. The end table was placed so it fit next to the left arm, awkward for the flow of the room but perfect if it was just one man who wanted his remote control and drink glass within easy reach. It looked new.

There was a small love seat against the wall that didn't look like it got much use. A framed Ansel Adams print hung above it. The only other thing in the room was a secretary, dark-stained oak and tall with drawers on the bottom and glass doors on the top. She pulled at the sloped middle section, and the panel easily dropped down to form the little writing desk. The cubby-holes along the back were packed with paperwork and odds and ends. She smiled. Everything else was so immaculate. This mess showed Timmons was human.

She left it open for Alice to see and continued her slow exploration of the house. He wasn't a reader – there were no books. He wasn't a gourmand – the kitchen was fully stocked, but not with anything exotic or flashy. She wandered into the little alcove that led to the back door. A curtain was pushed aside to show the heater – the pilot light was out, which explained why it was so chilly inside the house. Next to it was a stackable washer-dryer that was clearly a do-it-yourself place-ment. She peeked behind it and laughed. It looked like he'd tapped right into the kitchen plumbing and hadn't bothered with the specialized electrical outlet. So not a by-the-book kind of fellow. She added that to the picture of him she was starting to form and turned to the back door. It had a standard lock, but no other security. A row of shoes sat on the flowered linoleum – worn work boots, a pair of suede Oxfords, and some funky tennis shoes.

She continued through the house, examining everything and slowly working her way back toward the bedroom where Timmons lay. When she finally got back to that threshold, Kurt was on his hands and knees by the body.

'I think we're almost ready for Larry to move him. But if

you come over this way . . .' He motioned to the lamp near the poor man's head and shoulder.

Sheila maneuvered around the body as best she could to see where Kurt was pointing on the lamp. It was heavy and brass. And clean. Kurt rotated it and they both leaned in closer to look.

'There's nothing on it,' Sheila said.

Kurt hefted it higher so she could see the bottom. She shook her head. That was clean, too.

'Well, then what the hell killed him?' Kurt said. 'I thought it was this thing. But it'd be covered with . . . well, covered with him, that's what. This kind of beating, blood and tissue'll be naked-eye visible.'

Sheila swore. She'd also assumed they had the murder weapon. Instead, it must have just toppled over during the struggle. She could see the outline of the base on the faded nightstand surface, which now held only a cheap alarm clock and a cell phone. She glared at the damn lamp, and Kurt gave her a look that was a little too full of pity for her tastes. So she glared at him, too.

'We'll be fine. We know it's a murder, we know he was beat to death. That doesn't change. So we just keep on.' She rose to her feet and eyed Kurt's sweaty face, then pointed at the phone. 'Let's make sure we try to get into that after it's dusted for prints. Now I'm going to go get Larry. It's about time we moved this poor man.'

Hank hadn't slept this late in years. There was no office calling him for help. No kids jumping on the bed demanding breakfast. No dog whining to go outside. No Duncan singing along too loudly to Johnny Cash. He figured he'd start missing the first two by tomorrow. The last two . . . would take a lot longer.

Now he just luxuriated in the quiet of Jerry's house. He tried three different kinds of gourmet coffee in the Keurig and found a replay of last night's St Louis Blues hockey game on the satellite TV. It was the perfect background noise for the research he needed to do. He opened the laptop he'd found upstairs in a pile of Jerry's slightly out-of-date computer equipment. He would have brought his own, but it had disappeared right before he left home. He suspected Maggie had hidden it so he couldn't bring work with him. He had to give her credit for trying.

He went to the Closeout Castle website and then the secretary of state's searchable business database. There was nothing interesting with either one. He thought for a minute and then pulled up the federal PACER search page and entered his sheriff department login. He typed in the corporate name, and then slowly put down his beer. The Castle had filed for Chapter 11 bankruptcy three years ago. It was quickly withdrawn, but the fact that the process had even been started meant Lew's company wasn't in good shape.

He dug around some more, but he could only find a few brief mentions on small websites. So he turned to Tina Hardy, who had lived in and around St Louis before moving to Columbia. Hank was just starting on her husband when Jerry walked in.

'Hey, man. How was work?'

'Eh. Fine. Two conference calls that were deadly boring. But good for business. At least they weren't on video. I hate it when the clients want to do those. Then I have to put on a real shirt and look all attentive.'

Hank laughed. Jerry was standing there in an ancient, stretched-out 'Liquor Guns & Ammo' T-shirt. And cargo shorts, despite the fact that it was November.

'Honestly,' Hank said, 'I'm a little surprised that you don't just work out of the house.' He waved a hand up at the vaulted ceiling and four upstairs bedrooms. 'You got plenty of space.'

'Oh, I tried that. Not a good idea. Turns out I was a little too close to the fridge, and the beer, and the five hundred TV channels. I never got anything done.' He pointed at Hank. 'Unlike you. What are you doing? You are most definitely not supposed to be sheriffing.'

Hank sighed. 'You talked to Maggie, didn't you?'

'Yeah. We had a conversation. It was very informative.'

Hank rolled his eyes.

'I was given strict – and, I must say, somewhat limiting – instructions about what I'm supposed to do with you,' Jerry added.

'What's that?'

'Show you a good time – but not a time that involves too much booze, or any college students of any sort.'

Hank burst out laughing.

'I told her she should've come, too,' Jerry said. 'She said she couldn't leave the kids with just her dad. "The house would burn down" were her exact words, I believe.'

'That's for damn sure,' Hank said. 'Dunc is . . . a lot of help, to be fair. But he's also oblivious to a lot of things. Like bedtimes and balanced meals and kitchen cleanup.'

Jerry smirked. 'Sounds like me.'

Hank looked around the immaculate great room. 'You have a maid, don't you?'

'Hell, yes. There are no new leaves to be turned with me, my friend. Once a slob, always a slob.'

'Yeah, I remember Mount Laundry on the floor of our dorm room.'

Jerry ignored that and fished two beers out of the fridge. He flopped down on the couch and handed one to Hank. He squinted at the entertainment center. 'Dude, you've only got half the sound on. Watch this.' He poked at the remote and an action movie appeared on the screen. Two minutes later, a car-chase explosion made the whole house shake. Hank toasted him with his beer bottle and wondered how he could install something like this at home.

SEVEN

Some of the driveways on the street were long, but all of the houses were visible from the road, which was nice. Not like farther out in the county, where property could be a dozen acres and the house set so far back that you had no idea what you were getting into – if you could even get through the gates to begin with.

No one had been home in the house next door to Mr Timmons. Instead of going to the house beyond that, Sam decided to try across the street. It had a pretty clear view of the dead guy's front yard. Hopefully somebody saw something. He trudged up the gravel drive and knocked on the sturdy glass storm door.

The wooden front door immediately swung open. A very short, small-framed older lady peered out at him through the glass and demanded to know who he was. So it was going to be one of those kinds of interviews. He was in full uniform with his Branson County Sheriff's Department badge clearly visible. And based on the speed with which she'd answered the door, the woman had obviously seen him coming up her driveway, which meant she'd been watching the commotion at Timmons's place, too. But she was going to act like she hadn't. Fine. He could play that game.

'Hello, ma'am. I'm very sorry to bother you. My name is Samuel Karnes, and I'm one of your county sheriff's deputies. We are looking into an incident across the street, and I was wondering if I could ask you a few questions.'

Her gaze switched from him to Timmons's house and back again. He could see her reflex inclination to tell him to get the hell off her property battling with her nosy-neighbor curiosity. The Chief always told him, 'Help people want to help you.' He gave it a try.

'I'm sure, ma'am, that you also have some questions for me. Any law-abiding citizen surely would. After all, we're your tax dollars at work. If I could just come in for a moment, we could talk about it.'

He wanted to see what kind of view the lady had from her front window. That would let him judge how much she really was able to see as she monitored the neighborhood, which he was positive she did on a regular basis. He put on his best smile. The woman frowned more. Then she pushed the storm door open.

'Only 'cause I can't hear you through this glass.' She shuffled back a few steps, leaving Sam to catch the door before it smacked his shoulder. He stepped into the little entryway and seemed to fill the entire space. He felt awkward until he realized it was causing the lady to back away and move farther into the house. She led the way into the kitchen, where the one window was fairly high up. She had solved this problem by putting a bar-height table right next to it. It was almost as tall as she was. He wondered how she got up on to the high bar stool, then smothered a smile as he saw the little stepladder next to it.

He shifted to get the right angle and was able to tell that from her perch, she could see all of Timmons's front yard and halfway down the street. Jackpot. He decided to act like she hadn't seen a thing.

'First, ma'am, I wanted to explain what we're doing over there across the street. There was some concern about Mr Timmons's welfare, and so we're checking on that.' He wanted to get everything she knew before he told her about the murder. 'So I'm sure you understand that we'd want to talk with folks in the neighborhood, especially anyone who might be particularly observant. I don't suppose you know anybody like that? Any of your neighbors?'

'My neighbors all work. Then they come home and don't do nothing. Or they barbecue, real loud. And late. Those ones over there do.' She jabbed a finger at a house two doors down that was set much closer to the road. 'It's so a body can't get any sleep. Music going all the time.'

'What about Mr Timmons? Is he noisy, too?'

'Oh, no. He keeps to himself. Keeps his house up nice and don't make a ruckus ever. A very good neighbor.'

'He's retired, correct? Does he have any regular habits?'

Her eyebrows rose in outrage. 'I wouldn't know that. We're not familiar. What gave you that idea, young man?'

'No, no, that's not what I meant.' He felt like she'd just rapped his knuckles with a ruler. 'I just meant – do you ever notice him leaving at a certain time? Or does someone come over to his house every week? Does he have a grandkid visit? Things like that. That's all I meant. Ma'am.'

'Oh. All right then.' She shook a finger at him. 'Because no one's ever accused Madge Lerman of being familiar.'

Sam was quite sure that was true. He smiled encouragingly, and she thought for a moment. Mr Timmons did go out every Tuesday and Thursday morning about nine in the morning, and sometimes on Saturdays. He went out other times, of course, but those times were consistent every week. He was always gone about two or three hours and then came home. As for visitors, there weren't many. Although about two months ago, his car was in the shop and someone came and picked him up for those Tuesday-Thursday times. A gentleman about Mr Timmons's age. In a red Cadillac. Her slow nod showed what she thought of such showy transportation.

'And he did once say something about a son. I got the impression he weren't local, though. Maybe that's where he is, going to visit his kid. And he just forgot to stop the mail.'

Sam congratulated himself. Madge Lerman was exactly what he thought. Eagle-eyed.

'When did you notice the mail start to pile up?'

She thought for a moment. Maybe five or six days ago. And that was unusual. He was usually very prompt about collecting it every day. She would sometimes meet him on the street, as she was also that kind of orderly person. Sam seized on the easy transition.

'Now I need to ask you about anything that was not orderly – anything unusual you saw during that five- or six-day time period. Any unknown people on the street at all?'

Ms Lerman thought about that and started counting things off on her fingers. There was the mailman, of course, but they knew him – a nice black gentleman who always waved. Then there were the Carvers at the end of the street, who were having some sort of repair work done, so there had been trucks coming and going for that on Friday and again Monday. And then there was the barbecue. She couldn't remember which night exactly, but it went to all hours. Loud and smoky and crowded and the barbecue itself out front like this was a no-account trailer park. Which this neighborhood most definitely was not.

'I can't believe they do that. Isn't there some law against doing things like that, out where the whole neighborhood's got to be exposed to it? Don't we have rights? You should do something about that. I've called plenty. I'm glad you're concerned about Mr Timmons and all, but that's the real problem over there.' She crossed her arms over her chest. 'So I'll let you all know when he comes home, and you go deal with those trashy people instead.'

Sam stiffened. He couldn't get out of it now. He had to tell her.

'I, uh, I appreciate your offer to help, Ms Lerman. But . . . we do know where Mr Timmons is.' Her face scrunched up, all puzzled. He fumbled for the words. 'He . . . I . . . I came this morning to check on him . . . and I found him deceased in the residence.'

He took a big gulp of air. She gaped up at him.

'He's dead? Is that what you're saying? He's been over there laying dead and nobody knew?'

She swayed a bit and Sam reached out to steady her. She smacked his hand away, but kept wobbling. He dodged the second swat and took hold of her elbow. Then he helped her up the little stepladder and eased her on to her padded bar stool. He got her a glass of water, left his card on the table, and fled before she could ask how exactly her very good neighbor had died.

The unfortunate Clyde Timmons was on his way up to the pathologist's office in Springfield. Even the voluble Larry Alcoate had been struck speechless at the state of the poor old man's body as he loaded the gurney into his rig. He merely pressed Sheila's hand in between his own two cold ones and then drove away. Stupid man, turning supportive when there was no need, she thought as she swiped at her suddenly itchy eyes.

She gave herself a minute before she walked back into the house and to the bedroom, where Alice and her fingerprint kit had joined Kurt. There was no room for Sheila. She made a sour face that they both ignored out of habit and long experience. She wandered into the spare bedroom, which held nothing but the furniture, an old army coat hanging in the closet, and the faint smell of lavender in the dresser drawers.

She didn't think she could face inventorying the kitchen contents at the moment. She decided to walk the property perimeter and had stepped back on the porch when there was a commotion down the street. Deputy Orvan came jogging along the gravel shoulder of the road and waved her over.

'There's a mailman down there wigging out. I told him it would be a bit until he could get through, and he started ranting about Clive Timmons. Is that the dead guy?'

'*Clyde*. Yeah. You didn't tell him the guy's dead, did you?'

Orvan shook his head.

'Is it the regular guy on this route?'

'How would I know?'

She sighed. 'Is he black?'

'Yeah. Why, does that narrow it down?'

'In this county, yeah. There's only two.'

She walked down the street and found Rodney sitting in his mail truck. He was quite agitated.

'Sheila. Thank God. You'll tell me what's going on. This is about what I told Tyrone, isn't it? What happened to Mr Timmons?'

My, did his voice carry. And his window was down, of course, so he could reach out from the standard-issue boxy white mail truck to stuff mailboxes. She told him that he needed to come sit in her squad car. He spread his arms wide – there was no way he could leave his load unattended. They compromised by him driving closer to the scene and leaving his truck under the hopefully watchful eye of the deputy who'd relieved that bastard Hoch. Then she sat the portly mailman with snow white hair in her passenger seat and pressed a bottle of water into his hands.

'Rodney, honey, I need to ask you some questions. So I need you to calm down. Can you do that for me?'

He took a big swig and nodded. 'Is he OK? Mr Timmons?'

'No, he's not. He's died.' She waited to continue until Rodney had gulped even more water. 'So I need to know some things. What was the first day you noticed that he wasn't collecting his mail?'

'I've heard of this happening,' Rodney said. 'Older customers passing away, and us being the only ones noticing. Us mailmen.' He sniffed a little. 'I never thought it would happen to one of my folks, though.'

Sheila gripped the steering wheel and prayed for patience. Rodney was a sweet man. She and Tyrone had known him forever. His flair for tangents was one of his more endearing qualities. Except today. Today, she needed him to focus. She repeated her question. He thought out loud, going through the aspects of the last week that had lodged in his memory, and finally decided that it was the same day that he'd later had steak for dinner. So, Saturday. Yep, that was the first day there'd still been mail in Mr Timmons's box.

'And he never picked it up again,' Rodney said with more sniffles and another gulp of water. He'd almost drained the bottle. Sheila didn't know what she'd do when he did – it seemed to be the only thing holding him together.

'How well did you know him?' she asked. 'Did he come out and chat?'

She knew many people, especially older ones living alone, certainly did. Tyrone had a devoted following. They baked him cookies at Christmas and made sure he had sunscreen during the summer. He knew who had new grandbabies and financial troubles and too many Amazon orders.

'Not especially,' he was saying. 'If he happened to be outside, he'd surely say hello and ask how I was. But he wouldn't make a point of it, you know? Not like some. I got one lady at the end of my route who rushes out—'

She cut him off. 'So in the times you did talk, what did he say?'

'Oh, we'd jaw about the weather. That's always an easy subject. And he had a garden – round the back, I think. Gave me a basket of tomatoes once. He'd get a gardening catalog. That was always good for a chat. I'd tell him about that wife of mine killing her flowers, and he'd tell me about his vegetables. Oh, I hope he doesn't have a crop going right now . . .'

He drained the rest of the water bottle, his hand shaking the whole time. She noticed her own clenching the steering wheel and turning her knuckles pale.

'It's November, Rodney. I'm pretty sure there's nothing in the garden right now.'

'Oh, well, that's good. It'd break my heart if a crop he worked hard on went to waste.'

If only a neglected garden was the biggest tragedy out here today.

'You mentioned a gardening catalog. What other mail did Mr Timmons get?'

Rodney's hands slammed down into his lap, smashing the plastic water bottle with a sharp crunch.

'Mrs Sheila Turley. I can't tell you that. That's sacred.'

She glared at him.

'OK, not sacred, exactly. But it wouldn't be professional. Mail carriers don't go talking out of turn. You, of all people, know that.'

'Oh, yeah? And I also know that you all share which houses get the heaviest packages or the most overdue notices. So don't give me that.'

He glared back at her. 'Why does it matter anymore anyway? Just leave the poor man be.'

She did not want to tell him about the murder. It would be all over the county before poor Timmons even made it to the morgue.

'You're just going to need to trust me, Rodney. Trust me when I say that the best thing you can do for Mr Timmons right now is help me. I promise you.'

He pressed his lips together and blew out his cheeks. 'All right, dearie. I trust you.' He looked out the window over to the bulging mailbox. 'And that load isn't going to help much, if I recall correctly. It's mostly all junk that everybody gets. Nothing specific about it.'

'What did Timmons get that was specific?'

Her hands strangled the wheel some more as Rodney thought on it for a bit. Then he started to talk, and hallelujah, it was worth the wait. By the time she'd hurriedly dug out her notebook and taken down everything he said, she knew where he banked, where his son lived, what company sent him sleep apnea machine replacement parts, which charities he donated to, which local clubs sent him newsletters, the name of his doctor, and that he was partial to mail-order fruitcakes at Christmas. It was all information that could potentially be in the house, but scattered through messy paperwork or, God forbid, in that chaotic bedroom somewhere. The mailman had at the very least saved her tons of time, and at most, saved the whole investigation.

'Oh, and about the son – Mr Timmons said something once that made me think they don't get on very well. Maybe about him coming to visit, or not coming to visit? I can't remember what it was, but I definitely got that impression.'

She almost kissed his grizzled old cheek. She was stopped by a cautionary finger wagging.

'Now, you keep that promise, young lady. And you tell your husband a thank you for getting you out here so quick. You're both good people, and I'm lucky to know you.'

He hoisted himself out of the squad car and trundled back to his mail truck, still clutching the water bottle in his hand.

EIGHT

A big smoker dominated the front yard. Plastic chairs were scattered around what could – if you were being nice about it – be called a lawn. A portable fire pit sat too near the porch. The house needed a paint job and a lot of new siding. The windows were the old crank kind and most of them were open. Sam hoped that meant they heard things.

He walked past the one parked car and up the dirt driveway, swinging wide so he could maybe get a look into the backyard. It appeared to be all high weeds, which would explain why the barbecue was out front. He redirected toward the front door and gave it a strong knock. It was mid-afternoon, but based on the Chevy in the driveway, somebody might be home. He waited a minute and then knocked again. That got him a thump and a curse from inside the house. It took another minute for a face to appear in the nearest window. It was distorted by the screen, but Sam could still tell it was not happy. The door creaked open.

'What the hell do you want?'

It was a man probably in his mid-thirties who was average height and a little on the skinny side, with brown hair, white skin that didn't see much sun, and a beard that didn't hide the belligerent scowl he was aiming at his visitor.

'Hello, sir. I'm looking into a matter down the street.' Sam pointed at the squad cars in front of Timmons's house. 'And I need to ask you a few questions, just about anything you might have seen going on here on the street. That's all.'

The guy clearly didn't trust him. Or like him. Or believe that

Sam was only interested in other people's business, and not his. He shifted his body to block more of the open doorway.

'Did you know him?' Sam pointed again. 'Mr Timmons, who lived in that house?'

The dude rubbed the sleep out of his eyes and finally looked down the street.

'Damn. What'd he do?'

'He died, actually.'

Now Sam had his full attention.

'We're just trying to figure out when it happened, if anybody had visited him beforehand, that kind of thing,' Sam said quickly. It still felt like the guy was two seconds from slamming the door in his face. 'You seen anything over there in the past week or so?'

The guy rubbed at his beard and thought.

'I don't think so. I work nights, and then sleep all day.' That last bit was said with a pointed glare. Sam just smiled. 'I guess I'd see him poking around in his yard every once in a while, but not since it's got colder.'

'What was he like?' Sam said.

The guy looked at him like he was an idiot. 'Do I look like I'm friends with an old geezer down the street? How the hell would I know?'

Sam chided himself. That hadn't been a good way to phrase it.

'I just meant – did he throw parties? Did he decorate his house for the holidays? Did he get lots of visitors? Did he go peeling out down the road when he left? Stuff like that.'

'Oh. I see.' He shrugged. 'There never really were other cars parked there. And he didn't do no stupid blow-up snowmen or nothing like that.'

Sam subtly shifted his foot forward on to the threshold. It would stop the door slamming all the way shut. 'Did he complain about your barbecues?'

The dude stiffened up instantly. 'What the hell do my barbecues got to do with it? There's nothing . . . wait, it's that bitch, isn't it? You talk to her?'

He stabbed a finger at Ms Lerman's house. Sam pressed on.

'That's why I'm asking. Did Mr Timmons complain like she does?'

'Oh. Nah. He never did. I never talked to him about anything, actually. Didn't even know his name until you showed up.'

Sam scanned the street. 'What do you know about your other neighbors? Anything?'

He shrugged. 'Some of them bitch about me smoking.' He gestured at his hulking smoker and then over at Ms Lerman's house. 'The old prune is the worst. She doesn't like anything, including fun and good food.'

Hmmm. 'Do you know how she gets along with everybody else?'

'Oh, she's a bitch to everybody. Those folks over there had a broken-down car on the street that they couldn't move for a while and she was over there all the time. And that house with the bushes, she bitches at them for not trimming. I wish it'd been her you found dead.'

Well, that was honest. Sam stopped his tirade.

'Did she get on Mr Timmons at all?'

The dude rubbed at his face again. 'I don't remember seeing her over there or nothing. But like I said, I sleep days.'

'Where do you work that there's a night shift?' Sam wanted to know more about this neighbor, but he was also genuinely curious. Branson was not a twenty-four-hour town.

'I'm a security guard. I do graveyard at the Gallagher Enterprises warehouse.'

Sam's eyes widened. He was unaware that the biggest real estate developer in the county had a warehouse. 'Oh. Is that a good gig?'

It was OK, said the guy, whose name turned out to be Frank Hord. Kind of boring, but the pay wasn't bad. They talked about that for a minute and then about the smoker's abilities with different types of meat. That topic softened him up for what Sam planned as his last question.

'Oh, hey,' he said as he turned to go. 'You got any room-mates or anything? Who are awake during the day and might have seen something?'

He had two. Sam walked away with names and phone numbers. And a venison barbecue tip he planned to try as soon as possible.

*   *   *

'Dude, I do not feel like going out. This is perfection right here.' Hank spread his arms to take in Jerry's massive living room.

'And it'll be here in the morning,' Jerry said. 'But Wednesday night at the brewery only comes once a week. And they'll have the Mizzou basketball game on in a little bit. So that's where we're going.'

'That sounds like a bar with happy-hour specials and lots of people. I don't want to do that.'

'It's adults, don't worry. It's not a college kid hangout.'

That was not a denial, Hank thought. He gave Jerry his best apathetic stare and was met with a grin.

'Go put on a nicer shirt. We've got to make it in time for dollar pints.'

Hank snorted. 'Why? You're not exactly on a college budget anymore.'

'It's the principle of it. If cheap booze is possible, you have to take advantage. It's one of the tenets of life.'

Hank refused to move off the couch. He hadn't been in the mood to socialize since the teens' car accident. They weren't ever going to be able to again. Why should he? He settled deeper into the soft leather seat.

'Plus,' Jerry said, 'I'm buying, and I refuse to spend more than ten bucks on your ass.'

That broke him. He chuckled in spite of himself and trudged off to his room to change clothes. A half hour later they walked into a brew pub with polished brass fixtures and soaring ceilings. Behind a glass wall, large, burnished copper tanks sat busy fermenting more of whatever Jerry was about to foist on him.

He started to insist on a soda, but Jerry had already managed to grab the bartender – despite the three-deep crowd at the bar.

'You come here pretty often, don't you?'

Jerry ignored him and snagged the two pints the bartender set on the polished bar. Hank took the stout and they moved away toward the tables. Hank headed for a booth in the corner, but Jerry stopped at a tall one right in the middle of things and refused to move any farther. Hank glared at him.

'Dude. You're going to have a good time, and you're going to interact with the server, and you're going to stop looking like you're eating a lemon while passing a kidney stone. I'm prepared to work hard all night to make it happen. And you know how much I hate workin' hard. So start drinking and make it easier on me.'

He took a huge swig of his IPA and tried to flag down a waiter. Hank sighed and attempted to make himself more comfortable on the hard chair. He sipped at his stout and pulled out his phone. When Jerry turned around and saw, he snatched it before Hank could stop him.

'Your reaction time's gotten bad, old man,' he said. 'I'll just keep this for the evening. No hiding behind a screen. Time to be a social human person.'

Hank scowled. Jerry responded with a smug smile and resumed trying to place an order for mozzarella cheese sticks. With nothing to do, Hank was forced to look around. It was a nice establishment, he had to admit.

There'd certainly been nothing like it when they were going to school here. He chuckled to himself. Even if there had been, they couldn't have afforded its regular prices. Penny pitchers were more their speed, especially with the cost of living in the dorms and then the rent on their apartment once they moved out of the tiny room in Hudson Hall.

There were very few in tonight's crowd who could be pegged as college kids. It seemed to be mostly young professionals coming in after work. Business casual clothes and 'I'm available' expressions. He and Jerry seemed to be on the older end of things. He hoped that meant they'd be left alone.

'Hi.'

Great. She'd even snuck up on them, coming up from just beyond his left peripheral vision. Some trained observer he was.

There were two of them. Probably about thirty years old. He contemplated fleeing for the bathroom, but Jerry nixed that idea with a swift under-the-table kick that about kneecapped him, so he was in no condition to go anywhere for a while. Jerry immediately engaged in conversation. Hank stuck to nursing his beer and randomly nodding. When was the damn basketball game going to come on? Then he could act like he was here for that, and not for the pickup potential.

At least Jer was carrying the conversation. They were all

chatting about some road construction project and the nightmare traffic.

'What do you think?' the brunette asked him.

'Um, I'm in from out of town, actually. So, I just have this guy drive me around.' He pointed his pint glass at Jerry, who flashed a smile that Hank knew wasn't intended for him. The brunette shifted a little closer to Jerry and smiled back.

'So are you here in Columbia on business?' the one with blonde hair asked Hank while eyeing her friend.

He shrugged. 'Not really. I just haven't seen him in a while. Thought I'd come up and stay a few days.'

She nodded. 'What about your wife?'

She'd noticed the wedding ring.

'She had to work,' he said.

'My wife's at work, too. Rachel,' she pointed at the brunette, 'made me come out tonight. Said she needed a wingman.'

Rachel was currently leaning closer to Jerry and laughing. Hank wanted to slap a sign on him that said 'Just Survived Horrible Divorce – Approach With Caution'. Instead, he finished off his beer.

'Yeah, I'm starting to think that's my function tonight, too,' he said. 'What does your wife do?'

She worked at Jesse Hall, the university's main administration building, and had to be there tonight to coordinate an event. So that left the blonde, whose name was Lisa, at the mercy of Rachel and her desire to go out. 'She wouldn't take no for an answer.'

'I know how that goes,' Hank said, pointing at Jerry while trying not to look directly at the high-wattage flirting.

Lisa laughed. 'And what do you do?'

Jerry's attention shifted so fast Hank almost jumped.

'No, no,' he interrupted, airily waving his hand at them both. 'None of that. No work talk. He's here on vacation, and isn't allowed to even think about it.'

Hank was shocked he'd even noticed their conversation. He was a little irked. It wasn't like talking about his job would send him into a funk right there in the middle of the bar. Probably. He started to say something, but Jerry kept the diversion going by ordering another round and then leaning forward conspiratorially.

'Besides, it's more fun to tell stories about ol' Hank during college. Did you know he set fire to the dining hall our sophomore year?'

Well, that couldn't stand. Hank corrected the story to include Jerry's significant role and the two of them were off and running, trading anecdotes until the basketball game came on. After that, the whole bar turned into a raucous party. The season was young, and hopes were still high. Mizzou fans knew to seize the moment while they could.

NINE

I t was dark and cold and quiet when Sheila let herself into her office. She needed to get several things done before she headed back out to the scene to meet Kurt at seven a.m. She fired up her computer and turned on the little space heater she kept under her desk. It was time to track down Lonnie Timmons.

She'd asked the morgue up in Springfield not to notify the next of kin. She wanted to gauge the estranged son's reaction herself. And find out if he'd been anywhere near Branson in the past week. Until she had proof that he hadn't been, he was at the top of her suspect list.

She settled in with her travel mug full of hot tea and started pulling up databases. Rodney had remembered a Cedar Rapids return address, so she started there. That Iowa city had nothing, so she widened her search and found him in Des Moines. Which was only a six-hour drive away. Not a quick jaunt, but certainly doable.

He had past addresses in Independence and Lee's Summit, both municipalities near Kansas City. There was a gap of time in between, though. She poked around some more and still came up empty, so she switched over to the fun part and ran a criminal background check. Bingo. Lonnie Timmons had been a guest of Jackson County, Missouri, five years ago, and then again two years later. Both times the convictions had been for

theft, but the mere months-long sentences had the feel of plea
deals. She wondered what the original charges were. She dashed
off email requests to the two police departments for their investigative reports, and then pulled out a new notepad. Ten minutes
later, she had a loose chronology written down. It was at least
enough to be able to ask some questions when she got the junior
Timmons on the phone.

She left a message just before seven, identifying herself and
saying only that she needed to speak with him. He called back
immediately.

'Why you calling me?'

'Lonnie Timmons?' she said.

'Yeah. What do you want?'

'I need to ask you what your father's name is, sir.'

'Why?'

'Sir.' This time her tone had steel in it. She did not have time
for twenty questions.

'OK, fine. His name's Clyde Timmons. He lives in Branson
County, which you obviously know, since you're the damn
county sheriff. What do you want me for? Did he get in trouble
or somethin'?'

That was one way to put it.

'We're trying to sort some things out, and I need to ask when
the last time was that you talked to him.'

Lonnie started to protest, but then seemed to think better of
it. 'I don't remember exactly. A while back.'

'I need you to narrow it down. Does that mean a week ago?
A month ago? A year ago?'

He thought for a little bit too long. She made a note to get
a warrant for his phone records.

'I guess maybe it was about six months ago.'

'And when did you last see him in person?'

More silence. The phone line was crackling with irritation
in both directions.

'I don't see how this is any of your business.'

'What kind of relationship do you and your dad have?'

Lonnie let out a derisive snort before he could stop himself.
Sheila waited.

'Why don't you ask him?' he finally said. 'I'm sure he'd be

happy to share his opinions with you. I'm not going to talk about this anymore. If he's in trouble, he can get himself out.'

Sheila heard rustling that sounded like him moving toward the hang-up button.

'Sir, your father has died.'

The rustling stopped.

'Huh. How about that. Well. Huh.'

He fell silent. Sheila waited, but he stayed quiet.

'Where are you now, sir?' she finally said. 'Is there someone who can come be with you?'

He laughed a little. 'I'm not *that* broken up, lady. I don't need any hand-holding. I'll be fine.'

She pressed him. She wanted him on the record. He told her he was at his apartment in Des Moines, but he could easily be lying. She'd check that when the warrant came through for his cell phone records.

'What was it, a heart attack or something?'

'It wasn't. Your father was murdered. We found him yesterday.'

There was a long intake of breath. She waited. It took fifty-two seconds, according to the wall clock, for him to speak.

'Are you sure?'

'Oh, yes. We're quite sure. We've started a homicide investigation.'

'Oh. So, uh, you got any suspects?'

It was a perfectly reasonable question, but the way he said it pricked at her. Like he was really asking, 'How worried should I be?' She told him she couldn't comment on any of that and asked if he would be coming down to Branson.

'I don't have to, do I? It's not like I'll be doing a funeral.'

But oh, did she want to meet this guy. She tapped her pen against the desk.

'I certainly understand that. We'll just settle up all of his assets, then? We have procedures with local charities to—'

'Wait? What? No, no. I'll be there. Don't do anything. That's mine.'

Greed. Such a useful tool. She smiled and assured him that her department – which had no authority to do that without going to court first – would be happy to wait for him. He told her he could be there by tomorrow.

'Wonderful,' she said. 'I look forward to meeting you.'

That got her another snort and a curt hang-up. She laughed, because she hadn't been kidding. She was quite eager to meet the errant son who hadn't bothered to ask normal questions about where or when his father was murdered. She looked at the time and realized she was late to meet Kurt at the scene. On the way out to Nighthawk Lane, she made a call to the Des Moines PD watch commander and asked if he had someone available to do a quick observational drive-by for her. When she gave him the name, he used the term 'low-life asshat' and said he'd be happy to help. She finished the drive with a smile on her face.

Bill Ramsdell sat slouched in his squad car. Sam could hear some sort of podcast as he tapped on the window. The glass slid down and Bill blinked at him.

'You OK, man? You look a little out of it.' He handed over the coffee he'd picked up on his way out to the Timmons's house. The poor guy's face lit up, and he downed half of it before speaking.

'Graveyard's bad enough. But graveyard where you're just sitting in one spot the whole time? Torture. Worse than water-boarding, man. I will never complain about patrol again.' He opened the car door and stiffly climbed out, still clutching his coffee like a life preserver.

'So I'm guessing nothing happened?' Sam said, sipping at his own coffee. There was no breeze, so the trees were still and the house itself looked almost peaceful, if you didn't count the crime scene tape all over the place.

'Nah. Not a thing. I did a walk-around every hour or so. No street traffic – except two people got home about one a.m. over there.'

He pointed at the barbecue house. Sam nodded. Those must be Frank Hord's roommates. He'd go over and talk to them this morning.

'And about an hour ago, the lights came on there.' Bill nodded subtly in the direction of Madge Lerman's house. 'Been watching me ever since. Like constantly. A little creepy, if you ask me.'

'Yeah. I talked to her yesterday. She's definitely the neigh-borhood busybody. Apparently she's always complaining, or telling folks what to do. No one on the street can stand her.'

Bill made a scoffing sound. 'I don't blame them.'

They stood for a minute in the cold pre-dawn air and worked on their coffee.

'How much longer you on graveyard?' Sam asked.

Only another week, Bill said, then he'd be back to days. Everyone rotated through, so that no one was stuck on that duty all the time. That was the one good thing about Sheila's overtime crack-down, he said. It was less likely that deputies would be pressured into picking up those crappy shifts for others. Some of the younger guys got taken advantage of that way.

Sam laughed. He knew all about that. Bill was a decent guy – he'd never done it. Somebody like Hoch, on the other hand, did it all the time and then somehow finagled primo day shift overtime. Sam thought about that for a moment.

'So, uh, that's a good point, about the graveyard overtime. What do you think about the new policy, like, as a whole?' He cringed inwardly. What a terrible segue. Thank goodness Bill seemed too tired to notice.

'Meh.' Bill shrugged. 'It looks all fine and dandy on paper. Course, that's her specialty, isn't it? Sitting there in her office and working stuff out on paper – not being out in the real world. What's she going to do later this winter when people start calling in sick? How're you going to cover those shifts without overtime?'

Sam was pretty sure that Sheila had a plan for that, but he kept quiet and just nodded as Bill continued.

'And don't think folks haven't thought of that. They're thinking it's the way to prove their point. Turn things back to the way it was.' He gave Sam a look out of the corner of his eye that said a lot more than his words were doing. 'Some folks, anyways. Folks that don't like new things. Or new people.'

He fell silent and started swishing around the dregs of his coffee. Sam stared at the ground. He hadn't realized it was quite that bad. He knew the overtime ban wouldn't go over well. But now it sounded like there was some kind of actual organized sick-out in the works. Which would be a direct challenge to

Sheila, and to Hank. And Bill, good guy that he was, was standing here telling the deputy known to work closely with them both. He forced his gaze back up and looked at Bill.

'That's interesting,' he said slowly. 'Definitely something to think on.'

Bill nodded. 'You should. I wouldn't want you caught in anything.'

An engine rumble came from down the street and they both turned to see Kurt drive up in the department's crime scene van. Bill moved to lift the perimeter tape so Kurt could get closer to the house. Sam grabbed the other end and the van crunched down the gravel driveway. Kurt was almost done unpacking equipment when Sheila pulled up. She hopped out of her cruiser and approached them with a smile.

'Good morning, gentlemen. How is everything?'

Bill reported on his boring night of guard duty and asked when she wanted him back in the evening.

'Oh, Lord no. You don't have to do this two nights in a row. I'll get somebody else. You just report for your regular patrol shift – although I might need you to also cover a little farther east than normal if I pull that deputy off to come sit here.'

'I can do that, no problem,' Bill said. 'That's a lot better than having to sit still outside a dead man's house.'

She smiled sympathetically and told him he could go home. As he opened his car door, he looked once more at Sam, who could only respond with a tight nod as Sheila stood right next to him. Bill hung a U and sped away. Sheila turned and smacked her hands together with a grin. Sam took a step back.

'Why are you in such a good mood?'

She told him about finding the low-life son. That put a smile on Sam's face, too.

'We need some context, though,' Sheila said. 'We've got to track down some friends. Somebody who can tell us something about this guy. Alice is still cataloging all the paperwork, but she did find a few mailings.'

She pulled out her notebook. The local Salvation Army, the Missouri Botanical Garden, the United States Bocce Federation.

'Can I take those?' Sam said. He told her about the red

Cadillac that nosy Ms Lerman mentioned. 'I can ask around at those places, see if anybody knows that kind of car.'

'Good idea. And I'm going to go talk to his bank. See what I can wheedle out of them before the warrant comes through.'

They agreed to touch base at lunchtime, and Sheila turned to go into the house.

'Oh,' Sam said. He'd meant to ask her first thing, but he'd forgotten. 'What'd Hank say?'

She stopped and patted at her hair for a little too long before she turned back around to face him. He gaped at her.

'You haven't told him, have you? You didn't call him?'

'I did not. He is on vacation.'

Sam's mouth was still hanging open. He snapped it shut. 'Are you nuts?' he said without thinking.

She stiffened and her nostrils flared alarmingly. He held up his hands.

'No, I just mean – he'd want to know. You know him. He'd totally want to know about it.'

'I know that,' she said. 'And I thought about it. And decided that we can brief him fully when he gets back. And that will be fine.'

She arched an eyebrow. Which meant that the discussion was over. Sam decided the safest thing to do was hustle his ass back to the car and get started on those newsletters. And make sure he was nowhere near when Hank came home and found out there'd been a murder and nobody'd told him.

TEN

She lived in a newish condo development off Columbia's Old Highway 63. Hank parked down the street and watched it for a bit. People in surrounding units left for work, hustling out with lunch bags and attaché cases. Lots of solitary middle-aged people. Probably divorced. The whole condo development gave off that vibe.

He watched Tina Hardy's quiet unit from the obscenely

comfortable BMW. Jerry had offered him the Acura, and it had
taken everything Hank had to say no. The coupe was less
conspicuous and the majority of his day would be surveillance,
so he'd quickly grabbed the Bimmer key and left before he
changed his mind. Now at least he could sink into the leather
headrest and cushy lumbar support while he waited for an empty
street. And his aching head needed the comfort. They'd closed
down the bar after so many beers, Hank had lost count. Damn
Jerry. He squinted in the feeble winter sunlight and sipped his
coffee. Finally, things cleared out enough and he got out of his
cocoon and walked to Hardy's door.

The potted plant on the doorstep was dead and the doormat
was dusty. There was no answer when he rang the bell – he
hadn't expected there would be. He stood for a minute and
then fumbled and dropped the BMW key fob. He knelt down
to pick it up and quickly looked under the mat. No key. He
shifted and sent the car key sliding across the step toward
the plant. That let him reach for it with one hand while
balancing his other on the plant stand. He felt around the
bottom water dish and tilted the plant to the side. Bingo. A
standard size key was taped to the bottom of the pot. He
yanked it off, grabbed his car key and rose to his feet. He'd
have to think seriously about whether he was actually going
to use it, though. If he was in uniform, he could just let
himself in. This not-acting-in-an-official-capacity approach
was a pain in the ass.

He got back in the car and after tooling around the neighborhood, headed toward downtown and the county courthouse.
Parking was a bitch, not only because of the government crowd,
but also because the area was only a few blocks north of the
university. Infringing college students always nabbed any
parking spots they could get. He finally found a spot, squeezing
the BMW in between a cargo van and a battered SUV and
praying it didn't get scratched.

The courthouse was too grand a setting for the grubbing he
needed to do. It had soaring three-story columns along the front
and a domed roof. He made his way to the clerk's office and
immediately found Hardy's divorce case number. He requested
the file and sat down to read.

It was standard in its awfulness, her divorce. It was interesting to learn about it in such a sterile way. Hank was usually right in the middle of it – taking the report of a man whose car had been keyed by an angry wife, or stepping in between yelling spouses, or calling the domestic violence helpline as a woman sat and sobbed on the curb while her handcuffed husband was bundled into a cruiser. Thankfully there wasn't anything that bad in the file of Tina and Darwood Hardy. The divorce decree sat on the top and underneath were filings that divvied up the couple's assets. A house in an older section of Columbia that they'd sold outright, dividing the proceeds right down the middle. A retirement account that he'd tried to hang on to, but a judge had split that in half, too.

He kept flipping through, going further back in time. And then he froze. There was a protection order. Tina claimed Darwood had threatened her, trashed her home office, and kidnapped the dog. The order required him to move out of the house and take an anger management course. This was almost a year ago. The order had been in effect for six months and hadn't been renewed. That didn't make much sense. Had she let the guy move back in? Or did they just amicably decide to throw in the marriage towel and go their separate ways?

Somehow neither of those possibilities felt right. Hank returned the file, extracted his car from its tiny space, and drove over to the house the Hardys had sold. This time as he parked on the street, he hoped that there were neighbors around. He got lucky immediately. A gentleman across the road and two doors down was out raking leaves. Hank introduced himself as a friend of Tina Hardy's family.

'She hasn't been in touch lately, and I just thought that since I'm here in Columbia, I'd ask after her,' Hank said. He'd decided to pretend that he thought the Hardys still lived in the nice single-story brick ranch with a detached garage. 'Have you seen her around lately?'

'Oh, they haven't lived there in about six months,' the old man said, leaning against his rake and pushing his wool hat farther back on his head.

Hank tried to look surprised and mumbled something about writing the forwarding addresses down in the wrong order.

'I think they sold it as part of the divorce. Because then they were both gone, just like that.' The man snapped his fingers.

'Was she the only one living in it for a while?'

'You mean, did she kick him out?' he chortled. 'She sure did. They had a huge ruckus one night. So much yelling and crashing around. Folks heard it all up and down the street. She had somebody come out the next day and change the locks. She still always looked jumpy after that, though.'

'Did he ever come around again?'

'Oh, we'd see him on occasion. A lot of times when she wasn't there. Honestly' – the old man shook his head and sighed – 'both of them were just ripe for the divorce – always snipping at each other in the yard, or going out alone. There was no happiness in that house, I can tell you that.'

Interesting. He asked a few more questions, but the old guy wasn't able to tell him much else. He started wielding his rake again and then paused.

'You ought to go talk to Lorna.' He pointed at the house right next door to the unhappy Hardys. 'She had a front row seat to the whole thing. Didn't much appreciate the view, either.'

Hank thanked him and immediately headed across the street. Lorna's door opened before he'd finished pushing the doorbell.

'I've been watching you through my ring,' said the woman, who was that certain kind of slender that made her look much taller than she really was. She had perfect posture and gray hair pulled back in a loose bun. Her hands were bare.

'Not *a* ring. That Ring.' She pointed at the doorbell, which was one of those video monitoring systems. 'It catches a fairly wide section of the street. What were you talking to Tom about?'

Hank gave her his family-friend line. Lorna Shelton, unfortunately, was a much sharper tack than Raking Tom had been.

'If she hasn't lived here in so long, why do you care what we've got to say? Shouldn't you be asking her current neighbors if they've seen her?'

Hank shifted uncomfortably on the front step. His head still hurt and the piercing look she was giving him wasn't helping. She was seeing right through him not only to his hangover but also to the pack of lies he was carting around. He looked over at the Hardys' old home for a moment and made a decision.

'You're right. And I plan on it when those folks come home from work. But here's the thing. It's not just that her family hasn't heard from her. It's that no one has heard from her. She hasn't shown up for work in weeks. There's been no contact.'

He raised his eyebrows, hoping Lorna's astuteness would do the rest. It did.

'Oh, dear. So you want to know more about the ex-husband, don't you?'

Hank nodded. Her spine straightened even more, which he wouldn't have thought possible. She'd made a decision. She gestured around the side of the house.

'If you'd come around the back . . .'

Hank stepped away so she could come out the front door. She closed it behind her and led the way toward the backyard.

'They lived here for about six years. When they moved in, they were just normal. An ordinary couple, you know. They didn't seem to be newlyweds or anything. They had that sense of . . . being established.'

'And what were they like, individually?'

Lorna thought that over. Darwood was friendly in passing, but certainly wasn't the chatty type. He always had his satchel and his books and that sort of thing and seemed to be more interested in getting to whatever more important place he was going than he was in talking to the neighbors.

'He thought very highly of himself, but he's certainly not the first college professor I've known who's like that,' she said.

Tina was the one who brought over cookies at Christmas time and asked about Lorna's grandkids. It was like she knew she needed to be the one to soften her husband's sharp edges. She was quiet, but not shy. Just someone who came across as thoughtful and deliberate. She was originally from the St Louis suburb of Chesterfield and moved to Columbia after she met and married Darwood. That was about ten years ago. She worked a couple different places in the time she lived next door, always as some kind of executive assistant, although Lorna unfortunately couldn't remember which places.

'She just seemed to like to move around. Like she'd go in

somewhere and kind of master it, and then need something new. So she'd switch jobs. She was looking for a new one when everything started to change. That was about a year and a half ago.'

By now, they were in Lorna's meticulously landscaped backyard. She stopped and considered the Hardy house for a long moment before speaking again. He got the feeling she was gathering things she'd sensed during that time but had never put into formal thoughts, let alone words.

They never went anywhere together. They kept different schedules. The whole place seemed shuttered and miserable, which was a silly thing to say about a house, but it was true. Every once in a while she would hear arguments, voices that were tight and angry. But the yelling only came once. It was a Sunday night about this time last year. Chilly. But their windows were open. There was crashing and swearing and such inside the house, and then Darwood had come bursting out the back door. He was disheveled, which was quite odd. He was always fastidious about his appearance – very professorial at all times with his pressed jeans and blazers. But that night, he wore sweats and a grungy sweater and carried a baseball bat. He raged around a bit – there really was no other way to describe it – and then went back in the house. That was when Lorna went for her phone to call the police. But then, just as she was about to dial, he came out the front. Instead of the bat, he was holding the dog. It was Tina's little Pekinese and she was going crazy. Darwood got in his car with the dog and sped off.

'And I just stood there with the phone in my hand. I didn't know what to do. He was gone, so I felt a little silly calling the cops at that point.'

Hank cringed. If only she had. Then there'd be a police report. Concrete documentation of what sounded like a knock-down-drag-out.

'But then I thought, well, what if she's not OK? So I went over.'

He stared at her in surprise. She hadn't seemed the type to insert herself directly in something like this. She pointed toward the Hardy back door.

'I was in my kitchen and so I came out my back door and

walked over to hers. It was wide open still. The kitchen was a war zone. Broken dishes and things all over. I called her name and she came out from the front room. And *she* was holding the bat. And I thought – well, my first thought was *Good for her*, to be honest – but I thought that I should still maybe call the police, or an ambulance or something. But she said no. She said it was fine. And there wouldn't be any more problems after that.'

Lorna turned and looked at Hank directly. 'And there weren't. He came back a few times that I saw, but you could tell it was just to move his things out, and it was when she wasn't home. And then the house went on the market this spring.'

By that point, she was working for Lew, Hank thought. He asked.

'Her last job? It was at some retail company, working for the president. She seemed to enjoy it, said she was still trying to get the lay of the land, so to speak. I don't think she ever told me the name of the company, though. I'm sorry.'

'That's OK.' Hank smiled. 'Have you heard from her since she moved?'

'No,' she said with a smile. 'We were friendly neighbors, but we weren't friends.'

Lorna seemed to be a person with a clear-eyed view of interpersonal relationships, including ones she was part of. That was a pretty rare thing.

'I think she was looking forward to making a fresh start of things. She didn't say as much – and she didn't talk about the divorce process at all – but I got that feeling. That she was relieved to be leaving the house behind.'

Hank asked a few more questions, but Lorna couldn't tell him much else about Tina Hardy. He started to walk back to the street but then thought of something. He turned back.

'What about the dog? Did Darwood bring it back?'

'Little Ginger? No. He told Tina he didn't have her. Kept insisting that he didn't know where she was. As far as I know, she's never seen the poor thing again.'

ELEVEN

Every once in a while, something good came out of working in a small town. Sheila hoped this was one of those times. There was only one branch of Timmons's bank in Branson. It was known for its friendly and personalized service. Hell, they even handed out doggie treats in the drive-thru if your pet was in the car with you. She'd heard that Hank's Guapo had quite the reputation amongst the tellers. She doubted it was because of his good behavior.

She bypassed the line at the window and headed for the manager's office. Pete Vanderlan met her at the door.

'I saw you drive up, Ms Turley. Hard to miss that car. Are you here on official business?'

She said yes in a serious enough tone that he showed her right in and shut the door behind them. She took a seat in front of his desk and pulled out a sheaf of papers.

'Uh-oh. Someone's in trouble. Serious trouble, for you to be coming by in person. Usually, we just get those subpoenas in the mail.'

He plopped down behind the desk and pulled his keyboard forward.

'It's not a civil subpoena, Pete. It's a search warrant. Signed by Judge Sedstone late last night. I need to look at somebody's accounts. And safe deposit box, if he's got one.'

Pete's toothy grin disappeared. He smoothed down his tie – which had to have been a Father's Day gift, it was so atrocious – and leaned forward eagerly. 'What did he do?'

'He got murdered.'

Pete's jaw sagged. 'Oh, my. Good Lord. How awful. One of our customers. Oh, my.' He paused and tried to collect himself. 'Who was it?'

'Clyde Timmons.'

'Oh, dear. He was a lovely gentleman. Always came in, never used the drive-thru.' He started to type with shaking fingers.

'He had three accounts with us. Checking, savings, and a CD. He and Nell paid off their mortgage nine years ago. Just before she passed away.'

He had to stop. Several sniffs and a tissue dab later, he was able to keep going. He didn't have much routine interaction with Mr Timmons, but had always enjoyed working with him on loans and such. He stopped typing. There was one thing Ms Turley might be interested in.

'Mr Timmons did make an early withdrawal from the CD. Which was quite surprising. Not consistent with his saving profile at all. Twenty-two thousand dollars.'

She moved to get a look at his computer screen. The money had been moved into his checking account after incurring an interest penalty.

'Where?' Sheila said, pointing at the line item. 'Where did it go?'

'I have no idea,' Pete said, sniffles forgotten. 'He insisted on it in cash.'

Well now. 'How much did that transfer leave in his CD account then?' she asked.

'Less than twenty thousand.'

'And that account is pretty much his major savings, right?'

'As far as we go, yes. He could have money somewhere else, but – and I don't mean to sound pompous here – if he's had everything with us since taking out a mortgage forty-nine years ago, plus several auto loans and his everyday banking business, then I think it's safe to say that, yeah, we probably have his only savings.'

Sheila squinted at the computer screen. Didn't they have alerts for stuff like this? Elder abuse training? For when old people unexpectedly withdraw large amounts of money? She started to say that, and then thought of a different way to come at it.

'Can you tell how the CD thing occurred?' she said. 'Like, at the window out there? Or was it through online banking?'

'Oh, it was here. I tried to talk him out of it. Even made him take a cooling off period. But he came back and insisted.' He stood. 'Let's go out to the girls. They'll be able to tell you more.'

Sheila barely kept from rolling her eyes at his word choice as she followed him out to the two teller windows. There was no one in line at the moment. Pete got all toothy again and was surely about to drop the word 'murder' like the bombshell it was. Sheila quickly laid her hand on his arm and asked to go behind the glassed-in counter. He let her in with some grumbling and left to go copy the warrant paperwork for his files.

The two women – one in her mid-fifties with short salt-and-pepper hair and a blonde in her late twenties, both white – looked like they were about to sit down for a particularly good *Law & Order* episode.

'You were in with Pete an awful long time,' the blonde one said. 'Are you investigating something?'

'Yes,' Sheila said. 'It's about one of your customers, and—'

The gray-haired one interrupted. 'Did they steal money? Embezzle, maybe?'

She had to smile. It made sense that financial crimes would be the first thing to occur to these two. She, on the other hand, would immediately think of violent death if police asked her about someone. To each their own.

She said no, there had been no theft, just a death. She gave them Timmons's name and showed them a photo of him and his wife that Kurt had found in the poor man's bedroom. She'd had to take it out of the smashed frame. Both ladies nodded immediately.

'Oh, yes,' said the older one. 'He's a regular. Been a customer since who knows when.'

He didn't like the ATM, she said. So mostly he came in to withdraw the kind of small amounts that most people would use the outside cash machine for.

'I think he was lonely. We gave him someone to talk to.'

'What did he talk about?' Sheila asked.

'Oh, all the usual things – the weather, the traffic, the tourists. Nothing real personal,' the older one said, then paused. 'He had started mentioning an activity lately. He'd taken something up. Tennis? No, it wasn't that. But something in a group, that he was enjoying very much. Shoot, I can't think what it was.'

'Did anyone ever come in with him?' Sheila asked.

The woman tapped her chin. 'No. It was always just him, since his wife died. Although he did mention his son once.'

Sheila smiled encouragingly. She didn't want to taint the older woman's recollection with a skewed follow-up question, so she forced herself to stay quiet. The teller thought for a moment.

'It was something negative,' she finally said. 'Like, "My son is coming to town, and he always needs money." Something along those lines.'

Sheila asked about the CD withdrawal. The older one pointed to the blonde, who was still holding the photo and tracing over Timmons's face with her finger. She hadn't yet said anything. The older one elbowed her. 'I remember you telling me about that one, Allison. You going to say anything here?'

'Shush. I'm replaying it in my head.'

That drew a shrug from the older one that was half-exasperated and half-indulgent. Finally, Allison was ready. She handed the photo back to Sheila.

'A week or two ago he came in, and I was expecting him to just get out his normal forty bucks. But he didn't. He told me he needed to cash out part of his CD.'

'For twenty-two grand?' Sheila said. 'Shouldn't that raise some red flags, with his age and all?'

Heck, yeah, Allison said. She asked him all the questions on the elder abuse form, and then still didn't give it to him. She walked him right over to Mr Vanderlan's office instead.

'Did he tell you anything about why he wanted to take out that much money?'

Allison shook her head. 'He just kept saying it was for the best. And he looked sad and happy at the same time.'

'That doesn't make sense,' the older one said.

'Well, that's how he looked. If you hadn't been busy flirting with that podiatrist at your window, you would've noticed.'

The older one got red and changed the subject. 'Did something happen when Mr Timmons died? You all don't usually come in here when our clients pass away.'

Sheila told her without including any details. The two women reached for each other.

'I need you both to think once more, just about any little

thing that you can remember regarding Mr Timmons. Even if you don't think it's important.'

She let them sniffle for a minute and was just about to move to the door when the older one spoke.

'There was one day, maybe a bit before the CD withdrawal, when he came in and did get his normal forty bucks. Then he walked away and I remember I laughed, because he didn't grab his lollipop like he always did.' She pointed to the big glass bowl on the customer side of the counter. 'I grabbed one and was going to go give it to him in the parking lot. But a car pulled up quick as anything, and Clyde climbed in and they raced off.'

'I don't suppose you remember what kind of car?' Sheila said.

'Oh, yes. It was a cherry red Caddy.'

Darwood Hardy taught in the English department. He did one general freshman course, but his specialty was some esoteric, horrible-sounding literature from a place Hank was pretty sure wasn't even a country anymore. He was, according to the faculty web page, 'the world's foremost expert'. Hank rolled his eyes. Then he put away his phone and got out of the car. He'd deliberately parked on the far eastern edge of campus so he would have to walk through it. He strolled through Lowry Mall and passed by Ellis Library, where he'd spent many an evening working on research papers during his last two years of school.

Things had boomed on campus since then. There was a student recreation center that was a cross between the Taj Mahal and an Olympic training facility. There was a new quad, south of the old quad. There were actual non-nauseating dining options in the student union instead of just limp fries and greasy pizza. But Lowry Mall was still paved in bricks, activists still tilted at windmills in Speakers' Circle, and some of the oldest academic departments still occupied their premium spots in grand buildings around the center of campus.

He headed for Tate Hall, which housed the English department and sat just to the southeast of the original quad behind Jesse Hall. He stopped and stared at the administration building's bright white dome and remembered Jerry's guffaw as they made their way inside that night during their senior year. He walked a short way around the huge building to get a better view of the dome and noticed a bounce to his step. Even with all the changes, this place made him feel good. The vise around his chest had eased since he got to town, and now as he walked around the campus, he felt a little twinge of normal. Not quite as off balance and suffocated and desolate as he had been since the crash.

He walked through the double doors and asked the first person he saw. She directed him down several hallways. He ended up in front of the Foremost Expert's closed office door. There were no posted office hours. He sighed. Now he'd have to find the department secretary. He was about to head back down the hall when the door opposite swung open. A woman who was the right age to be a grad student popped out with her arms full of books.

'Oh, hi. Can I help you?'

He must look pretty out of place to be offered assistance that quickly. He asked about Dr Hardy.

'I think you just submit your papers online.' She smiled indulgently. 'He won't be back until next semester.'

'Uh, no, I'm not a student. I just needed to speak . . . where is he?'

Her opinion of him switched instantly from charming old fart-slash-nontraditional student to idiot adult.

'Out of the country. It's listed in all the department information. He's only teaching the one class here and it's all done online.'

'Wait. Out of the country? For how long? I mean, when did he leave?'

'I have no idea. August, probably?'

He was gobsmacked. If that turned out to be accurate, Foremost Expert was eliminated as a suspect.

She shifted the books she was holding. 'He's been over there all semester. He's teaching his famous "Protest Literature behind the Iron Curtain" class.'

She turned to leave but the way she'd said 'famous' made Hank stop her.

'Do you not like him much?'

She shrugged as best she could with twenty pounds of Southern Gothic writers in her arms. 'He's . . . very sure of himself.'

Conceited.

'And . . . talkative.'

Verbose.

'I see. Ah, thanks for your help. I appreciate it.'

She nodded and walked off down the hall. He stood there and tried to get his investigative bearings. He'd have to check Hardy's customs records to make sure, but if the guy had been in Eastern Europe all fall, he hadn't bundled his ex-wife into the trunk of a car and dumped her body off the Missouri River Bluffs. Or something similar. He could have orchestrated her disappearance and used an accomplice here in town, Hank supposed. But it wasn't very likely. It definitely didn't make him as good a suspect as someone with a confirmed presence here in town. So now Hank was forced back where he hadn't wanted the investigation to go – to Lew and his scraped knuckles.

TWELVE

Sadly, it didn't appear that Mr Timmons belonged to a church congregation. Or a synagogue. Or even a Buddhist temple. Not that there was one of those in Branson, but still. Sam would have taken any of them. They were easy to get in contact with, and they knew things about their members. All he had on Mr Timmons was a library mailer, which just meant that he'd probably donated at some point. And a bocce ball newsletter from some nationwide organization. He sighed and then thought hard.

Several of the local resorts had bocce courts. There was no public one, as far as he knew. He started a list and an hour later was standing at the front desk of the Stoney Mount Resort, one of many that dotted Indian Point, a jut of land that extended into Table Rock Lake just west of Branson. It was a collection of one-room cabins rentable on a weekly basis. He looked around the empty lobby and rang the bell. And out popped Jermina Templeton. Dear Lord.

'Sammy Karnes. Well, I'll be. You haven't been around in forever. I heard you was a cop, but I didn't believe it.' She looked him over as he stood there in his uniform and then batted her overly made-up eyes. 'Guess I was wrong. You fill that out real good.'

He hadn't realized his former classmate worked here. If he had, he would have started his canvass somewhere else.

'Hey, Jermina. How long you been working here?' He wasn't going to ask how she was doing. That would lead to a long and painfully detailed update about people he'd been deliberately avoiding since they all graduated from high school. And slinky, rumor-starting, innuendo-slinging Jermina was at the top of that list.

'Oh, just a month or two. I was up at Calico Cabins before that. But it wasn't, uh, the right fit for me, so I moved on.'

Which meant she'd been fired.

'You know me,' she said, leaning over the counter and winking at him, 'I'm always looking for better opportunities.'

Sam suppressed a shudder. He explained that he needed to know if Branson residents were allowed to use the resort's bocce courts.

'What's those?'

Dear Lord.

'One of the amenities. For guests. Is there anybody else I could talk to? Where's your manager?'

She snapped out of her come-hither lean in a huff. 'He ain't here. All you get is me.'

What about a maintenance worker?

She considered that. 'There's some old guy who wanders around. With, like, garbage bags and stuff.'

He decided to take that as permission to go look for the man. He hustled out, pretending not to hear her ask for his cell number. He wandered around for about ten minutes before he found the 'old guy', who was actually only about Sheila's age – she sure would have had something to say about that if she was here.

The man started chuckling the second Sam said 'bocce'.

'Did the manager finally get pissed off enough to call the cops? That's hilarious. It's just a bunch of old men looking for a place to play.'

'So people have been trespassing?' Sam asked.

'Technically, I guess. It's a group of them, and they just pop up out of the blue. They never come when actual guests are using it. But I gotta tell you, that's a rare thing. It's not like it's a hoppin' attraction here. Most guests go for the tennis courts.'

'So you don't mind?'

'Nope,' said the man, whose name was Mike, according to the name patch on his shirt. 'Heck, they even rake the sand back into shape most of the time.'

There were six or seven that he'd seen, Mike said. All men. All probably about seventy years old. They usually snuck in about twice a week. He'd only seen them arrive once, and they came all together in two cars. Parked up in the guest lot to make it look like they belonged. He couldn't remember what kinds of cars they drove. And he couldn't describe any of the men beyond 'old, white, and half of them bald'.

'Pretty sure they've come at night, too. 'Cause sometimes in the morning, the court will be altered a little bit. Could be guests, I guess, but like I said, it's not a hot ticket here.'

Sam gave him a business card and asked him to call immediately if he saw the group again. Mike clearly thought he was overreacting.

'They're not in any trouble,' Sam said. 'I just need to talk to them about something. The welfare of one of their group. It's not about any kind of trespass at all.'

Well then, he was happy to help, Mike said as he pocketed Sam's card. He went back to work, and Sam fled before Jermina could come corner him again. Next up was the Piney Cove Resort out off Stormy Point Road, which had a very old lady at the front desk who thankfully didn't flirt. She just smiled and nodded and showed him into the manager's office. That guy had no idea what Sam was talking about.

'Our bocce courts are for guests only. We have signs posted all over. I can take you out and show you, if you want.'

Sam did want, so they hopped in a golf cart and puttered

down the hill at the posted five miles an hour. The little road wound past small motel buildings with about five rooms each and numerous little parking lots, with a few stand-alone cabins tucked in between. A bunch of sneaky old men would have no problem pulling cars into some of these spaces without being noticed, he thought.

They arrived down at the bottom of the slope, where the swimming pool, one tennis court, and a kiddie playground clustered in a nicely landscaped area. Off behind the pool were two bocce courts. They climbed out of the golf cart and walked over.

'All of this is pretty much closed for the winter,' the manager was saying. 'We usually open it all up again in late April and—'

Sam held up his hand and the manager stopped mid-sentence. He was staring at the two long, narrow, perfectly parallel courts. The left one's crushed gravel surface was lumpy and had damp spots. The right's was flat as a board and spotless. Even the faint rake lines were straight as arrows.

'Why would these look so different from each other?'

The manager had no idea. He called maintenance as they stood there and was told that no one had done anything to the whole area since they shut it down three weeks earlier.

'I . . . I suppose you might be right,' he said, all flustered. 'People sneaking in is the only reason it would be like this. This is horrible.'

Sam thought leaving a resort asset to become a wintertime cat litter box was rather more horrible than trespassers maintaining what they obviously considered a precious amenity. He turned to look at the nearest cabin.

'Are any of these occupied?'

The manager stopped wringing his hands long enough to respond. 'No, I don't think so. I don't know. Let me check.'

He got on the phone again, but Sam didn't wait. He walked to the nearest one and got no answer to his knock. He tried two more before he got lucky. A woman in her early sixties opened the door. Behind her was a man who had to be her husband. They had that thing couples get where they slowly start to look like each other. Like two halves of the same unit. He nodded politely and asked if they'd seen anyone down by the pool lately.

'Oh, just the bocce bunch.'

Sam's eyebrows shot up. The woman blushed.

'Sorry. That's just what we started calling them. They came when? Three nights ago?'

She looked at her husband, and he nodded. That would be two nights before Mr Timmons was found, Sam thought. He invited them both to have a seat out on the little porch and tell him all about it. They'd arrived Saturday to celebrate their fortieth wedding anniversary. This was where they had honeymooned, and they thought it would be a kick to come back. It'd turned out to be not quite as great as they remembered it, the husband said in a wry tone. The place was practically empty and a little run down. Which was why it was so odd to see a group of old men show up.

'I don't know if they walked in or drove. They just kind of materialized. They looked like they were raking or hoeing or something, and then they started playing. They did it for a couple of hours with some sort of battery-operated lights, and then they left. Seemed to be having a great time,' the husband said. 'I was tempted to go out and ask to join them.'

Sam asked for descriptions and got a frustratingly vague catalog of four men who were various combinations of bald, short, thin, tall, chubby, and average. He sighed.

'Was there anything distinctive about any of them?'

Both halves of the couple considered that.

'Well,' the wife said slowly. Sam could practically see her conducting a lineup in her mind. 'One of them did have a lot of hair. Like, young-man thick. All gray, of course, almost white. But very thick. Came down over his forehead a little bit and was longish on top, but short in the back.

'And before you say it' – she poked her husband – 'it wasn't a toupee. He kept running his hand through it, making it all mussed up. He wouldn't have been able to do that if it was a toupee.'

'Oh,' the husband said. 'That's actually a good point.'

'Actually?'

'You know what I meant. Just—'

'Anything else?' Sam cut in.

'No,' she said, giving her husband an I'm-better-at-this-than-you look.

The husband sat up straighter and thought desperately about how to even the score. Sam had to hide a smile.

'I think one of them was named Owen,' the husband finally said. 'I heard that name a couple of times.'

Excellent. Sam took out a business card and asked them to call if they saw the group again. The wife took it, rose to her feet, and then stopped.

'Oh, and now that I think about it,' she said, 'when they left, they didn't walk up the drive toward the main entrance. We would've seen, or at least heard them if they went that way. Does that help?'

It sure did. Sam sidestepped the resort dude, who was hovering way too close, and walked quickly toward the stand of trees behind the bocce court without even bothering to ask permission. The guy scurried along after him until Sam told him to stay put.

'You need to stay right here. If there are tracks, you could ruin them.'

He could tell the man definitely didn't like being told what to do by some young kid. But he also wasn't going to disobey somebody in uniform, thank goodness. Sam walked on into the oak trees alone. He moved forward, the weak winter sunlight not doing much to illuminate the ground as it filtered through the branches. He turned on his flashlight. The blanket of leaves decreased the possibility of footprints. But these guys were old. They couldn't have hiked in from too far away. There had to be a place to park a car.

Ten minutes later he found it. Two vehicles had used the little turnout, from the looks of the tire tracks. The dirt lane ran along the back of the resort property and curved around again toward the main road. It'd be easy to get in and out if you knew it was here. He scoured the area and found one clear footprint. He took a photo of the unusual-looking tread and then went back over the ground where the cars had parked. It looked like there had been some waiting around. He caught a flash of white out of the corner of his eye. Hallelujah. Someone was a smoker.

He carefully bagged the two cigarette butts. He knew it was pretty much impossible that the department would spring for DNA testing or anything, especially without a concrete link between the homicide and the bocce guys. But at least he'd walk away from this sorry resort with something to show Sheila.

THIRTEEN

Sheila had farmed out as much as she could. Deputy Gabler was checking with all the local senior centers to see if Timmons attended any, and Orvan was tracking down red Cadillac registrations. Otherwise it was all up to her and Sammy – everybody else was needed on patrol. She refused to let herself think the thought that kept pressing against the back of her mind. They would be able to handle the workload, she told herself. She didn't need to call in anyone from out of town.

Her cell flashed with Kurt's number.

'Please tell me you found the murder weapon,' she said.

'Ah, no. But there's some guy outside the Timmons's house making a big stink. Ted's trying to stop him coming in.'

Sheila hung up without responding and started her squad car. She'd parked in the Branson Events Center lot and had been about to call the pathologist for an autopsy update. That could wait. She needed to get out to the house and meet the prodigal son.

She pulled up to find Ted Pimental standing opposite a scruffy white boy with a half-hearted mullet haircut and an array of artistically challenged tattoos. Pimental, normally the most relaxed guy in the department, was standing stiffly with his hands on his duty belt. Sheila rested hers near her gun as well as she walked up.

'Lonnie Timmons?'

He whipped around.

'Are you the one I talked to? This asshole won't let me in. That's why I drove all the way down here. You said I could get in, get my assets.'

Pimental raised a disbelieving eyebrow.

'I did not tell you any such thing,' Sheila said. 'I did say that your father's assets would be reviewed. We haven't yet found a will, so we don't know how Mr Timmons wished to dispose of them.'

Lonnie's arms straightened at his sides and his hands balled into fists. He took one step toward Sheila, saw the look on her face, and moved right back to his original position.

'You need to cool down, buddy,' Pimental said. 'Because otherwise you're about to be arrested.'

'I'm his only kin. I have every right to go in there.'

'Your dad doesn't have any siblings? Any nieces or nephews?' She'd started the process of pulling Clyde's birth certificate with the county health department, but answering her questions through that route would involve additional genealogical search work. She'd rather find out right here and now.

'He did have a sister. My Aunt Leslie. She died a long time ago.'

'And your mom?'

His anger finally cracked, a little. A quick flash of sadness crossed over his face.

'What was your relationship with her like?' Sheila asked.

'OK.' He shrugged. 'Normal. What do you want me to say? She was my mom.'

'What about your dad?'

He scowled. Sheila and Pimental waited, silently pressing in on him from both sides.

'He was an asshole. Always judging and bitching about stuff.'

'Just with you, or with other people, too?' Sheila said.

'Everybody. He was always a hard ass.'

Sheila asked for examples. He didn't have any regarding other people. When it came to himself, though, the guy was a fountain of grievance and complaint. Daddy dearest wouldn't loan him money to make rent, wouldn't pay to fix his car, wouldn't let him crash here at the house.

'When was the last time you asked him for money?'

It had been about a year ago. He called and left a message. 'The bastard never even called back.'

'And have you talked to him at all since?'

'Once. About six months ago.'

'And when did this all start – your dad not helping you out?' she said, considering her phrasing carefully.

'It was always "Make your own way, boy" since I left home. But he at least used to let me come and stay. I could crash here if I needed to.'

'And when did that change?'

'When Mom died. He went from hard ass to asshole,' he said. Then his brain caught up with his mouth. 'But I wasn't, like, holding a grudge or nothing. I didn't kill him. I wasn't even in town.'

He turned toward the house and started to fidget. He looked from Pimental to Sheila, both still bookending him from less than two feet away.

'I think I better stop talking.'

She expected better judgment from someone with his criminal experience, frankly. He should have shut up several questions ago.

'We are going to need your contact information. For when we have information for you – you know, since you're next of kin. Could you write it down?'

She pulled out her notepad and laid it on the hood of her car. He flipped it open, took the offered pen and leaned over to write his cell number, holding the paper down in the chilly breeze. With her insistence, he also listed two possible places where he might be staying.

'I don't want you leaving town, understand?' she said, handing him her business card. 'You need to change where you're staying, you call and tell me.'

She finally stepped away and Lonnie stomped off toward the old two-door Chevy parked across the street.

'You get the car's license number?'

'Oh, yeah,' Pimental said. 'I'll run it as soon as he leaves.' He pointed at her car. 'And I'm guessing you want Kurt out here to dust your hood for prints?'

She grinned at him. 'And the notebook. It's got a plastic cover. Should've picked up some pretty good ones.' She raised one shoulder in a half-shrug. 'I just want to confirm he is indeed the wayward son. And have them right here ready for comparison with anything they lift from inside the house.'

She moved toward the house. Pimental lifted the crime scene tape for her and then walked the short distance to his own squad car. She stopped on her way to the front door and watched him. His limp had gotten so much better; you wouldn't even notice it if you didn't know to look for it. He was just about back on full duty after the spring shooting that had almost severed an artery in his leg. He'd been so far out in the backwoods that it was a miracle they'd gotten him to the hospital in time. She shook her head to clear it from silly tangents and hollered for Kurt. She got Alice instead.

'He's up to his elbows in that mess in the bedroom closet. I'll do it.'

She reappeared with a latent kit and a wool hat over her short, spiky gray hair. She trotted over to Sheila's cruiser, where she was delighted with the plastic notebook.

'You need anything out of this?' Alice asked.

'Nah. It's brand new. You can bag the whole thing.'

She was turning to go into the house when Pimental called her name. He carefully maneuvered himself out of the cruiser and stood looking over the car roof at her.

'That car he was driving? It got a parking ticket four days ago. In Branson.'

Darwood Hardy, Foremost Expert, lived in a condo complex that housed the same kind of middle-aged, middle-class professionals as his ex-wife's. He did not, however, keep a house key hidden on the front porch. Hank was actually glad. He didn't want the temptation. It was bad enough having Tina's key, which felt like stolen property in his front jeans pocket. He still wasn't sure he would use it. He had no badge in this town and no open investigation of his own to legitimize his trespassing.

He used the same story he had in their old neighborhood as he went door to door in Darwood's condo development, professing surprise when people said that there was no Mrs Hardy living there. Nobody knew much about the Foremost Expert, either. He kept to himself, didn't have many visitors, and was always polite out by the mailboxes. All tidbits that were completely ordinary and totally unhelpful.

Hank walked back to the BMW and pulled up Lew's company

on his phone once he was settled in the driver's seat. The satellite map showed several warehouses on the land off Paris Road just north of Interstate 70. It would be nice to know which one held the Closeout Castle main office. He called Fin.

'Oh, heavens. You can't go out there now. Lew is there.'

'I thought you said he wouldn't be in the office today?'

'I didn't think he would be. But he called a few hours ago and said his meeting in Jeff City got pushed to tomorrow, so he'd be working late at the office tonight.'

Hank sighed. He'd been hoping to catch the employees at the end of the day, chat them up, see what they thought of their boss and the absent Tina.

'So sorry,' Fin was saying. 'I hope this doesn't mess things up. Does it ruin your schedule?'

Hank smothered a laugh. Investigations didn't really run on a schedule, he explained. So putting it off wasn't a big deal. He could just pick up again in the morning. He heard Fin breathe a sigh of relief. And now, he told himself, he could spend some time poking around online for more information about both Lew's company and Darwood Hardy. Or . . .

'Hey, Fin? What are you doing tonight?'

When he told her what he was thinking, she was totally game. She told him she'd be ready by six o'clock.

FOURTEEN

Two more resorts had suspicious bocce court usage. The guy at the corporate-owned facility thought it was hilarious, but said he'd have to report it to New York anyway. The owner of the family-run place said he'd handle it with a shotgun if he ever caught them on his property again.

'Sir,' Sam said, 'we do not recommend you do that. Really. You can call nine-one-one. But please do not go shooting at somebody who's just playing bocce.'

That got him a harrumph and a lot of muttering about trespassing and the sacred rights of property owners. Sam nodded along and managed to get in one more plea to call law enforcement before the man stomped off and slammed the door to the office behind the registration counter. Sam trudged out to his car. His initial delight at figuring out the bocce ring had gradually turned into frustration during his long day of resort canvassing. If only he had even one identity, he could confirm whether Mr Timmons was part of the group and start to learn more about the guy.

Now it seemed likely they'd have to do a press release asking the public to come forward with information about the victim. He stopped short just as he was about to climb behind the wheel. Now that he thought about it, that reporter hadn't been around. Which was weird. He usually showed up at crime scenes. Especially murders.

Sam thought about that as he drove back to the office. Sheila had called a meeting for six thirty. He wasn't sure why they didn't just talk on the phone. She usually wasn't one for wasting time traveling all over the place just so people could meet face to face. He arrived at department headquarters in the county seat of Forsyth just in time. Trying to calm down that old 'property rights' motel owner had put him further behind than he thought. He walked quickly to Sheila's office, only to find it empty. Was she in the conference room? Geez, put her in charge of the whole office and she started getting all official and bureaucratic. He went down the hall, opened the door, and instantly felt guilty.

There were stacks of paper all over the table. Derek Orvan sat at one end and Sheila was in the middle. The white board behind her was covered with writing. The room smelled like pastrami.

'I had the Whipstitch Diner make us sandwiches.' She gestured at a box in the middle of the table. 'I figured we could eat while we worked.'

They dug in as Sam told them about the late-night bocce matches throughout the city. Derek almost choked on a French fry, he laughed so hard. Sheila shook her dry-erase marker at him and then wrote the men's descriptions on the board. Then she pointed to a date and time written in the upper left corner of the board. Four days earlier, at two fifty-two p.m. That was when a car driven by Lonnie Timmons was ticketed on a down-town Branson street.

'So he was in town around the time we think Mr Timmons died?' Sam asked.

'Well, the car was. We don't know for sure who was driving it. It's not his – it's registered to a woman in Des Moines. Lonnie told me this morning he's been out of state the whole time. He said he just got into town this morning. Driving that car.' Sheila smirked. 'I don't believe him. And I don't trust that he's not going to take off. So he's currently under surveillance. Pimental's following him around in his wife's Subaru.'

Derek flashed Sam a look that communicated the same thing he was thinking – that kind of surveillance meant a lot of over-time. Both of them quickly looked away before Sheila could see anything. Derek turned to her and laughed.

'Lucky Ted,' he said. 'That makes my day only the second-most-boring of everybody on this case.'

He gestured at the piles of paper.

'I've pulled every red Cadillac sedan registered in Branson County. There are twenty-two. Then I pulled the driver's license of the registered owners. I'll do the surrounding counties if I need to, but I thought we should at least go through these first. And I'll tell you right up front, there's no "Owen" in the bunch.'

'That'd be too easy,' Sheila muttered.

They spread out the DL photos. No one was under the age of fifty-five. The only two women got put to the side. Sam rifled quickly through the rest, but there was no head of thick gray hair on anyone. That left them with one pile for 'bald', another for 'short', and a third for 'tall and skinny'. And of course there was overlap.

'We might as well go through and just call everybody,' Derek said with a groan.

Sam hadn't realized he was slowly drumming his pen on the table until Sheila leaned forward.

'You got something, Sammy? You have that look. What are you thinking?'

He felt his face go red. He didn't want to question anything, but he was wondering.

'It occurred to me,' he said slowly, 'that the *Branson Daily*

Herald guy hasn't been around. So there's been no news story about the murder. And maybe if there was, people would come forward – you know, who knew the victim?'

Sheila nodded. 'I noticed that, too. He always shows up. Since he hasn't, though, I wanted to get as much done as we can without the public – and the killer – knowing. He left the house closed up and looking normal. If he hasn't seen news that Timmons was found, he might not have his guard up yet.'

'Eh, that does make sense,' Derek said, 'but man, it'd be a lot easier if we had a helpful public just calling us with information.'

Instead, they spent the next several hours calling Cadillac owners. They were able to reach almost all of the bald ones, and none knew Mr Timmons or played bocce. Sam was halfway through the list of short dudes, mostly leaving messages, when someone actually answered the phone.

'Oh, yes,' the woman said. 'Ward knows Clyde Timmons. They've been friends for years.'

Sam snapped out of his bored slouch, startling both Derek and Sheila. He waved the driver's license printout at them and grabbed his pen.

'When was the last time your husband saw Clyde, do you know?'

'Well, now, let's see. They had bocce on Monday. So it was probably then.'

Sam smacked the table in glee and then tried to calm down.

'And that bocce – what time of day do they play?' he said in what he hoped was an even tone of voice.

'Oh, it's always in the evening. They go out and do that, and then coffee or whatever. You know, old retired men gabbing like a gaggle of geese.'

The days of the week varied for their bocce meetups, she said. She'd stopped paying too much attention. It kept him active and out of her hair, and that was all she cared about. But say, why exactly was the sheriff's department calling about all this? Was everything all right with Clyde?

The phone was loud enough for everyone to hear. Sam paused. Sheila shook her head.

'Is your husband home, ma'am?'

There was a resigned sigh and some rustling on the other end of the line. Then they heard a muffled 'sheriff's office' and a sharp gasp. Sheila leaned back in her chair like she was getting ready to watch a good movie.

'Who is this?'

Sam identified himself.

'And what do you want?' The voice was cautious – and worried. Sheila raised an eyebrow.

'Go out there in person,' she mouthed at Sam.

He nodded and told Ward Ullyott that he would be at his house within a half hour. Once his was off the phone, Sheila rose to her feet.

'We need to see his reaction when we tell him Clyde's dead.'

They raced from Forsyth over the Bull Shoals Lake bridge and down Highway 76 to Branson, where the Ullyotts lived in a neighborhood well south of the Strip and near to Lake Taneycomo. Sam drove while Sheila sat beside him jotting questions in her notebook. Orvan followed in his own squad car, every mile he went adding to her overtime expenses.

But she'd seen the look on his face as she and Sam got ready to leave the conference room. She'd stood there and, God forbid, thought about what Hank would do in this situation. He would consider the feelings of those around him – not the department budget. So she told the lanky deputy that his work had led to finding this guy, and he should be in on the interview. And Sammy had to be, since he was the only one who knew about this bocce nonsense. And neither one of them was going anywhere without her.

So it was a damn caravan that pulled up outside the Ullyott house just after eight o'clock. She gestured for Sam to do the knock. The door opened immediately. Ward was a short, somewhat chubby white man with rosy cheeks and thinning gray hair. He cringed when he saw all three of them.

'May we come in, sir?' Sam said. 'We're really sorry to bother you this late in the evening, but we do need to speak with you.'

Nobody did polite quite like Sam. Always the perfect blend of earnest and firm, she thought. Ward moved aside and they all trooped into the house, a nice split-level with country décor and lots of flowery curtains. The front room was crammed with furniture, not in a messy way, just an overstuffed one. A fire crackled in the fireplace and the mantel was covered in awards, plaques, and medals and other tidbits in shadow boxes. They sat in stiff wingback chairs and sipped their coffee. Ward didn't touch his. Sheila thought it was interesting that he hadn't asked them any questions.

'We need to ask you a few things about the bocce,' Sam began.

Ward's cheeks went from rosy to tomato. He clasped his hands together.

'I'm not sure what you mean,' he said.

His wife looked at him like he was daft. He carefully avoided looking at her, focusing instead on Sam, who repeated his question with different phrasing.

'I do occasionally play bocce,' Ward finally said.

'Who do you play with, sir?' Sheila said.

Both she and Orvan had notepads on their laps, but she wasn't taking her eyes from Ward's face. Orvan had been conscientiously writing the whole time. Maybe it was useful having him along after all.

Ward slowly gave them names. Timmons was second-to-last of six.

'When was the last time you saw Clyde Timmons?' Sheila asked.

Ward seemed like he knew right off, but paused and acted like he was thinking about it. Sheila didn't have time for this. She leaned forward.

'Sir, we know that you've been sneaking around to different resorts in the area and using their bocce courts without permission.'

His eyes popped wide and all the color left his face. Off to the side, she heard the wife mutter in confusion.

'So, please,' Sheila continued, 'just answer the question.'

He hung his head. Sheila wasn't sure whether it was embarrassment over getting found out, or an effort to avoid revealing something much worse than a bit of minor trespassing. When he finally looked up, his eyes were unreadable.

'It was last Thursday. We played at Meadowview Lodge.'

'Were all the players there?' Sam asked.

No. Adam Moreno was out of town, Ward said, visiting family in Texas. Wouldn't be back until next week. Orvan carefully made a notation in his notebook.

'Is that the last time the group met to play?' Sam said.

Ward shook his head. 'We played on Monday at Piney Cove. But Clyde didn't come. I don't know why.'

'Have you tried to contact him since then?' Orvan asked.

'I gave him a call the next day, but I didn't get a hold of him.'

'Excuse me.' Belinda Ullyott, who was plump and fairly tall and could pass for Mrs Santa Claus, set her coffee cup down with a clink. 'What is this all about? It sounds like all six of them were being idiots. Why are you asking about just Clyde? Has something happened to him?'

Both deputies shot quick glances at Sheila. She nodded to let them know she'd be taking this one, but she didn't take her eyes off Ward.

'Clyde was found dead in his home yesterday. He'd been murdered.'

Ward's mouth sagged open. His color got even more pale, which Sheila wouldn't have thought possible. His wife gasped and gripped the arms of her chair.

'Who would kill Clyde?' Ward said hoarsely.

'That's what we're trying to find out, sir,' Sam said. 'So we need to know everything you can tell us about him.'

The man started nodding like a bobblehead. It took thirty seconds and a sharp nudge from his wife for him to actually start talking. He'd known Clyde for about five years. They met at the Roark Creek Diner, where they both had a habit of going for breakfast on half-price Tuesdays. That meal deal eventually drew together the six of them. They'd get together there and shoot the breeze for hours. Clyde was a shy one. He never said too much. Never even mentioned he had a son until several years into their meetups. Seemed to be a bit of a falling out there. Once, he forgot his wallet and Clyde had immediately put down cash for them both.

'Said he was glad to treat me, instead of giving it to his

ingrate, laggard son. I got the impression that the kid had been pestering him for money.'

Orvan asked if anyone had ever met the son. Ward hadn't, and didn't think anyone else had, either. How about any other of Clyde's friends? Ward shrugged.

'I never did. He didn't have many interests. He'd retired from the sawmill. That work did a number on him. His joints weren't too good, especially in his arms and hands. I don't think he kept in touch with anybody from there. He wasn't a churchgoer, so there weren't any folks along those lines. He was just . . . he was just somebody who was fine with his own company.' Ward wiped at a tear that started to run down his cheek. 'He didn't need much. A simple guy. He'd always kid me about my Cadillac. I loved driving him around in it. He'd say that his little car was just fine, and I'd say that his old bones deserved a cushy ride every once in a while.'

'How was he at bocce?' Sam asked. Sheila settled back in her chair. She wouldn't have turned the interview to that subject so quickly, but she wasn't going to interfere with his decision.

'Terrible.' Ward smiled. 'We all are. Just a bunch of lousy beginners.'

They'd only been doing it for about two months. Dick Maher had gone on a cruise and played it on the ship. Said it was a gas. At first, Ward thought that was probably because Dick was drunk the whole trip. But once they all started getting the hang of it, everybody agreed it was a pretty good time.

'We started doing it in Dick's backyard. It could've worked, but his wife's, ah, difficult.'

Mrs Ullyott rolled her eyes and muttered, 'Amen to that.'

'She suggested we go someplace else,' Ward continued. 'So we tried it here at our place, but it was too sloped and rocky. We decided to sneak into the Ol' Mountain Resort to see what a proper court looked like. And somehow that turned into doing it all over. Two nights a week – three if we could swing it.'

Orvan wrote down all the locations Ward said they'd used. Sam had found all but two, Sheila noted.

'Did you get chased off any of them?'

'Nope,' Ward said, pride plain in his voice. 'They never caught us.'

'Are you sure?' Sheila said. 'Nobody was mad at you? Nobody followed you?'

Ward didn't think so.

'What about within the group? What's that like? Anybody not get along?'

Ward lifted his hands and then dropped them limply back in his lap. 'No, ma'am. We're just a bunch of old men who're happy to be mobile enough to leave the house, and together enough to carry on a conversation. Nobody's antagonistic. Especially Clyde. I don't know how anybody could want to hurt him.'

They stayed to get the contact information for the rest of the bocce group, but otherwise, Ward wasn't capable of anything more. His wife showed them out. As Sheila stepped out on the porch, Sam hung back. She glimpsed the woman's hand on his arm and heard her whisper.

'One of them *is* a troublemaker. Ned Hodges. Talk to him. He doesn't like when things aren't run his way. He can get very angry. That inside, seething kind of angry. Ward doesn't tend to pick up on that kind of thing. But I do. Talk to Ned.'

Sam thanked her and traded looks with Sheila on the way out to the squad car.

'I guess that makes it easy to decide who we're going to see next,' he said.

'Oh, yeah.'

FIFTEEN

'S o we're just walking right up and letting ourselves in, correct?'

Hank nodded and handed her the key. Aunt Fin stared at him for a moment and then climbed out of the BMW. She smoothed her tweed skirt and walked briskly toward the condo. Hank followed along behind her, trying to look like nothing more than a tag-along relative. It took all of his self-control to squelch the bounce in his step. Because this was brilliant. It was completely plausible that Fin, the wife of Tina Hardy's boss, could have a key to her home and would need it to check on things during the woman's absence. Not necessarily likely. But certainly plausible. And that was what they would say if anyone stopped them and asked about it.

Hank hadn't stretched the truth this much since college. He and Jerry had talked their way into some crazy places, including the nuclear research reactor and the dazzling white dome of Mizzou's main administration building. That last one had been the high point, both literally and figuratively. All that stopped once they graduated and he became a police officer. Now, though, there was a little of that old tingle in his spine as Fin unlocked the front door and they stepped inside.

He nudged the door closed with his elbow and handed Fin a pair of nitrile gloves. She just stared at them.

'We don't want to contaminate anything,' he said quietly.

Her eyes widened in understanding. Hank helped her get them over her arthritic fingers and they stepped from the small entryway into the front room. The furniture set was sleekly modern and a little too big for the space. He supposed it had come from the house they'd divvied up. Things were fairly tidy, except for a half-full oversized mug sat on the coffee table and a pair of heels dropped near the couch.

They both moved farther toward the back, where they found the kitchen and a half-bath. Fin pointed with alarm to a stack of dirty plates in the sink. Hank bit back a chuckle. The only thing that would prevent Fin from doing the dishes was kidnapping or death. Most people weren't so fastidious. And he'd seen some – in both the city and the rural Ozarks – who lived in filth that would make pig slop look neat.

He turned away from Fin's worried look and opened the refrigerator. And felt his face morphing into the same expression. The milk was expired and starting to get chunky. The cream cheese was moldy, and the bagged salad was long past putrid. He closed the door and headed quickly for the stairs. There were two bedrooms on the second floor. Tina was clearly using one as storage. It was littered with moving boxes, framed art prints, bed linens, unnecessary kitchen accessories. All things she hadn't dealt with yet from the old house. The leftover baggage of a married life.

Tina had clearly spent her energy on the other room. Everything was new. The bedroom set was perfectly sized for the space and the linens a gracefully feminine silver and dusty purple. The bathroom accessories matched perfectly. Hank stood in the small space and stared at the scatter of makeup and lotions on the counter. Nothing seemed missing. Wouldn't there be if Tina had packed a suitcase and gone somewhere, like Lew said she had? He had Fin take a look.

'Oh, yes. She wouldn't go somewhere without some of these things at least. This one, especially.' Fin pointed at a jar of some kind of cream. 'This is quite expensive and you use it daily. You wouldn't have a spare one of these in a travel bag like you would a mascara or something. If she'd gone somewhere, she would have packed this.'

Hank nodded. He stepped back so Fin could leave and give him enough space to open the medicine cabinet. It contained a bottle of hydrogen peroxide, a box of bandages, an unopened pack of razors, and two toothbrushes. He wished he could bag them for DNA analysis right now. He closed the cabinet and walked back into the bedroom. Fin was closing the drawer to the nightstand.

'There's only a paperback book and some Kleenex,' she said. Her shoulders slumped and she sank wearily on to the bed. 'I just really thought we'd find more . . . something that would tell us what's happened.'

'I know this is tough, Fin. But we'll keep at it, OK?'

Hank held out his hand to help her up – he really didn't want her sitting on anything. She waved him off and started to heft herself to her feet on her own. The sound of tearing paper stopped them both. Hank pulled her away from the bed and knelt down. He pulled back the bedspread and lifted the mattress away from the box spring. A file folder had been stuffed between the two and the top few pages had gotten wedged in a way that tore them when Fin's weight shifted the bed. He pulled the file out and laid it on the floor.

'That's from the Castle,' Fin said.

Hank was dying to just walk out with it. That would make his life a lot easier, but it could torpedo a potential criminal case. He thought for a second, then pulled out his phone. He and Fin spent the next half hour photographing every piece of paper. Then everything went back exactly as they'd found it. They took off their gloves and let themselves out of the condo with what Hank was hoping looked like the nonchalance of people who'd just stopped by to water the houseplants.

'Those were financial documents,' Fin said once they were back in the car.

'Was there any reason for her to have them?'

Fin shook her head. 'I can't think of any. Maybe the small office accounting, but not anything else.'

Hank started the BMW and pulled into the street. 'Then there's something in them that's important enough to hide.'

Sheila decided to divide and conquer. She sent Sammy to interview Dick Maher, the man who got everyone interested in bocce in the first place. Derek Orvan was given the last group member, Owen Lafranco. She kept the bad-tempered Hodges for herself. Except that he was perfectly pleasant. He offered her coffee and admitted the trespassing as soon as she brought it up. She wasn't ready to discount Mrs Ullyott, however. A woman's take on a group of men was usually accurate and always valuable.

He handed her a mug and smiled. 'It's awful late at night to be investigating a bunch of old men who aren't doing anybody any harm, isn't it?'

She nodded. 'I'm actually here to ask about one of them in particular – Clyde Timmons. How well do you know him?'

'As well as any of the others, I suppose. Why?'

Sheila told him. He almost dropped his own mug.

'Murdered? Oh, my Lord.'

He last saw Timmons the same night as Ward Ullyott had. He was kinder about Clyde's bocce skills, but also mentioned his friend's poor physical condition as a result of years working that sawmill job.

'Did you know him when he worked there?'

Hodges shook his head. He'd met Clyde when he was waved over one morning at the Roark Creek Diner, where a little group of men was talking. He hadn't known any of them before that. They were all retired and had a lot of time to burn. That's why the bocce was so much fun.

'Did you ever get caught?'

'Not outright,' he said. 'I think some of them figured out that something was up. Especially the Meadowview Lodge. Their lights came on the last time we were there. We hightailed it out of there before the guy saw us, though. We haven't been back there since.'

'Who picked which place you'd go on which night?'

'Usually me or Dick Maher. We rotated them as best we could.'

'And no one else minded that they didn't get to pick the locations?'

Hodges laughed. 'No. Everybody's pretty easygoing.'

'Anybody ever have a disagreement with anyone else?'

'Ah, I see what you're getting at. No, ma'am. We all got along just fine. It was just about shooting the shit and then goofing off with the bocce. None of us would ever have hurt Clyde.'

'Do you know of anyone outside your group who might have wanted to?'

Hodges thought for a minute and slowly put down his mug.

'Clyde and I were pretty alike in circumstances, I suppose. I'm a widower as well. We didn't talk about it much – what is there to say? – but some things we'd chuckle about together. Like how hard it is to cook dinner for yourself every night. Or do the laundry without ruining something.'

Sheila tried to force a smile, but she was tired and he was talking about missing his live-in maid, so it came out tight and grudging. He was staring into his coffee and didn't notice. She held her tongue and let him meander to what she hoped was some kind of point.

'We also were similar in our kids. In that we don't speak to them.'

Sheila sat a little straighter. He looked up, directly at her.

'We'd talk about that, every once in a while. That son of his was a trial. A lazy, disrespectful, drug-doing thug who stole from Clyde repeatedly. Has a temper, too. Busted up some furniture when Clyde let him in the house last month.' He pointed a wrinkled hand at Sheila. 'That good-for-nothing bastard is who you need to be talking to.'

*   *   *

Papers covered the floor and the printer kept spitting out more. The file under Tina Hardy's mattress was more voluminous than he'd realized as he was hastily taking photos of the pages. Once he'd taken Fin home and was back at Jerry's house, he had quickly decided he needed to print hard copies and attack it that way. He took the final pile of documents into the formal dining room, with its massive – and probably never used – oak table and started dividing everything into stacks. Financial data, inventory lists, an investor prospectus.

Everything looked great. He didn't get it. The Castle was doing good business. The sales figures were healthy and looked persuasive in the investor pitch materials. Documents showed lists of vendors and how much they'd sold to the company, with prompt payments sent in return. There were payroll figures and health insurance costs. Why would Tina feel these documents needed to be hidden under her bed? He sorted everything into categories and discovered there were several email printouts mixed in with the rest.

The earliest was three years ago, from someone with a free email account labeled *muncie2652*: *Communicate only through the phone or by email at these addresses. Report agreed-upon numbers.*

The next was sent six months later from the recipient of the earlier one, *bilbobaggins*: *Need more staffing. Looks bad.*

Then a response from *muncie* asking for ideas: *I know somewhere to ask.*

Another *muncie* message said: *We can spike sales at Christmas. Needs to be big.*

On the face of it, all the emails were innocuous. But they could mean other things, too. He raked his hand through his hair and tried to remember. The bankruptcy. He grabbed his phone and pulled up the notes he'd taken when doing research on Jerry's laptop. The Castle's withdrawn bankruptcy petition had been just weeks after the date on the first email.

Hank looked over at the rest of the documents, now haphazardly scattered all over the table. Then he considered the otherwise bare room and made a decision. He went into the kitchen and while a Hot Pocket thawed in the microwave, he rooted around in Jerry's cabinets until he found a roll of masking tape.

He took them both back to the table and ate while taping the email pages to the dining room's big blank wall. He needed a timeline and this was how he'd grown used to doing it. What he wouldn't give for a white board right now. Something he could scribble notes on. Which was Sheila's influence. He smiled. He did miss her for this. Investigating something without her felt like working a construction project while missing a hand. Possible, but a hell of a lot more daunting.

A half hour later, he had the financial documents in chronological order and was able to see that Closeout Castle got a cash infusion of three million dollars just four weeks after that first *muncie* email. That must be the first outside investment. He taped the paper to the wall.

All he had left on the table was what looked like a hurriedly photocopied original – not a digital copy like everything else. It was an unsigned lease agreement between a real estate investment trust and Closeout Castle for twenty-five hundred square feet of space. Probably Lew's proposed new store. But the second page was missing. Hank was going through the photos on his phone to see if he'd missed printing the second page when Jerry walked in. He stared at the wall and then at Hank.

'If you start putting up newspaper clippings and attaching string in between all this, I'm going to report you as a serial killer.'

Hank sighed. 'I'm not quite to that point yet, man.'

Jerry took a swig of beer from the longneck he was holding.

'It does look like you're investigating something. You know that's against the rules.'

Hank shrugged.

'You're going to get me in trouble with Maggie,' Jerry said. 'I'm supposed to keep you from working. What'd you do, bring all this shit with you?'

Hank shook his head. And then he explained. It took long enough that Jerry had to get another beer. He brought Hank one, too.

'And so this,' Hank finally said, waving his bottle at the wall, 'is where I'm at. I think Tina's suspicious that something's going on at the company.'

Jerry walked the length of the timeline as Hank went back

to his phone. Everything was too damn small to read this way. He sighed and kept flipping, zooming in when he needed to. He'd gone through almost everything when he found it. He enlarged it to fill the screen, because he didn't believe what he saw. Closeout Castle wanted to lease a location in Branson.

SIXTEEN

S am could see why Dick Maher's hair was so memorable. Super thick and longish in front, it was highly unusual for someone that old, and it was hard not to stare at it. The man invited Sam in. He'd obviously been relaxing on the couch with a novel and a glass of whiskey. The room was cozy with a fire going in the gas fireplace and framed photos everywhere. It looked like he had a large family and many years of service at Lansfield Pharmaceutical.

Mr Maher waved Sam to a seat and sipped at his drink as he went over the four years he'd known Mr Timmons. He had the same take as Mr Ullyott – Timmons was a shy man who didn't share much. He had a good sense of humor and was always kind to folks.

'He didn't come to . . . well, we had a get-together on Monday and he didn't show up, which is unusual for him. I tried calling him the next day, but didn't get an answer.' His eyes widened. 'Oh, shit. Is that why you're here? Did something happen to Clyde?'

Sam broke the news. Mr Maher gasped and dropped his glass. It hit the edge of the coffee table and upended all over the floor. Sam leapt to his feet, but wasn't fast enough to avoid getting whiskey on his boots.

'I'm so sorry, my boy. Let me get a towel. I can't believe this. Clyde . . .'

He shuffled toward the kitchen just as a woman in a housecoat came down the hallway. She was halfway through a snippy reprimand when she saw Sam.

'Who the hell are you?'

That seemed pretty obvious to Sam as he stood there in his uniform. He started to identify himself, but Mr Maher spoke over him.

'Clyde's dead. Somebody killed him.'

The lady froze. Then she stomped over to Sam and waved a trembling finger in his face.

'Are you sure?'

Sam took a step back. 'Mrs Maher? Yes, ma'am. We're sure.'

Her hand dropped to her side and she turned to her husband, now carrying a dishtowel. They were the same height, about five foot eight, and the same shade of fading tan. Must be the cruise ship trips, he thought. She had short hair that was probably usually curled but lay flat on her head right now. She ran her hand through it, told Mr Maher to clean up his mess, and started shooting questions at Sam.

'C'mon, Roberta,' Mr Maher said. 'You never showed any interest before. You wouldn't even let them all come over.'

'Why would I want six ancient men tottering around my backyard? Who knows what could happen? One of you could've fallen and cracked your skull.'

Sam winced. She kept going until he cut her off. He told them that he knew about the bocce trespassing. Mrs Maher got furious, and Mr Maher got laughing.

'You found us out? Well, good for you, son,' he said. His smile faded and he sniffed. 'It's not funny now, is it? But it was. A great time. It made us all feel young again. Daredevilish, you know? But we weren't doing anybody any harm, not really. Are you going to have to ticket us or something?'

'No, sir.'

'You should.' Mrs Maher glared at her husband. 'I can't believe that's what you were doing. What idiots.'

Sam was starting to feel a little bad for the guy. 'We aren't interested in the trespassing. I just need to know if any property owners found out and were upset. And I need to know very specifically the last time you saw or talked to Mr Timmons. You said it was at a get-together. Was it bocce?'

Mr Maher nodded. It was a bocce game last Thursday at Meadowview Lodge. Their next one was at Piney Cove, but Clyde didn't show up. They'd always meet at the diner and carpool, so they had fewer cars attracting attention. He used his cell phone to call over to Clyde's house, but there was no answer.

'Had he ever done that before – not come?' Sam asked.

'No, not at all. He'd had a cold the time before, though, so we figured he was just taking a sick day, so to speak.'

'Do you remember anything else about the Thursday game?'

'Well, let's see . . . Clyde was pretty quiet that night. Barely said anything. Not that he was much of a talker in the first place, but he was especially quiet that night. Like I said, he had the sniffles, so I just chalked it up to him not feeling well. I was hoping to see him next time at the diner for breakfast, ask how he was feeling. At our age, you don't want things like that to linger too long. But now . . .'

He took a shaky breath and bunched up the wet towel. His wife scowled something fierce, and Sam started to feel bad that he'd have to leave Mr Maher to face her wrath on his own. The man walked him to the door and patted him on the shoulder.

'Don't worry about me, my boy. I'm used to her. You concentrate on what happened to poor Clyde.'

Sam nodded and stepped on to the porch. Facing the street, he noticed a bag full of balls and a pair of shoes tucked in the corner that he hadn't noticed on the way inside.

'My bocce stuff,' Mr Maher said with a shrug and then a sly grin. 'She won't let me keep it inside. What she doesn't know is that having it out here makes it easier to sneak out and go play without her knowing.'

He gave Sam a wink and closed the door. Sam walked slowly back to his car, thinking about old men and marriages and bags full of bocce balls.

'Hey, I got some news.'

Sheila straightened in the driver's seat. 'Is he trying to leave town?'

'Nah,' Ted Pimental said. 'He checked into that crap motel over near Bull Creek. And I looked – there's no back window to the room. He's not going anywhere I can't see him do it.'

Good. It was past eleven o'clock and Sheila was hoping she

could finally go home. She didn't need an absconding dirtbag at this point in her day.

'Anyway,' Pimental was saying, 'I called the registered owner of the Chevy Cavalier this afternoon and left a message. She just called me back. And ol' Lonnie here didn't have her permission to take the car.'

Sheila let out a delighted gasp. 'Really?'

'Yep. She's never even set foot in Branson, so she sure wasn't down here to get that ticket four days ago. Says she had the car parked in a lot because her license is suspended. So she hadn't used it in a month and didn't know it was gone until I called.'

'Please, please, please . . . tell me she's going to report it stolen.'

'Oh, yeah. Apparently they date off and on. They're "off" right now, so that's good timing for us.'

Sheila couldn't keep the glee out of her voice as she agreed and jotted down the information. 'Sit tight. I'll call you right back.'

She dialed the Des Moines PD watch commander number that she'd used that morning and got the same guy again.

'Pulling a double shift,' he said. 'Sounds like you are, too.'

'Yeah,' she said. 'It's about to pay off for me, though. I hope. Have you had a vehicle theft report come through tonight for a 2005 Chevy Cavalier?'

He scoffed. 'Maybe. Probably not something they'd flag me to right away.'

Sheila explained what was going on. He perked up right away and she could hear a computer keyboard clicking.

'Yes. Dispatch just took a call. Pissed off woman. 2005 Chevy. Lonnie Timmons.' His smile came through the phone line. 'I'll have somebody take a phone report ASAP and email it to you. You say you have eyes on him?'

'He'll be in handcuffs sixty seconds after I get that paper-work,' she said. 'And I plan on taking a very long time to process him. I need to sweat him on my homicide case.'

There was more typing on the Des Moines end of the line.

'How about a probation hold?' the watch commander said.

'He's got a piss-ant shoplifting conviction here, but it means he's on probation. Any new arrest would—'

'Violate that, and let me hold him a lot longer,' Sheila finished. 'You've made my day.'

'Mine, too,' he said. 'I'll send you all the paperwork.'

She thanked him and ended the call. Then she thought things through for a minute before calling Pimental back. Lonnie Timmons was a possible killer so backup would be a wise move, regardless of which deputy was making the arrest. It was an especially smart decision with Ted, who still wasn't completely steady on his feet. Sheila sighed. For that very reason, sending reinforcements would look like she didn't have confidence in him, which was the last thing she wanted. She drummed her fingers on the steering wheel in frustration. Managing people was a pain in the ass. Her phone chimed with the email notification from Des Moines. She took a deep breath and dialed Pimental.

'We've got more than we even thought we would.' She explained what Des Moines told her. He let out a whoop.

'I'm real close,' she continued. 'I'll be there in twenty.'

Silence.

'I just want to see his face when you put the cuffs on him,' she said.

Now she heard a chuckle. 'All right,' Pimental said. 'I'll wait.'

Sheila started her cruiser and sped toward the Po-dump. Technically it was called the Po-dunk Motel, and it had twelve rooms that had all seen illegal activity at one time or another. Its revised name had been bestowed by Hank when she took him on his introductory tour of county hot spots. That had been the first time she'd thought that maybe they actually would get along OK.

She made it down there in fifteen minutes and roused the manager to get the set of ancient master keys. Then she stood plenty out of the way as Pimental pounded on the door, trying to angle herself so it wasn't obvious she'd drawn her service weapon. Pimental pounded again.

'I ain't coming out. You got nothing on me,' Lonnie screamed from inside the room.

'You're wanted for car theft,' Pimental yelled. 'You come on out, or we're coming on in. And you don't want that, pal.'

There was a lot of swearing and some crashing glass. Pimental gestured for the keys. Sheila's stomach churned. She didn't want him to be first in. The last time he was first, he'd almost died. Pimental signaled more forcefully. The look on his face made it plain that he knew what she was thinking. She held up her hand in a wait-a-sec motion, exchanged her Glock for the Remington shotgun in her car, and then tossed Pimental the keys.

'Last warning, Lonnie,' Pimental hollered as he twisted the key in the lock.

The room's window exploded and glass rained down on the pavement. Pimental leapt to the side and Sheila raced forward along the row of rooms until she was pressed up against the wall on the opposite side of the window from Pimental. He had his gun in one hand and the keys in the other. She shook her head. They needed more people. No deputy was going to get injured on her watch. Pimental shot her a disappointed frown. She shook her head again and radioed for backup. Then flinched as something came flying out of the window. A clock radio hit the pavement and broke into a hundred pieces. Then came a crappy particle board dresser drawer that split apart on impact. Another followed, and then a chair. Pimental rolled his eyes.

'We don't know if he has a gun,' Sheila mouthed.

Pimental pointed at the room remnants and then his Glock and then the window. Sheila got his meaning loud and clear. *If he had a gun, he'd be using it instead of furniture.* She gave him a glare that was interrupted by a pillow sailing in between them as it went through the broken window. Another one followed seconds later. Pimental was starting to laugh. The manager was screeching about the room deposit from the far side of the motel. Sirens were becoming audible down Highway F. They all needed to shut up because she was trying to hear something. She inched closer and heard grunting and then a scraping sound. She chanced a quick look and saw the TV moving closer to the window. She moved to a full-on angle and saw that Lonnie had both hands full wrestling with the flat screen.

'Now,' she shouted, and moved directly in front of the window with her shotgun raised. Pimental kicked at the door and broke through the knob and the flimsy interior chain. The TV froze.

'You got two guns on you, Lonnie.' Sheila had to shout to be heard over the god-awful din. 'You throw that TV at us, and things are gonna end very bad for you.'

Pimental moved closer until he was level with Timmons and had a clear shot at the man instead of the TV. The mullet swung back and forth as Lonnie looked from deputy to deputy.

'Put it down slow,' Pimental said.

Timmons's face twisted and his shoulders slumped. He let go of the TV and it fell the four feet to the floor with a sharp crack. Sheila steadied her Remington.

'This is aimed straight at your fool chest,' she said. 'So you're going to let Deputy Pimental handcuff you. Or I'm going to get to practice my center-mass target shooting. You got it?'

The mullet nodded. Pimental holstered his gun and told Timmons to put his hands on his head. Sheila aimed her shotgun downward once Ted moved closer to Timmons. He wasn't gentle as he pulled each arm down and cuffed the idiot behind his back. Then he hauled Timmons out the door and walked him over the smashed window glass to where she stood.

'He's all yours,' she said. 'Book him on every charge you can think of.'

Pimental shifted his weight off his bad leg and smiled.

'With pleasure.'

SEVENTEEN

They had just started the coffee pot when Hank walked in the door of the disappointingly pedestrian Castle offices. No turrets or drawbridges anywhere. He'd expected more of Lew. There was just a little sitting area and then a few desks separated by a low wall. There were two doors in the back that Fin had told him were the offices for Lew and Marco. In between the two was one more desk. The surface was cluttered with the standard office equipment and a few picture frames, but the seat was empty.

He shifted a small bouquet of flowers from hand to hand and waited for someone to notice him. Finally, a woman with short red hair at the nearest desk glanced up.

'Oh, goodness. I'm sorry – I didn't see you walk in. Can I help you?'

He smiled. 'I'm here to see Tina Hardy.'

He now had not only the redhead's attention, but everybody else's as well. There was a younger guy with floppy college hair wearing a tie and a woman who looked to be in her late fifties with reading glasses perched on top of her teased hairdo. That must be Human Resources Doreen. Excellent.

'Tina isn't here,' the redhead said slowly.

'Oh.' Hank tried to look disappointed. 'I'm sorry. I thought she said she would be back today. I must've gotten my dates mixed up.'

Doreen stood up. 'She said she would be back? Really? We haven't heard anything.'

'We've been starting to get worried, actually,' the redhead said. 'She's been gone so long.'

They all stared at him.

'I haven't heard from her lately, either,' Hank said. 'She told me a date a while back, and I must've written it down wrong. I, um, I wanted to welcome her back. We, um . . .'

He held up the flowers and gave what he hoped was a sheepish smile. All three of them broke into grins and Doreen actually clapped.

'Oh, yes,' she said. 'How wonderful. After that horrible husband. Where did you two meet?'

That's what Hank was afraid of. Specific questions.

'Don't ask him that,' the guy said.

Hank sighed in relief. Maybe this guy assumed they'd used a dating app and current etiquette dictated that you didn't admit to that? He had no idea what dating was like nowadays, thank God. So he needed to turn the conversation away from that subject area quickly.

'About her ex-husband – he hasn't come around, has he?'

He took a concerned step closer to the low dividing wall. 'Because he, um . . .'

He trailed off, hoping someone would take the bait. Doreen didn't fail him.

'Has a temper? Oh, yeah. She's told us. He did come here a couple of times right after he moved out of the house. But he hasn't been back since.'

'Oh, good,' Hank said. He looked around. 'She sure does like working here.'

'That's good to hear,' the redhead said. 'Sometimes it's hard to tell with her. That's why we were so glad that she decided to take that vacation. She was all stressed out.'

Hank voiced vague agreement and then glanced at Doreen, who suddenly had a perturbed expression.

'Oh, honey, don't mind me,' she said when she realized he was looking at her. 'I just wish she'd filed the right paper-work with me. Her going away without it just made my job harder, but never you mind. It's Lew's fault, really. He should've sent her to me real quick before, instead of telling me after. It's murder on the payroll coding.'

Hank hid his delight. Lew was coming up in the conversation, and he hadn't even had to be the one to do it.

'Bosses, right?' he said. 'My department head just does whatever he wants. He forgets to track things or schedule people. And don't even start on budgeting. He's got no clue.'

'That's why you need an accounting department,' the young guy said with a grin.

'Will you stop with your "business school" stuff?' The redhead pivoted in her office chair and jabbed air quote marks at the kid.

'I didn't say anything about business school, but since you brought it up – go Tigers.' He made a face at the redhead. 'And, I gotta say, you all should've had somebody who knows accounting a long time before me.'

Hank was pretty sure he heard the redhead mutter something about being 'full of himself' as she turned to Business School.

'We move plenty of inventory, so there's nothing to worry about,' she said. 'So stop criticizing.'

Hank hadn't taken his eyes off Business School. A look

flashed across his face as she spoke – skeptical and secretive at the same time. The kid's eyes flicked quickly toward the window and then back. Interesting.

'You both need to go back into your corners. Lord, cats and dogs get along better,' Doreen said. She returned her attention to Hank. 'When you see Tina, would you tell her to call me?'

'Of course,' he said and then gestured toward her desk. 'Say, could I leave her a little note? Just, you know, so she's got something cheerful to greet her on her first morning back.'

Doreen thought that was a great idea and waved him right through. She even gave him an envelope 'for privacy'. He jotted down a generic, unsigned hello, left it sealed on her desk, and walked out of the office with a smile on his face and Tina's day planner in his pocket.

'So you want to tell me why you thought it'd be a good idea to trash that motel room last night?'

Lonnie Timmons sat slouched in the hard plastic chair, his ankle chained to the floor of the interview room. His hands were bandaged – the little snowflake had scraped his poor fingers while heaving Po-dump motel property through broken glass. Sheila placed her pen on her notepad and waited. Eventually, he shrugged.

'I didn't like the décor.'

'That's a real big word for you. I got another one – reimbursement. You're going to owe the motel for everything you ruined.'

He rolled his eyes.

'But we both know that's the least of your worries.'

He just yawned and stared at her. This wasn't his first rodeo. She asked where he'd been in the days before Clyde was found dead. He launched into a long-winded, and frankly ridiculous, tale that involved meeting people, several Uber rides, a hangover, and buying bananas. She sighed.

'Let's talk about when you were down here a month ago to see your dad.'

He stiffened, just a little.

'You busted up some furniture. Hmm, that seems to be a thing with you, doesn't it? What you got against coffee tables?'

He let out a splutter of laughter before he could stop himself.

'And what,' she continued softly, 'did you have against your dad?'

Now every inch of him, from the mullet to the soft-soled jail shoes, tensed up.

'You told me that the last time you talked to him was six months ago. That was a lie. You saw him a month ago.'

His look said, *Yeah, so?* She decided to go out on a limb.

'You're really hurting for money. And he wouldn't give you any. Who do you owe, Lonnie? Because it's one thing to be late on the rent. But you're not going to drive six hours and beg a man you don't like, just 'cause you got overdue bills. You're going to do that 'cause you got some serious, break-your-kneecaps debt. So who do you owe?'

'I'm not telling you shit, lady.'

Now she was the one who shrugged. Then she jotted a few things in her notebook and examined her pen for a long moment.

'I talked with quite a few of your dad's friends yesterday,' she finally said. 'They're devastated that he's dead. They were close, you know. All said what a great guy he was. Good sense of humor. Kind and thoughtful.'

Lonnie's snort was snide and derisive at the same time. 'Then that means they didn't know him. He was a dick.'

'I think they knew him better than you. You don't see him in Lord knows how long and then you come down last month, vandalize his place and smack him around and—'

'I didn't lay a hand on him.' He hit the table with his fist and then yanked it off into his lap as Sheila raised a sardonic eyebrow. 'I asked him for money, yeah. He said no, so I left. I might've kicked at the table on my way out. But I didn't touch him.'

Nobody had claimed he did, actually. She was just throwing out different kinds of bait, seeing what he would snap at. She kept the questions coming quickly.

'Why ask him for money if he didn't like you?'

'I knew mom and him had retirement money. I figured he couldn't have used it all up yet.'

'Why do you need it so bad?'

'I gotta get square with . . .' He stopped and shook his head.

She had to keep pressing. The second she gave him any time to think, he'd lawyer up and that would be the end of it. She tried a different angle.

'Would this person have killed your dad? The one you owe? Could they have gotten in the house and killed your dad?'

From the astonished look on his face, that clearly hadn't occurred to Lonnie. Sheila hadn't considered it, either. Because it was ridiculous. It was far more likely Lonnie killed his old man than some two-bit Des Moines loan shark or bookie or whoever. But when his surprise turned to fear, Sheila started to broaden her thinking. If Lonnie's astonishment had turned to agreement – if he'd jumped right on her theory – then she'd be even more certain he'd killed Clyde. What better scapegoat than a mysterious moneylender? But that wasn't what he was doing. Which was very interesting.

Hank was just about back to the BMW when incredibly had thing pulled into the Castle parking lot. Marco Cortello climbed out of his Infiniti sedan and gave him a hearty hello. Hank scanned the area – no one else was outside, but Lord knew who could be looking out the office windows. And what if he went inside saying he just saw Lew's nephew? That would throw the whole place into high alert. He forced himself to smile.

'What are you doing here on this blustery morning?' Marco asked as they shook hands.

Operating under false pretenses. Pilfering personal items. Manipulating people.

'Oh, nothing much. I just stopped by to see Lew, but he's not here.'

'Yeah, I think he has off-site meetings all day.'

'I couldn't even leave a message with his assistant.' If his cover was going to be blown, he might as well try to get some information first. 'She's out, I guess?'

Marco nodded and his face turned grave, but in a way that looked more rehearsed than genuine. 'A family illness. We're not sure when she'll be back.'

'That's too bad. I'd imagine she's pretty integral to operations around here.'

Now his face went blank. 'Yes. I suppose so.'

The wind gusted and leaves skittered across the asphalt. Marco took a step toward the building. Not so fast, buddy. 'Things sound pretty busy. Lew said you guys are thinking about opening another store?'

Marco nodded. 'Sales are doing pretty well. And we've got another investor coming on board. I'm trying to talk Lew into using some of that money to start selling on the internet. But he keeps refusing.'

Marco's tone stayed even, but his whole body stiffened and one hand curled into a fist before he stuffed it into the pocket of his immaculately cut wool overcoat.

'I've always wondered about that,' Hank said. 'Do you know why?'

Marco half-shrugged, his shoulders still tense. 'He believes it's a treasure hunt. And that it can only be done in person at a physical location. We slumped there for a while, and that's when I started pounding on him to build a website. But the stores have come back strong, especially one we've got just off the highway. So I have no grounds to argue with him on that. But I still think we need to sell online. Especially since we've nailed down one vendor whose stuff sells like hotcakes.'

Hank phrased his next words carefully. 'That must be tough, to have two different philosophies about the business. Especially after working together for so long.'

A tight smile, and the other hand went in the other pocket.

'Well, he is the owner. I just sit around and look pretty.' He made a more blatant move toward the building. Hank wished him a nice day and backed off. For now.

EIGHTEEN

Man, did he wish he could have been there last night for Lonnie Timmons's arrest. Sam had heard all about it from Ted Pimental, who was still jazzed about it this morning. It sounded like it'd been quite the show. And it sure made Lonnie look guilty of his dad's murder. He thought about that for a minute. Lonnie was definitely the most obvious suspect, but there was something about the bocce group. He couldn't put his finger on it, but it was there. Maybe he should go back over the notes from all the interviews. He wondered if Derek Orvan had written up his report of the Ullyott interview yet.

He desperately wished they had a better time of death than just a range that included everything from sometime Saturday-ish to Monday morning. The pathologist had already said that with the cold indoor temperature caused by the furnace being out, it would be impossible to narrow down the time of death beyond that. Which was going to make it hell nailing down people's alibis. He pulled out his notebook and started to make a list. His cell rang and he hit answer with his eyes still on the paper.

'Hey, Sammy.'

Sam froze. It was Hank. Was he back in town? Had he heard about the murder? Had he talked to Sheila? Did Sheila still have a job? What the hell should he do?

'Uh . . . hi, sir. Um . . . how's Columbia?'

'It's good. It's been nice to see my friend up here.'

OK, it sounded like he was still out of town. That was one question answered.

'How are things down there?' Hank asked.

Oh, God. He couldn't breathe. He stared at the notebook full of murder suspects and started to get dizzy.

'Fine.' It came out as a squeak.

'How's that house burglary case?'

The what? He dragged his focus back several days to the couple who were probably padding their homeowner's insurance claim. 'Oh, that. Yeah. Good. I'm almost done with the report, which goes over lack of receipts and documentation and stuff on some of the items.'

He stopped talking. He was afraid to say more. He just knew Hank could tell through the phone that he was withholding information. That he was lying, more like. Should he tell him? What would he say? *Oh, by the way, there was a murder and Sheila deliberately didn't tell you about it.* His stomach started to hurt.

'That sounds great.'

Hank was talking. Sam forced his racing thoughts to stop so he could hear what the Chief was saying.

'. . . need you to check out an address for me. I'll text it to you. It's near one of the outlet malls.'

Sam seized on it. 'Sure. I can do that. No problem.'

'I just need to know . . . well, I don't know what I need to know,' Hank said. He had that thoughtful tone where he was talking and thinking at the same time and didn't know where exactly his brain was taking him. 'Look and see if there's any activity inside. Let me know what other businesses are located in the general vicinity. And don't be obvious about it. Can you do that for me?'

'Yeah. I can get it done pretty soon. I'll let you know what I find.'

Sam stopped. It was now or never. He took a breath.

'Thanks, Sammy. I appreciate it. I gotta go. I'll talk to you soon.'

The air stuck in his throat and he just sat there as Hank hung up. He finally managed a gasp and then dropped his head into his hands. He wished to God he'd never picked up the phone.

The irony of lying in wait wasn't lost on Hank. It always struck him as one of the more cowardly offenses that one could commit. And now he was doing it – parking behind a Dumpster in the Castle parking lot and waiting for Business School to come out of the building. He could call it a stakeout. But it wasn't. He wasn't watching to see who the kid met for lunch or where he lived. He was going to accost him. Politely and subtly, sure. But it was an ambush all the same.

He had pegged the correct car right off, which was why he had the unfortunate Dumpster position. The small five-year-old Subaru sat in the spot closest to the loading dock and the trash. The other vehicles in the lot were two pickups that he'd seen warehouse workers come out to for their bagged lunches, Marco's spotless Infiniti, a nice black Ford SUV that had to belong to the redhead, and a lavender-ish Camry that he would bet money belonged to Doreen. So that left the used Subaru as the most likely recent-college-grad option.

And the kid knew something. That look on his face said that the company's finances didn't add up. And the window he couldn't help glancing toward looked out at the warehouse Hank was now parked behind. Now he had to hope that another Castle employee was willing to go out on a limb, too. By confiding in a complete stranger. One who just lied to the entire office. Hank sighed. There was no going back from that now. He'd just have to talk his way past that deception. He went over several ways to do that before Business School finally came out of the building. He followed the kid the few miles to a Subway and waited until he got his order and sat down before he went inside. He didn't even bother pretending it was an accidental encounter.

'Hi. Can I sit down?' Hank gestured to the empty chair across the table.

Business School gaped at him. Hank took that as a yes and sat down.

'I need your help. I don't know what's going on at your company and I'm worried that it's something that is going to get a lot of people hurt.'

The kid just stared at him with a mouth full of sandwich.

'I've been asked to look into the state of the company, because of concerns like the ones you're having,' Hank continued. 'To really do that, I need your help.'

The kid put down his six-inch spicy Italian.

'Who the hell are you? Do you even know Tina?'

Hank danced around that one. 'Not in any kind of a relation-ship way. I was hoping to talk to her today, but she's not back.' He wondered if he'd said a single thing today that was completely true. He was pretty sure he hadn't.

'I'm trying to find out what's going on with the financials and the budgeting and all that. But I need to do it on the quiet, you know? I need to do it in a way that protects people's jobs and . . .' He trailed off and hoped that Business School's imagination would fill in the rest. It did.

'Wait – what? Our jobs? Shit, I just got this one.' He slumped back in his chair. 'I don't want to have to go looking for another one.'

Hank nodded sympathetically. That wasn't an act, at least.

He started to explain what he needed and only got a few words in before the kid interrupted.

'So what's your name? And who exactly is having you look into Closeout Castle?'

Good for him, Hank thought. He should be asking questions in this kind of situation.

'My name's Hank. And one of the owners asked me to do this independent review. They didn't want anybody to feel put on the spot or anything. So that's why it would be great to get your thoughts. Figure things out without there being any fuss.'

The kid, whose name turned out to be Doug Pearson, took a bite of his sandwich. Then another. Hank waited. Half of it was gone by the time he seemed to make a decision.

'There's nothing in one of the warehouses. The one next to the office has stuff, but not enough for that to be even half of what's on the books. And the warehouse that's up near Brown Station Road – there's barely anything in it. I drove out and looked at it . . .' He trailed off and took a swig of soda.

'What made you do that? Did you think something? About the inventory?'

'It all matches up on paper. What I've seen anyway. But sitting next to a warehouse every day, it just doesn't seem like enough is coming in and going out to match those numbers. That's why I went out to Brown Station one day on my lunch break.'

Business School leaned forward. 'And Doreen said something. About how a couple years ago, we were really hurting, and then things just turned around and we started selling well again. We opened up Store Four and a bunch of investors came on board. She said it was sure nice not to struggle to make payroll anymore.'

'And that's the truth – you don't struggle anymore?'

'No. I know that for sure. There's always money. They kid that I'm the accounting department, but I'm really just doing bare-level bookkeeping. I do the vendor bills and the payroll.'

Mr Cortello did the rest, he said. Hank asked if Mr Lancaster or Ms Hardy ever handled any of it. 'Not that I know of . . . but I did see Tina staring out the window at the warehouse a couple of times that week before she went on vacation. Just like I'd been doing.'

* * *

There he was, standing in the lobby, looking extremely anxious. She'd never really dealt with him. Hank always did that. She couldn't even remember his name. But he clearly knew who she was.

'Chief Deputy Turley. They told me Sheriff Worth is out of town, so I need to ask you some questions about the homicide on Wednesday.'

She found herself patting at her hair and quickly pulled her hand away. He was *not* making her nervous.

'We have a deceased white male, sixty-seven years old,' she said. 'He was found in his residence by a deputy doing a welfare check.'

'He was beaten to death?'

'Is that a question? You seem to know the answer.'

The kid glared at her. 'I'd like to confirm with you what the morgue up in Springfield told me.'

She rested her hands on her duty belt and looked him in the eye. He was only a little taller than she was, early twenties, skinny, and obviously of Indian descent. She wondered if he felt as isolated and conspicuous in this county as she did.

'So he was beaten to death?' the kid kept pressing. 'Do you know when he was killed?'

'That is part of the active investigation.'

He sighed. 'Do you have any suspects?'

She gave him a dirtier look than she probably should have.

'What about Clyde Timmons's son?' he said.

What? How the hell did he know about that dirtbag?

'You arrested him last night. Is he a suspect?'

Lord, she wished Hank was the one on the spot right now. She cleared her throat.

'Lonnie Timmons is in custody on unrelated charges.'

The kid crossed his arms over his chest and stared at her. They stood that way for what seemed like hours. She wasn't going to be the first to break. Apparently he was thinking the same thing. They glared at each other until the outside door slid open and a scraggly woman with a mouth full of meth teeth stomped in, yelling about seeing her husband in the jail. The stalemate ended as they both swung around to see her given directions by the lobby attendant. Sheila tried to remember what other spokespeople said when she saw them on the news.

'We are actively investigating this crime,' she said slowly. 'We're devoting intensive resources to the investigation. There is no danger to the public.'

He said thank you in a way that clearly meant *Was that so hard?*

'So it wasn't random? A burglary gone wrong or something?'

There was no way she was going to admit that could be what happened. She didn't need a hysterical public.

'No. Not random.' She nodded and turned to go back to her office.

'Wait. Can I give you my card?' he said.

She said yes with what she considered great magnanimity. He reached into the back pocket of his jeans and then blushed furiously.

'I don't – crap, I'm sorry – I came straight from the airport. I don't even have my luggage.'

She raised an eyebrow. 'But you have a notebook?'

He straightened.

'I. Always. Have. A. Notebook.' He scribbled on a fresh page, tore it out, and handed it to her. 'Thanks for your time.'

She watched him leave the building and wondered when his article would come out in the *Branson Daily Herald*. Then she wondered who leaked him that info about Lonnie Timmons. Three days ago, there would've been only two or three folks disgruntled enough to bother. But with the new overtime policy, that list of candidates had grown exponentially. She stuffed Jadhur Banerjee's information in her pocket and headed back into her viper pit of a department.

NINETEEN

Tina had plans. A haircut, several lunch dates, a doctor's appointment. All supposed to take place when she was either 'on vacation' or 'out of town' with her 'ill mother'. Hank flipped the pages further into the future and found more of the same. A fully scheduled life. He did a quick Google search and then dialed a phone number, choosing the person he thought would be most likely to chat with a stranger. Two minutes later he knew that Tina hadn't shown up at the salon for her cut and color. He wasn't surprised.

He closed her datebook with a snap. It was time for a come-to-Jesus with Aunt Fin. She had to call the Columbia police. He still didn't know what the hell had happened to Tina Hardy, but he did know it wasn't good. If she'd left of her own accord, she wouldn't have planned out her calendar so thoroughly. And she would have taken those smuggled company documents with her instead of leaving them under the mattress.

Add to all that the financial irregularities at a company where Lew was the president, and Fin had plenty to justify calling the authorities. She no longer had to worry that she would be dragging her husband into something without any substantiation. Now he just had to convince her of that.

He laid Tina's calendar on the BMW passenger seat and started the car. He wanted a look inside the warehouses – both the one adjacent to the corporate office and the one a few more miles out from the city. He wondered if he could talk his way into those. That might be harder to do without outright lying. He thought for a minute. There was one place he could go without having to explain anything to anybody. He'd just be an ordinary shopper, browsing the aisles of Store Number Four.

He hit Interstate 70 and sped east toward Kingdom City, a collection of truck stops and hotels where 70 intersected with state Highway 54. The store sat just off the interchange near the Holiday Inn. The parking lot was practically empty. He sauntered in and took a look around. The sheer randomness of the merchandise was astonishing. Extension cords sat next to frying pans. Reams of copy paper were stacked next to bedsheets. It could be better organized, broken into categories. But maybe this was the point. Having to go through all of it to see what was in stock, which increased the possibility of coming across an impulse buy. Like the fondue pot he was currently looking at. That'd be fun to do with the kids. Oh, look, it even had auto temperature control. And it was only five bucks. He knew full well that his customer behavior was exactly what Closeout Castle wanted. But it was a cool little thing. And now he had a reason to engage with the cashier.

He wandered around some more first. As he got deeper into the store, he realized that it wasn't stocked to the extent he'd first thought. Only the front was bursting with inventory. Farther back, there were gaps all over the shelves and what items there were sat covered in a fine layer of dust. All of this matched what Fin said about the state of the business – slow, no foot traffic, people now doing this kind of shopping online. What didn't match were the fantastic sales numbers Business School was getting, and Lew saying that business was booming.

Hank walked up to the cashier, who'd been watching him from behind the counter. The young woman said hello and rang up the fondue pot on one of the two cash registers. As he pulled out his wallet, he asked if business was always this slow. She nodded and bagged his purchase.

'I'll bet things pick up around the holidays?' he said.

She nodded again and took his cash. He looked at her long dark hair and brown eyes, and then asked if there was a bathroom.

'No, sir. You must go to the gas station.' She pointed across the street.

'¿Tu hablas español?' he asked.

Her eyes went wide and she took a fearful step back. He held up his hands, palms out.

'No te preocupes. Todo está bien.' He repeated that she wasn't in trouble. She took another step back and he started to worry that she'd bolt for the door. She probably knew just enough English to get by – basic greetings, where the bathroom was located, how to get to the highway.

'Mis papeles están atrás en la oficina,' she said. 'Y soy legal.'

That broke Hank's heart. She was legal and she was still terrified. He shook his head. He told her that he didn't need to see her papers. He was a friend. He just thought she'd be more comfortable talking in Spanish. She nodded, but didn't move any closer. The language always reminded him of his mother, Hank said, leaning against the counter to make himself look less tall and imposing.

'*Mi mamá es de Mexico*,' he said. '*¿De dónde eres tu?*'
Where was she from?

She gawked at him. Guatemala, she said in a small voice.
He nodded encouragingly. How long have you worked here?
She eyed him, clearly not believing his reassurances. He didn't
blame her. He pulled out his phone and quickly scrolled through
his photos. That's my mother, he said, showing her a picture of
Mamá standing outside the house in California's Central Valley.
He searched further back and found a shot of the two of them,
sitting in a restaurant with his *abuela*. Her eyes lit up at the
sight of the little old woman with thick gray hair in a bun.

Her *abuela* lived with her, she said, in an apartment
down the road toward Jeff City. She supported them both. Hank
seized the opening. How much do you make here at the store?
Ten dollars, she said. That was just above minimum wage, so
there wasn't anything illegal about that. There were enough
employee options in mid-Missouri that the store manager could
have hired someone who spoke English for that amount of
money. So why didn't he?

He asked if she always worked alone, phrasing it like he was
curious to know whether she had help with stocking shelves or
ringing up purchases. She said she usually didn't. The only
other employee was the manager, and they rarely worked at the
same time. He usually opened or closed, and she handled
the middle of the day. The occasional times she did work
at the end of the day, all she did was turn off the lights
and make sure everything was locked up tight. She looked
puzzled about why he'd asked. What else would she do? Hank
could think of several things, like tallying what was in the cash
registers and sending sales reports. All things that would need
to be falsified if Store Number Four was indeed selling stock
that didn't exist to customers who were ghosts.

Hank was surely going to some special kind of hell for what
he had to do next. He leaned a little more on to the counter
and confided that he had a friend who needed a job and this
seemed like a good one. Were there other stores? Oh yes, she
said. She'd never seen them, but there were three others. She'd
be happy to give Hank the name of her manager so his friend
could ask about employment opportunities. His name was Vic

Melnicoe and he worked the closing shift today, from three to nine.

It was just after one thirty now. Hank thanked her and finished paying for the fondue pot. He asked for a bigger bag than the one she'd given him and she ducked into the back to get him one. As the door swung shut behind her, he caught a glimpse of the back room. It was almost completely empty.

Sam walked out of Donorae's with a hot cup of coffee in his hand and a smile on his face. He didn't want to get back in his squad car just yet, so he wandered down Main Street and stopped under the big trees next to the First Presbyterian Church. He leaned against the walkway railing and looked down the hill over downtown and toward Lake Taneycomo. He figured they wouldn't mind if he hung out for a bit. He replayed what Sheila'd told him about last night's arrest of Lonnie Timmons. It sounded like the dude just went nuts. And it sure made him look guilty. Lonnie and his temper could've come down here easy, argued with his dad, killed him, and then fled back up to Des Moines. So far, there was nothing to prove otherwise.

He took a sip of coffee and stared at the cloudy sky. What he saw, though, was a ransacked bedroom and a pulverized Clyde Timmons. And there was just something about it that didn't fit. It didn't seem like Lonnie was the kind of guy who would have the presence of mind to lock everything up on his way out. He'd be more likely to tear out of there immediately, with the doors left wide open and his car tires squealing. People would've noticed. But nobody did. So there was a certain amount of stealth.

He set his to-go cup down next to the railing and pulled out his notes from last night. The bocce players. He flipped through the papers but nothing jumped out at him. He stuffed the notebook back in his pocket. Hank would tell him to replay the interviews in his head. Let them unspool in his mind and see if he realized something that he hadn't caught while it was happening. He took a breath and closed his eyes.

They snapped open a minute later. He fumbled for his cell and punched Kurt's number.

'Have you found any bocce balls?'

'Huh?' the crime scene tech said.

'Bocce balls. Have you found any in Timmons's house?'

'What's a bocce ball look— well, wait. It doesn't matter. The only balls we found were in a pack of tennis balls in the laundry cupboard. So no, no bocce balls.'

Sam hung up and started to pace. If Dick Maher had a canvas bag to carry his bocce balls, then Mr Timmons probably did, too. And if you swung one of those things around, it would become a sixteen-pound club. He needed to get a hold of the forensic pathologist. He pulled up his contact list as he started to run back to his car, his coffee cup forgotten on the walkway.

The email subject line should have read *Low-life asshat*. But Sheila bowed to professionalism and titled it *Timmons arrest* instead. She clicked send and Lonnie's mug shot, complete with bloodshot eyes and scratched face, shot off to the Des Moines watch commander as a thank you for his help. He responded immediately.

This'll go up in our squad room. Make everybody's day. PS You go ahead and keep him. We don't need him back.

That was just the opening she was hoping for.

You have anybody to spare who could check the alibi he gave me? We think our victim was killed between sometime Saturday and Monday night. He claims he was at the Steam nightclub both Saturday and Sunday nights. And that he went shopping Monday at the Hy-Vee. Just those two locations. If we can blow that apart, no way will our judges down here grant him bail.

This time, she attached a photo of the trashed motel room. Again, the reply was immediate.

He's upped his game. No problem on the alibi check. I'll let you know.

Thank goodness. Because she sure as hell didn't have enough manpower to spare someone for a trip to Iowa. She didn't have enough to investigate things properly right here in her own county. Not having Hank made things much more difficult. Easier, too, of course. She wasn't having to talk him out of conspiracy theories or make sure that he wasn't putting himself in dangerous situations. But his absence made her realize how much of the workload he carried when they were investigating a homicide. Not that she'd ever admit it.

She swung around in her desk chair and contemplated her white board patrol schedule. She just needed to accept that this month's budget was blown. She'd have to try to make it up next month, she thought, as she turned to her computer and opened the file with the jail staff schedule. No one had access to this but her. Ever since that meeting with all the jailers, she had provided each one with only his or her individual schedule. Trading for overtime became more difficult if nobody knew when anybody else was working. Not impossible, certainly, but she needed to throw up every roadblock she could.

She looked at today's lineup and saw that Gerald Tucker would be working. She'd had to switch him to swing shift in order to make her other changes work correctly. He'd been working graveyard for almost a year, ever since Hank banished him to the jail after the *Branson Beauty* explosion. But that meant he'd been working too often with Bubba Berkins, and those two together were far more than twice the threat of Tucker alone. They covered for each other and left the jail understaffed, lied about inmate welfare, stoked resentment and insubordination, leaked information, and God knows what else. So she needed to split them up. Since Bubba was closer to retirement, she hoped that keeping him on overnight shifts might hasten his departure. Not that she'd been reading medical studies about how bad overnight shifts were for your health, or anything.

But she was under no illusion that Tucker would stop sabotaging Hank just because he didn't have Bubba anymore. She knew he'd keep feeding biased information to the county commissioners, who controlled their budget and loved to hear how she and Hank were mismanaging the department. Which they weren't, but Tucker was an old-school, good ol' Ozark boy, and there were folks who took his word as gospel just on account of that. She hoped that isolating him on this shift – with deputies like Molly March who had no bone to pick with Hank – would start to choke off his information pipeline.

She hadn't figured on quite this amount of anger about the overtime ban, though. It could turn into a real easy match for

Tucker to come along and light. And she couldn't think of any way to make it less volatile. All she could do was keep a very careful eye on things and hope that enough sensible deputies would be able to hold sway over the hot-heads.

She flipped through her spreadsheet and was making a few new adjustments when Sam texted to ask if she was in her office. She replied in the affirmative and moved to set the phone down when it rang with a number she didn't know. She clicked ignore and listened instead to the sound of those big ol' feet running down the outer hallway. Sammy burst in, fresh out of breath and waving his arms.

'It was bocce balls.'

She raised an eyebrow and waited.

'Bocce balls. The murder weapon.'

Now she sat up straight. She hadn't heard anything from the pathologist. 'Where'd you get that?'

'I was at the church . . . and I replayed it in my head . . . Mr Maher's foyer . . . and ball bags and . . .'

She made him stop, sit down, and start over. That slowed him down enough for her to untwist his loopy train of thought.

'And you talked to Dr Whitaker?' she asked.

'Yeah. Just now. He said that absolutely a bag full of heavy thirteen-inch-around balls, swung together, could cause those kinds of injuries. So it's got to be that the bag was the murder weapon. Plus' – he jabbed a finger at her excitedly – 'there were no balls in the house. And there should've been, what with him being so into the game. That's confirmation to me. 'Cause the killer took them.'

He finally took a breath and flopped back in his chair. Sheila knew she was gaping at him but she couldn't help it. It was brilliant. She was so proud of him. She was about to say so when he leaned forward again.

'And here's the other thing I think. There was a lamp right there that would've made a great club, right? Why use something else?' He waved his finger at her again. 'Because it meant something. Using the balls meant something.'

Now he was getting a little too far out there. 'You're reading too much into it, Sammy. It could've just been the killer grabbing what was handy.'

'The lamp was handy,' he said.

'Maybe not. Who knows where Timmons was standing when the fight started? The lamp could've been across the room.'

Sam started to look obstinate. She decided to let it go. At this juncture, it was pointless anyway. They couldn't prove which one of them was right until they figured out who the killer was.

TWENTY

Vic Melnicoe arrived right on time for his shift at Number Four. The sweet female clerk, whose name Hank realized he hadn't gotten, left in a battered sedan. He hoped that what he was about to do wouldn't end up costing her a job. He had a great vantage point from the gas station across the street, which was also busy enough to mask the fact that he'd been sitting there in the BMW much longer than an ordinary customer. And he had to say, this car was ruining him for surveillance in anything else. He'd never be comfortable in his cruiser again, with its lack of satellite radio, heated seats, and leather upholstery.

His plan was to wait a little for Melnicoe to settle into his shift and then go in and buy something else. He mainly wanted to get a sense of the guy before he called Fin. He had a feeling he would need every bit of information possible in order to convince her to call the police. He sipped at his industrial-sized gas station Diet Pepsi and watched the manager go into the back room several times. Then he planted himself in front of the second cash register. It looked like he was ringing up purchases, but there were no customers. In some other retail store, Hank would have thought he was working on online orders, but last-century Lew had no internet presence. The guy was bent intently to his task. It looked like a good time to interrupt.

Hank drove back over and walked in with a bounce in his step. He walked right up to the counter before Melnicoe had a chance to hide the paperwork next to the register. It appeared to be an inventory list. Some items were checked off and others weren't.

'Hi, there. How you doing today?' Hank smiled. 'I was wondering if you could help me. I'm looking for something for my little girl. I've been gone a while – business trip, you see – and I got one more sales call to make, so I'm in a bit of a hurry. You got anything I could grab real quick and take home to give her?'

Melnicoe blinked in surprise and took an involuntary step back under the force of Hank's monologue. He was in his late twenties and on the skinny side, with a curly brown nest of hair atop a thin, pinched face and big, wide-set eyes that continued to blink rapidly. Hank leaned in, placing his hands on the counter and moving his smiling face much closer to the stack of papers.

'Yes, um, of . . . of course,' Melnicoe stuttered. He took another step back. By now, Hank was practically hovering over the counter. He was able to get a glimpse of the register's monitor, which showed a purchase of more than three hundred dollars. A person could buy a whole aisle worth of merchandise for that kind of money. He wasn't able to see much else because Melnicoe moved away from the counter and walked hesitantly toward the aisles. He clearly had no idea what they contained. Hank was dying to stay put and keep reading, but had to follow in order to keep up his act. They wandered down two rows before finding a collection of stuffed animals that Hank had noticed on his first visit.

'We got these.' Melnicoe pointed.

Hank shrugged and asked if there was anything else. They searched another section while Hank kept up a steady soliloquy about his fake daughter and finally found a small collection of kid art supplies. Hank went back and forth for way too long, just to mess with the guy. He wanted him still flustered when they went back up to the checkout. He finally decided on a box of big sidewalk chalk and a bottle of bubble-blowing solution. At least his real kids could use them. They sure as hell didn't need any more stuffed animals.

As Melnicoe steered him toward the registers, he switched conversational gears.

'So I gotta be honest – I never noticed this place before. How long has it been here?'

'Three years.'

'Really? Well, who knew? Have you worked here the whole time?'

They reached the counter, and Melnicoe looked like he'd reached the end of his rope. 'Yes,' he said. 'The whole time.'

'Seems pretty niche. What'd you do before this? Same kind of thing somewhere?'

'It's not niche at all. It's retail. I worked at a Walmart before this.'

'Well, this is a lot more quiet, that's for sure,' Hank said. 'Any room for advancement?'

Melnicoe didn't even bother to answer that one. He grabbed the chalk and rang it up on the same register the Latina clerk had used, not the one he'd been working on when Hank walked into the store.

'Can I have the bubbles, please?' He held out his hand.

'Oh, yeah. Sorry. Just thinking about my next call.' Hank grinned and gave him the bottle. 'I sure appreciate your help. What's your name?'

'Vic.' He stuffed the items in a plastic bag while his eyes kept glancing at the other register. Hank wondered if he was trying to meet a deadline.

'There you go.' He shoved the bag at Hank. 'There's the door.'

'Well, thank you. I might stop by my next time through here and . . .'

He didn't bother finishing. Vic had disappeared into the back room. Hank chuckled as he walked out. His wallet was seven dollars lighter, but the shopping trip had been priceless.

The office coffee was sludge. Sam sniffed at it, then drank some as quickly as he could. He needed the caffeine. He couldn't believe he'd lost his latte. He was pretty sure he'd left it at the church, but he could've left it on the roof of his car, too. He'd certainly done that before. He choked down another swallow as Sheila walked in. She laughed at him.

'I thought you stopped drinking that stuff and only did fancy Donorae coffee now.'

He felt himself turning red and changed the subject.

'It's been a long couple days,' he said. 'I just need a little pickup before I start chasing down more on the bocce guys.'

She fed money into the vending machine and pulled out a bag of chips.

'And I want their balls,' she said.

Sam snickered. She waved a finger at him.

'I know exactly what I'm saying. I want all of their bocce balls. We're assuming that it was Timmons's that were used, but they each own a set. I want Alice and Kurt to process every single one of them. And if we find blood or other trace evidence on somebody's, then his more personal set of balls is mine, too.'

She tore open her chip bag and left the room calmly munching away, leaving Sam laughing into his coffee mug. He forced the rest of the drink down as he walked to the conference room, where it was nice and quiet, and placed a call to Plano, Texas, where the one bocce player not in Branson when Clyde died was visiting his daughter. The others were suspects, and Sam didn't know how much to trust what they were telling him, but Adam Moreno had no reason to lie. He came right to the phone when Sam asked to speak with him.

'Oh, Lord, it's so horrible. Poor Clyde. Ward called me yesterday and told me about it. I can't believe it.'

'Do you know of anyone who was angry at Mr Timmons?'

'You mean aside from his son? Well, hang on. I don't know that Lonnie was angry at him, just that they didn't have a good relationship. Didn't talk – things like that.'

That was all he knew about it until recently, Mr Moreno said. But he and his wife were down in Texas because their daughter just had a baby. The whole bocce group had known she was due soon, which had prompted several conversations about kids and grandchildren. One morning at their diner meetup, he and Clyde were the first ones there and got to talking.

'It was about how tricky it is – relationships with your kids. I'm real lucky. Mine still talk to me. And they've given me grandkids, which has brought us closer. I mean, I'd do anything to see those little guys. I wish Lonnie had a kid, maybe that would've helped his and Clyde's relationship. Maybe they both would've bent a little.'

'So they didn't bend? Is that it?'

Mr Moreno pondered that. 'I think so. Yeah, Lonnie was a shit, pardon my French. But Clyde wasn't willing to forgive.'

Sam frowned. Those two things didn't necessarily jell.

'Wait – it's one thing to be, uh, "a shit", so to speak. But when you say "forgive", it sounds like you mean something specific, not Lonnie's general, uh . . . lifestyle choices.'

'I guess I do mean that. When we were talking about Lonnie that day, Clyde referred to something. I don't know what it was exactly, but he said something like, "There are things you can't undo. He can never atone." Then he got all choked up and couldn't say anything else. My heart broke for the guy.'

'Did he ever talk about it again?'

Mr Moreno said no, Clyde never brought it up again. He was going to ask more that day at the diner, but didn't get a chance because everyone else in the group came in right then.

'Tell me about your group,' Sam said, switching gears. 'You've been getting together for five years? Did the bocce change anything? You all were getting together more often. You had this secret thing going. Was everybody into it?'

Mr Moreno laughed. 'Oh, hell yeah. We all loved it. It was this big dose of excitement in our pretty boring lives. Dick Maher is always a hoot, but when he taught us all how to play, he took it to a new level. He's like a social director or something. He'd map out the best way into the resort every time we hit a new place. He'd bring a cooler full of drinks. The only thing he wouldn't do is drive. He always hitched a ride with somebody because, well, Dick likes his whiskey.'

Yeah, he does, thought Sam, whose work boots still smelled like single malt. Their outings were some of the only opportunities for Dick to kick back and enjoy that kind of thing, Mr Moreno said.

'Dick's wife keeps him on a pretty short leash. She worked as a nurse supervisor before she retired, and she's got no sense of humor. She doesn't appreciate the joy we get out of our bocce raids. We were all disappointed when she found out we were sneaking out at night. Hell, man, we were terrified. That she'd keep Dick from coming – or that she'd call the cops.' Mr Moreno paused. 'Although I guess now with Clyde bein' murdered, our bocce isn't you all's priority, is it?'

'That's very correct, sir. I'm just trying to get to know about everyone in the group so I can get a better sense of Mr Timmons.'

And figure out which group member might have wanted him dead. Sam didn't say that part, though. 'What else can you tell me about Mr Maher?'

Dick was a retired salesman, Mr Moreno said. Some kind of medical equipment or something. It made sense, because he could talk a person into anything. Hell, he'd talked all of them into running around town under cover of darkness like damn-fool, oat-sowing teenagers, hadn't he?

'Did he ever get upset if one of you didn't show up?' Sam asked. 'Anything like that?'

'Nah. It's Ned Hodges who does that. He's the one who's strung a little tight. Don't get me wrong, he's a nice guy. He likes things just so, is all. Always sits in the same seat at the diner, always orders the same breakfast, always has to drive. We all wondered if he'd be able to handle the bocce, honestly. It's very by-the-seat-of-our-pants. He's had a few little agita-tions, but otherwise, he's been fine. You just got to take his quirks as they come. It's no big deal.'

Ned was a teacher. Retired, of course. Mr Moreno thought he'd taught middle school, maybe in Forsyth? Widowed, lived alone. Sam thought about what Mrs Ullyott had said as he'd walked out of her house the night before – that Ned was the one with a temper. He pressed Mr Moreno.

'That sounds more like irritation with keeping on schedule. Did he ever actually get angry at anybody?'

'He did light into Owen Lafranco one night. It was right after we started the bocce. Owen stepped away from the match for a minute to take a phone call, and Ned just lost it. He started yelling and got right up in Owen's face. Made the poor guy drop his cigarette. The rest of us were worried someone would hear the yelling and we'd get found out. It was over the top, I'll admit. I was a little worried Ned would have a coronary.'

Owen had taken it in his stride. He always did. He was pretty laid back, which Mr Moreno attributed to him never having married. No wife and no kids to drive the blood pressure up. He'd worked as a construction foreman for years, and now had knees almost as bad as Clyde's. But they both could still roll a decent bocce ball.

'Not like ol' Ward Ullyott. It's taken him a long time to get the hang of it. None of us are any great shakes, but Ward – whew, he's awful. His wife says his balance is off. He didn't tell her about the bocce, because he didn't want her clucking over him about his health. Oh . . . I suppose she knows now, though, doesn't she?'

Sam said she did, which made Mr Moreno doubt that she'd let her husband come out and play anymore. She was protective. That's why he loved his red Cadillac so much. She didn't mind him driving it, said it was safe enough. Remembering all the times Mr Timmons was seen in that car, Sam asked if the two of them were particularly close.

'Not necessarily. Ward is a . . . a helper, I guess would be the best way to describe it. You need a ride, he'll pick you up. You're short when the bill comes, he'll loan you the money.'

For instance, Mr Moreno continued, he bought the whole group bocce ball bags. Sam sat straight up with a jolt. Bocce ball bags. Mr Ullyott had ordered six spanking new bags made just for bocce balls. They were supposed to arrive next week. Sam sat back and pictured the canvas tote in Mr Maher's foyer. They were all using those kinds of temporary bags, Mr Moreno said. Bigger and loose, Sam thought, with enough room for eight bocce balls and enough material to get a good grip for swinging with enough force to bash somebody's brains in.

TWENTY-ONE

Fin was crying. Which Hank expected, but that didn't make it any less awful.

'So do you see why we need to call the police?'

She nodded. 'Absolutely. Tina hasn't left town of her own volition, that's for certain.' She picked up the phone. 'Let's do it.'

Hank let out a long, slow sigh of relief. It was time for search warrants and forceful, badge-in-the-face interviews. An hour later, the Columbia PD detective thought so, too. He leaned back in the nice leather easy chair in Fin's front room and snapped his notebook closed.

'I do wish you'd come to us earlier, Mrs Lancaster. Even if you did' – he shot Hank a look that would fit perfectly next to the dictionary entry for 'exasperated' – 'have a policeman looking into it.'

Hank ignored him. 'So you'll take a look at the business, too? That young man who works there has significant worries about the discrepancies between the account he has access to and where that money is coming from. And you've heard what Mrs Lancaster knows about the Castle being in financial trouble, even if no one else will admit it.'

The detective, who'd introduced himself only as Ghassan, rose to his feet.

'Of course we'll look at Closeout Castle. If Ms Hardy uncovered something illegal there, that would definitely be motive to . . . well, to do whatever it is that's been done to her.' He would immediately put out a missing person alert and search her condo, Ghassan said. 'And a late Friday afternoon visit to Castle corporate headquarters seems like a good idea. All sorts of things can happen to business records over a weekend, and we wouldn't want that.'

Hank couldn't keep the smile off his face. He was really starting to like this guy. He just wished he could tag along, but he knew that wasn't possible. He'd already encroached enough. He gave Ghassan the notes from his conversation with Business School and told him about the message he'd left on Tina's desk. The last thing they needed was to find that and launch a wild goose chase for a mysterious secret admirer.

'Damn, man,' Ghassan said. 'When you retire, you should go into PI work. That's some slick shit – oh, sorry, ma'am.'

Fin managed her first smile of the day. 'Sir, you've taken me seriously. That's all I care about. You can talk any way you want.'

He shook her hand, then as he shook Hank's he leaned closer.

'I know that you know more than you're telling me,' he said softly. 'If I only had the resources to do one thing at a time, what should I do first?'

'The office. And seal the warehouses. My bet is the inventory they have on paper isn't there in reality. Don't give them an opportunity to fix it. And the manager of Store Four. He's in on it.'

Ghassan stepped back and nodded. They showed him to the door and watched him walk out to his unmarked sedan.

'What do we do if they don't find the papers she hid under the mattress?' Fin whispered, even though the detective was out of earshot.

That would be very awkward. Hank had already started praying the Columbia cops wouldn't miss the documents. He didn't want to have to confess his condo trespassing in order to point them in the right direction.

'We'll just have to cross that bridge if we come to it.'

The address was burning a hole in Sam's pocket. And making his stomach churn. What was he going to do after he checked it out? Call Hank back? Maybe he could text a report. That would be a way to avoid an actual conversation. Because he wasn't going to be able to keep quiet about the murder if Hank directly asked him what was going on in the department. Sam would have to tell him. Then the shit would hit the fan. And Sam had no desire to be the one who triggered that mess.

He traded the department cruiser for his personal car, although he was still in uniform. That was as low a profile as he could manage with everything he still had to do today. He pulled in to the strip of stores, which were an annex of sorts to the outlet mall on Gretna Road. There was a ladies' clothing shop and an athletic shoe store for a brand Sam had never heard of. At the end of the row was the suite number Hank had texted him.

He pulled slowly through the parking lot and found a spot where he could see in the front of the store without having to get out of his Bronco. It had lines of shelving that made up long aisles running toward the back of the store. There was a counter on the right side that he assumed would be for ringing up people's purchases. It looked like there was a door in the back, but it was hard to see much more than that. Otherwise, there was nothing in the store. No merchandise, no signs, no cash register computers.

He pulled around the building to the back, which was even more boring than the front. There were a couple of Dumpsters and two cars – a Chevy Traverse and a Toyota Avalon. He wrote down both license plate numbers, but he couldn't run them because he wasn't in his squad car with its computer. He sighed. This had been a waste of time.

The white board was covered in black marker. Sheila's theories, connected by arrows to suspects, were linked by other arrows to a timeline of events. And the whole thing was decorated with a very liberal sprinkling of question marks. She sat down at the conference room table and rubbed at her aching temples. Usually putting it all on the board helped, but this time everything was just as muddled as when she started. It didn't help that they had a long time period when the murder could have occurred. And no clear motive.

She glanced across the table at the empty chair. That didn't help either. Hank not being here to hash through everything was really what was making her beloved white board ineffective. They'd been up against tough homicides before, but they could bounce things off each other. Now all Sheila had was peace and quiet. It wasn't getting her anywhere.

She needed to call him. It would come out in the *Daily Herald* tomorrow, and she didn't want him to see it there first. She actually never dreamed it would take this long to be publicized. She'd figured there'd be twelve hours – twenty-four at most – before she'd need to tell Hank about the murder. Somehow that had turned into more than forty-eight, and now things could get sticky. She placed her cell on the table in front of her and pushed his number.

He didn't answer – which astonished her, quite frankly. Not that she was any great thing, but this was the man who wanted updates if he had to take a mere few hours off. He'd had a morning doctor's appointment in Springfield a few months ago, and he'd called in four times before lunch. They hadn't even had anything more exciting going on than those dumb kids drag racing out near Taneyville. So when he was essentially forced to leave town for days on end and then finally got a call from the office, she expected him to grab for it like the workaholic's lifeline that it was.

She pushed the phone away and got up to pace the length of the board again. She hadn't yet put little dots on the timeline points so she added those, because she had no other theories left to write. She started on the right end and worked backward in time, carefully coloring in unnecessary circles. She ended with the date six months ago when Lonnie Timmons maintained he last saw his father. Then she drew an arrow to the day only last month when bocce player Ned Hodges said Lonnie came to town. Both things were definite changes in Clyde's life – Lonnie's urgent pestering, and the start of the bocce nonsense. Were those the only two?

She traced the timeline forward, then back again and beyond, extending her line farther to the left. Then she dug through her notebook and finally landed on what she wanted. The little group of old men had started meeting at the diner five years ago. Might as well write that on the board, too. She flipped through more pages and came to the other date she wanted. Nine years ago was when the Clyde–Lonnie relationship went all to hell after Nell Timmons died. Maybe the roots of this thing went that far back. Maybe one of these two moments in time would eventually explain everything.

TWENTY-TWO

There was nothing to do but sit and wait. He kept telling Fin that they wouldn't learn anything today. Even if the Columbia police did find something while executing their search warrants, they weren't going to call and update her. That wasn't how it worked. Sadly. Because Hank could really do with an update. So far, he'd resisted the temptation to drive out to the warehouses and see what was going on. Instead, he was sitting in Fin's kitchen, drinking tea and playing gin rummy. They were on their sixth hand when the landline rang. Fin answered it and waved him over. There was no speaker function, so he had to lean in close to hear.

'. . . need to know his schedule, Mrs Lancaster,' Ghassan was saying.

'Lew just told me that he would be back tonight. That usually means not to hold dinner for him.'

'And did he tell you where he was going?'

'He said he had a meeting in Jeff City.'

There was noise in the background, and Hank thought he heard someone say something about Marco Cortello. He pointed at the phone and then at Fin.

'Is Marco there with you?' she asked Ghassan.

'You bet he is. Sitting in the office lobby swearing six ways to Sunday that he had no idea Tina Hardy wasn't at her mother's.' There was some shuffling and the background noise disappeared. 'Mrs Lancaster, did you know that Mr Cortello has a degree in music theory? I've got someone looking more closely, but it appears he has no financial training. Were you aware of that?'

'I didn't know what he studied in college,' Fin said. 'But I do know that Lew hired him on because he was having a tough time and he was a hard worker. That was back when there was only one store and no more than a half-dozen employees. Marco kept working hard, and eventually Lew made him CFO. It was more a reward than anything else, I suppose.'

Ghassan groaned. Hank shook his head in dismay. A privately held company that kept its nose clean could get away with that, he supposed. Closeout Castle certainly wasn't that anymore.

'Cortello is telling us he doesn't know where Lancaster is,' Ghassan said. 'And we've checked where he was supposed to have his meeting, and he never showed. So I'm going to ask you again, Mrs Lancaster. Where's your husband?'

She turned to Hank with tears in her eyes and a look halfway between worried and furious. He reached for the phone but stopped and moved away just the slightest bit. If he were the one talking with the wife of a suspect – a potentially on-the-lam suspect – he'd be furious if someone interrupted. He couldn't let the fact that she was family ruin his judgment. He nodded encouragingly at Fin.

'I don't know, detective,' she said. 'I swear to you, I thought he was in Jeff City. I can try to call him if you like . . .'

That was an offer Hank would accept, if it were officially his case. Ghassan told her he might need her to do that later on, but not right now. Hank stuffed his hands in his pockets to keep from grabbing the phone. He listened as Ghassan asked where else Lew might be, what his hobbies were, whether he had a favorite bar.

'His only hobby is work. And the house – he likes to work on the house. He doesn't drink. He doesn't do anything else. The company is his life. He . . .'

She stopped and looked at Hank. She seemed to realize where that line of talk was headed and wisely cut herself off before she could gush about how Lew built his beloved company from scratch and would be devastated if anything happened to it. Hank nodded and mouthed a question.

'What would you like me to do, detective?' she repeated into the receiver.

Call if Lew gets in contact with you in any way, Ghassan said. Then the Columbia detective asked for Hank. He and Fin stared at each other in surprise and Hank took the phone.

'We're working on warrants for Tina Hardy's bank account and credit cards, but we don't have them yet,' Ghassan said. 'So we don't know if she's accessed them recently. We're canvassing her condo complex right now, but I need to know if you already did that, and if you found out anything.'

Hank hadn't done a true canvass, and he told Ghassan that. Then he stared at the kitchen wallpaper for what felt like an eternity but was probably only seconds.

'I do have something I need to mention,' he said. 'Mrs Lancaster and I did enter Ms Hardy's residence.'

Silence.

'Excuse me?' the detective finally said. 'You did what?'

Hank looked over at Fin, who pointed to herself and nodded, then snatched the phone out of his hand as he started to speak.

'Yes, detective. I let myself into her condo. I thought there might be something inside that would help me figure out where she is. I asked Hank to go with me. I was a little scared. He didn't really want to, but he did because he's a good nephew.'

All that came out in one torrent of speech. She took a deep breath and refused to look at Hank, whose jaw had dropped at the lie. She turned away from him and kept talking.

'We didn't touch anything, and he had us wear gloves, too, just in case. I'm sorry, sir, I was just so worried. I thought doing that would help me figure out whether I should call you.'

Ghassan said something Hank couldn't hear and then Fin handed the phone back to him. He glared at her.

'Mr Worth. Sheriff. I would say I'm disappointed in you, but why bother? Unfortunately you're not one of my teenage daughters – I can't ground you for bad behavior.'

Fin was pointing to herself again. Then she gave Hank a little shove. His glare turned to a glower.

'My Aunt Finella is a bit of an unstoppable force. She wouldn't take no for an answer.'

She nodded firmly and drew her hands apart. *Keep going.* He waved her away.

'There was nothing there that would indicate that she was abducted from that location,' he told Ghassan, hoping that switching back to the investigation would alleviate the detective's justifiable irritation about the search. 'Obviously, I didn't have any Luminol or anything, though. So your guys will be able to get a much better read on that than I did.'

A little understated flattery couldn't hurt. Ghassan fell silent and then covered his phone and shouted something unintelligible. A second later he was back.

'I gotta go. You keep yourself available, and you tell your dear Aunt Finella to do the same, got it?'

Hank said he certainly would, and hung up the phone.

'You did not,' he said immediately, 'have to lie to him for me.'

Fin tut-tutted and walked back over to their card game. 'They're not going to do anything to me. You – with your job – they could do all sorts of things to you. And that's not going to happen when I have any control over things.'

He half-smiled at her. 'And this assertive wonder woman is the person who just told a police detective that she was "a little scared" to go into Tina's house by herself.'

She shrugged. 'I'm old. I can say I'm scared of a cloudy day and they'll believe me. Old people get very little credit, and old *women* get no credit at all. About time it worked in my favor.'

She started shuffling the cards, doing it five times before she spoke again. 'I messed up the entire thing because I believed in him, or I was trying to protect him, or I don't even know what at this point. And now, because of me, the police are weeks behind on trying to find Tina. And my husband has disappeared – after lying repeatedly for who knows how long.' She took a deep breath. 'I'm going to get some fresh air.'

Hank watched her leave out the back door and got himself a glass of water. As the ice rattled out of the dispenser, he stared at his children's artwork on the fridge door. He walked into the living room, sat down, and dialed home.

'Hello?'

'Hi, Dunc.'

'Oh, hi. You having fun doing nothing up there?'

Hank thought about his last few days. 'Yeah. It's been nice.'

'You get Fin all settled back in OK? Did you see Lew? Did he look guilty? Like he's having an affair?'

Hank rested his aching head in the hand that wasn't holding the phone. 'I, uh, haven't seen Lew much.'

Dunc harrumphed. 'And Finella?'

'I've been staying in touch with her.' Again with the half-truths.

'Well, thank you for that, boy-o. Especially because she hasn't called me back. Typical.'

'Can I talk to the kids?'

'Yeah, sure. Just a second.'

There was some rustling and then the stampede of small feet. He listened to them fight over the phone and then Maribel said hello while Benny complained in the background. He asked her about kindergarten and then she handed the receiver to her little brother. Hank got two entire sentences out of him, which was pretty good for his current attention span.

'He wasn't supposed to tell you we've had chocolate chip pancakes every day you've been gone,' Dunc said when he got the phone back.

'With syrup, too, apparently,' Hank said. 'But you're the one who has to deal with them bouncing off the walls, so . . .'

'Oh, then we go for a walk. All four of us. Don't worry, I don't let them hold Guapo's leash. But I gotta do something since I'm not getting my miles in with you gone.'

Dunc and his miles. He walked between four and five a day, which was usually great because he took Guapo with him. But there was no way he was getting that far with a five-year-old and a three-year-old. His dream was to walk his age in one week – which would be seventy-two miles. Hank kept telling him that only an extremely fit crazy person could pull that off, and he was only one of those two things.

'Well,' Dunc said, 'you don't sound as down in the dumps as you did before you left, so that's good. Have you figured out how you're getting home yet?'

'I haven't, actually. I'm going to talk to Maggie later tonight when she gets off her shift at the hospital.'

'Just make sure you come back un-mopey. The house needs to be normal again.'

The old coot had a point, Hank thought as he said goodbye and hung up. Their home did need to be normal again. Especially with the drama that was about to start with the extended family. Hank hoped he wouldn't have to be the one to explain everything to Dunc.

He tapped at his cell to pull up Sam's number and saw that Sheila had called. He was about to dial her back when Fin appeared in the doorway.

'You need to come see something.'

Sheila's cell rang again. She declined it with a quick finger jab. It was the same unknown number that called earlier. She went back to what she'd been writing in her notes – instructions to Sam, who was busy digging into Nell Timmons's background. Derek Orvan had already spent the day doing the same with Clyde. So far, he'd come up mostly empty. Clyde had been a good employee at the sawmill, but nothing spectacular. Although nowadays, dependability and conscientiousness actually were pretty special, she thought. But Clyde retired nine years ago and hadn't kept in touch, so none of the information on his personality or habits was current. She sighed and started to read Orvan's reports.

The same number called again. She swore and picked it up.
'Ma'am?'
'Who is this?'
'Deputy March, ma'am. Molly March. Ma'am.'
Sheila dropped her pen. It clattered on her desk.

'Molly, are you all right?'

'Oh, me? Yes, ma'am. I'm OK. I mean, me personally, yes ma'am.'

Sheila quickly logged into her password-protected jail staff schedule. March was not on duty right now.

'I . . . well, ma'am, you said that I could call you if there were any problems. Like with the men deputies and all. On account of them giving me a hard time last month. This isn't that, but . . .'

The child was tying her tongue in knots trying to say whatever it was she needed to.

'OK, Molly, why don't we just slow down. How about you take a breath and just say what's on your mind.'

'Yes, ma'am. I thought you should know they're planning a sick-out.'

Sheila's hand, which had been hovering over her computer mouse, curled into a fist.

'The jail staff?'

'Yes, ma'am.'

'When?'

'Tomorrow. Starting with swing shift. And going on as long as possible.'

'Do you know who's organizing it?'

'Bubba is. He's been going around getting support for it.'

'Have you been asked to participate?'

'No. I figure they want to leave me as the only one on duty. Like for extra spite, you know?'

Sheila did know. Very well. They would find it hilarious that a young woman who was brand new to law enforcement and weighed no more than a bag of feathers was locked in by herself with dozens of the county's worst citizens. She patted at her hair as thoughts pinballed through her brain.

'What about Gerald Tucker? Did you hear him say anything, do anything regarding all this?'

She could practically hear Molly thinking.

'Well, he's not planning it like Bubba is, but . . . he sure ain't stopping it. He's just watching. Like, I don't know . . . like he's watching a movie where he knows the ending. Oh, man, that sounds dumb. I'm sorry, ma'am.'

That didn't sound dumb at all. It sounded like the most astute observation Sheila had heard in a long time. Tucker knew the end of this movie because he was the director. Bubba might be doing the legwork, but Tucker was behind it.

'Do you know if patrol is involved, too?'

'That's a good question, ma'am. And I don't. I been trying to figure out if they are, but all I know is the talk in the jail. I can't tell what they're doing on their phones.'

'But they are on their phones? A lot?'

'Oh, yeah. Lots since all this started yesterday.'

Which in itself was against regulations. She rubbed at her forehead, where a throbbing headache was developing. She told the kid to keep monitoring things like she had been, and call anytime day or night if something new developed.

'And tomorrow, report for duty just like normal. Act like you don't know anything about all this. But Molly, I guarantee you that you won't be there alone. Someone will be with you all shift, OK?'

A relieved sigh came through the phone.

'Thank you, ma'am. That sure helps.'

Sheila gave her a few more instructions and told her to be careful. When she hung up the phone, she dug two Advil out of her desk drawer and swallowed them dry before she could bring herself to look again at her staffing spreadsheet. Tucker and Bubba's names were at the top. Damn fools. If they'd tried to recruit Molly, she would've at least been conflicted about ratting them out to Sheila. But isolating her had made the decision to side with Sheila an easy one. Thank God. She might be able to contain the damage of this now that she had advance warning.

Tucker's insidious reach extended beyond the jail, though. He used to work patrol – for years, in fact, until his demotion to the jail. Then he lost the sheriff election to Hank. So now he was out to do as much harm as he could, to both Hank and the department as a whole. The overtime anger was just an opportune circumstance for him to capitalize on. And if he was able to use it to get patrol deputies off the street, that would really hurt. That's what the public saw and that's where the political damage would start.

Hank, when he approved her new overtime scheduling, had

said he could handle any blowback. But now that it looked like it would become a dispute played out in public, she didn't think he'd be able to. Especially since he wasn't even in town, damn it. She had to get a handle on the patrol numbers and try to figure out where each deputy stood. She pulled up the other scheduling spreadsheet and started to go through the names. Then she texted Tyrone to tell him they needed to cancel their dinner plans for tomorrow.

TWENTY-THREE

Nell Timmons had died of lung cancer nine years ago. Sheila thought this was somehow important to the investigation into her husband's murder. Sam frowned in concentration. He was sitting at his little kitchen table with his laptop. He'd decided to just come home after driving by that address for Hank. It was getting late, and going all the way back to the main office in Forsyth would be a waste of time. He could do the research here.

The *Daily Herald* didn't archive its obituaries online, which was totally irritating. He surfed around until he finally found Mrs Timmons's obituary on a catch-all death notices website. She'd been fifty-nine and died at home after a brave battle with the cancer. Up until her diagnosis, she worked for the White Tail Manufacturing administrative office, where she'd been for twenty years. She was known for her baking and her kind smile. She was survived by her husband of thirty-seven years, Clyde Timmons of Branson, and son Lonnie Timmons of Lee's Summit. She would be greatly missed.

It wasn't much, but the article did at least give Sam her workplace. The best source for anything else would be Lonnie, of course. But he wasn't in a real helpful mood at the moment. So Sam fixed himself a sandwich and hunkered down at the laptop. The company office was closed and would be until Monday, according to the voicemail recording. *Work around it*, the Chief would say. Sam drummed his fingers on the Formica tabletop and pondered. Then he started in again. A half hour later, he unearthed a partial list of employees courtesy of an old online park district newsletter. The company had sent a contingent to a community cleanup day, and, thank God, the newspaper had taken pictures and interviewed people. He started with someone named Jeanette Pistoresi because, well, there was only one of those in the phone book.

'Oh, goodness, yes, I worked with Nell. How long has she been gone now? Ten years? Why do you ask?'

'Just about ten years, yes,' Sam said, and then took a deep breath. He hated this part. 'I'm sorry to have to tell you, but her husband, Clyde, was found dead earlier this week. We at the sheriff's department are, um, just trying to figure out exactly what happened, and it's always helpful to know more about a person's history.'

'Oh, how awful. That poor man. I'll say a prayer. And anything I can do to help, sweetie. What do you need?'

'What was she like?'

'Hmm, well . . . she was a quiet soul. Very kind. She was in charge of the birthdays – you know, remembering when people's were, sending around the birthday cards for everyone to sign. And she'd bake the cakes. Oh my, was she a baker. Such delicious treats she'd bring in. Homemade candy at Halloween, cookies at Christmas. Always so generous.'

'And did she continue working after she got sick?'

'She tried to, but it got bad real fast. Her husband convinced her that she should quit so she could focus on her health.'

'What about her son?'

'I don't think he was around then. You'd need to talk to Mary Johnson or Bea Kircher. They worked with Nell the longest and might know more about that, because I seem to recall that there was something. But I never knew what it was.'

She hadn't stayed in touch with Mrs Kircher, but she knew how to contact Mrs Johnson. Sam carefully wrote down the phone number. He had her name – her photo was in that old newsletter – but Mrs Pistoresi had just saved him from having to spend hours rattling around online databases or calling the huge number of Johnsons in the county white pages. He thanked her profusely and placed his next call.

Mrs Johnson sounded much older than Mrs Pistoresi. She was shocked at Clyde's death. She'd worked with Nell Timmons the whole time Clyde's wife was with the company.

'Of course, the company changed hands so many times we didn't even know who we worked for at the end. Probably the Chinese,' she said. 'But you don't care about that. You want to know about Nell and her family. Let me think.'

She went quiet, and the silence lasted so long Sam wondered whether he should ask if she was still there.

'Nell started after her boy was old enough to be in school. She just had the one. I don't remember his name. But I do remember that he'd get into trouble every now and then as he grew up. The school would have to call her at work, that sort of thing. That was how I knew. But I never got the feeling that it was too serious. Just standard teenage boy stuff, you understand? I do know that it would always be her who was called – not Clyde. She told me once it was because he was hard to find in the far reaches of the sawmill, but I think it was because the boy preferred dealing with his mother. Clyde was a fine man, and a good husband. You might wonder how I know that and I'll tell you, young man. You sit next to a woman for twenty years and you'll know how she's treated by the people in her life. And he treated her good. He didn't hit her, and he didn't yell, and he didn't isolate. I saw all of that happen over the years with ladies who came through. But not Nell. They were a good, solid couple.'

'You think Lonnie preferred Nell over Clyde?' Sam asked.

'Lonnie, that's his name – thank you, young man. Yes, I think he did. Maybe "preferred" isn't the right word. Clyde was very quiet. If there was ever a work gathering, Nell would explain beforehand that he was shy, that he wouldn't be talking much. And it was the truth. He didn't. And I think he didn't talk much with Lonnie, either. Course, when it's your own kin, they're not likely to see that you're shy. A child might think you don't like them, or that sort of thing. I don't know if that's what happened with Clyde and Lonnie, but they always were a bit oil and water.'

Clyde was devastated by his wife's cancer diagnosis. He drove her to and from work every day and would take her to her chemo appointments, Mrs Johnson said. It pretty quickly got to the point where she wasn't able to keep working. So Clyde up and retired, too, to take care of her. Sweetest thing you ever saw. But it was a steady decline, and she was gone within a year. He didn't speak at the memorial service, but the boy did.

Sam bolted upright, knocking the laptop and rattling his dinner plate. 'He did? What did he say?'

'Oh, how much he loved his mother, how hard she'd fought the cancer. That kind of thing.'

Sam squashed the last bit of his sandwich in frustration.

'I'd love to know more about that, ma'am,' he said. 'Do you recall anything else he said, or anything Clyde said to him?'

She thought about it. Again it took forever. Sam passed the time pressing crumbs into his napkin.

'He said that his ma had always loved him for who he was. Which, I must say, I took to be a dig at his father. But then I knew the history, didn't I? He said how he was glad to have made it back to Branson before she passed, and he said he wished he could have her chocolate cake one last time. That got a nice chuckle from everyone. He also said he appreciated that so many folks came. There weren't that many, honestly. People from work, and some that had to be from Clyde's job at the mill. That was about it. They were private people, like I said.'

Clyde Timmons had come up to her afterward and thanked her for being such a good friend to Nell all those years. 'He was just so devastated. He shook my hand, and he said he couldn't believe it had happened so quick. I said it was normal to feel that way. He just looked at me like he was seeing right through me. Like he was still seeing Nell somewhere behind me.'

Mrs Johnson said she ran into him a few times in the years afterward and was surprised at how angry he'd get when she asked about Lonnie. Did she, Sam asked, know anyone who would want to harm him?

'Oh, dear. I didn't realize when you said he had passed away that it wasn't natural. Oh, dear. I see now why you were asking about the boy. If you'd asked me when Nell was alive if Lonnie could hurt his father, I'd have said no. But I don't know what happened in all those years since. If they kept drifting away, if Lonnie kept up those little digs, who knows?'

'You need to see this.'

Hank put his phone down on the coffee table. He couldn't read the look on her face at all. He quickly followed her out the front door and around the house to the back corner. A flowerbed extended about two feet out from the brick and ran the whole length of the wall. She pointed to one spot, where a fallen tree branch had flattened some kind of ornamental shrub and dirt had been scooped out and tossed aside. She nudged him closer.

Planted there was a leather purse. It was brown and strappy, and certainly not going to bloom in the spring.

'It's not mine,' Fin said.

He hadn't figured it was. He knelt down before he saw that she'd pulled out the wallet. He looked up at her and saw she was wearing gardening gloves. Small favors. She shouldn't have touched it at all. Her expression said she knew it and didn't give a shit. She reached down and flipped the bifold part open. Tina Hardy stared back at him. Hank looked at her shoulder-length dark blonde hair and brown eyes that squinted just the slightest bit, like those of anybody who wears glasses and is forced to stare and smile without them.

He slowly rose to his feet. Fin let out a trembling breath. He almost couldn't bear to look at her. Whatever suspicions she'd had, whatever dread she'd harbored, whatever thoughts she'd tried not to think in the dead of the night – they'd all just come true. Why else would Lew's secretary's purse be buried here? He wanted to tell her that it was possible someone else could have buried it here after taking Tina, but he didn't want her clinging to that slender shred of hope when their first instinct was most likely the right one.

'I'm sorry,' he said.

'I know.' She let her arm drop limply to her side. 'I saw the branch and came over to get it off my boxwood. The dirt was all bunched up and I tried to smooth it back out. The purse was just underneath. Not deep at all.' She took a deep breath. 'I hope this will help the detective find her.'

Hank wasn't so optimistic. It would certainly help prove Tina hadn't disappeared of her own volition, but by itself it wasn't pointing the way toward its owner. That kind of guidance would have to start with Lew.

'Let's get you inside. We'll get you a nice cup of tea and I'll call the detective.' He led her into the kitchen, started the tea kettle, and called Ghassan. After an impressive string of swear words, the detective said he'd send someone right over.

'You better not have fucked this up for me, Worth. If a judge tosses this—'

'She was wearing gloves. Working in her own garden. And I was nowhere around.'

Ghassan didn't sound very mollified, but he did stop yelling. Then he said he wanted to get a warrant anyway, just to be on the safe side. And Hank and Fin had better be there when his people showed up. Hank assured him that they would. He hung up and saw that Sheila had tried him again. Then the tea kettle started to whistle. He looked at his cell and then at Fin, pacing the length of the kitchen. He laid the phone on the coffee table and walked away. Maybe they could play a few more hands of gin rummy while they waited for the search team to arrive.

TWENTY-FOUR

Local Man Killed in Home
Branson County Resident Found by Authorities after
Mail Carrier Alert
by Jadhur Banerjee
Branson Daily Herald *Staff Writer*

Branson – A 67-year-old Branson resident was found beaten to death in his Nighthawk Lane home on Wednesday. Sheriff's deputies discovered Clyde Timmons, a retired sawmill worker, during a routine welfare check. He was found in a bedroom with massive wounds to the head after a concerned letter carrier reported that the mail hadn't been retrieved in several days.

The victim's son was arrested Thursday night; however authorities declined to comment on whether he is a suspect in his father's death. Lonnie Timmons, 35, is currently being held without bail on suspicion of auto theft, resisting arrest, disturbing the peace, and property damage. He was taken into custody just before midnight at the Po-dunk Motel after causing substantial damage to one of the rooms.

'That bastard just went nuts,' said motel manager Nicki Kirk. 'The cops come for him all normal-like, just knocking. No SWAT or nothing. And he started throwing things out the window. Busted all the glass and ruined the whole room.'

The younger Timmons has an extensive criminal history, including convictions for theft, property damage and burglary in both the Kansas City area and Des Moines, where he currently lives.

'He's just bad news,' said ex-girlfriend Gayle Petkovich. 'He's got a temper he can't control.'

Petkovich reported her car stolen Thursday evening, which she believes is what led investigators to Lonnie Timmons's location in Branson. The 2005 Chevrolet Cavalier was impounded by the sheriff's department early Friday morning.

Branson County deputies and crime scene personnel remained at the house, which is in an unincorporated section of the county, on Friday morning. Residents of the quiet neighborhood remain shaken by the killing.

'This is crazy,' said Eric Hampton. 'We never had anything more than a couple houses getting egged when there were teenagers on the street. That's it. And now we got a murder. Just crazy.'

Madge Lerman lives across the street and said she hasn't slept since learning of Timmons's death.

'This is just awful,' she said. 'We get no protection out here. It's pretty much lawless.'

Sheriff's department logs show that the area is routinely

patrolled. Chief Deputy Sheila Turley said the crime doesn't appear to be random.

'There is no danger to the public,' she said.

The department is devoting extensive resources to the investigation, she said. It is the third murder in the county's jurisdiction this year. In February, 18-year-old Mandy Bryson was killed on board the Branson Beauty *paddlewheel showboat. And in May, another homicide occurred on wooded property near the northern county line. In addition, a man was found stabbed to death in an apartment within the Branson city limits last month.*

Timmons spent 40 years working at Bull Creek Lumber Mill. He retired nine years ago.

'He was kind of a shy guy,' said company vice president Tim Fosmire. 'He came in every day and did a good, conscientious job, and just kept to himself.'

He was known for sharing the bounty of his home garden, Fosmire said, bringing in baskets of tomatoes and other produce.

'Some guys come back to visit after they retire. Clyde never did. I always pictured him sitting quietly in a lawn chair watching over his garden.'

Neighbors agreed that in Timmons's low-key way, gardening was his passion. He also enjoyed taking care of neighbor Paula Garber's cats when she was out of town, she said, and was famous for putting out huge bowls of candy every Halloween. He was also well-known for retrieving his mail without fail from the white metal mailbox at the end of his driveway.

The letter carrier who grew concerned about Timmons's overflowing mailbox declined to give his name.

'I did what anyone would do,' he said as he worked his route Friday. 'Mr Timmons was real regular getting his mail, so when he wasn't, I just got worried. I thought maybe he'd had a heart attack. I never imagined he was murdered.'

The article looked out at her from the phone screen as she sat in the dark kitchen. It was five a.m. on Saturday, and Sheila was in full uniform. She put the cell down on the tablecloth and took a contemplative sip of coffee. The word was now out about the murder. That meant the department would be flooded with calls from panicked old ladies afraid for their lives and from nosy conspiracy theorists certain they knew who the killer was. That was what always happened.

She read the *Daily Herald* story again. The one small corner of her brain that still thought like a normal human took time to be proud of Rodney. He'd given a good little comment. Hadn't even sounded wordy, which was amazing. She'd have to get Tyrone to read it, maybe grab an actual newsprint copy to hang up in the post office.

She poured herself another cup of coffee and wondered how the reporter kid knew about the car and Lonnie's ex-girlfriend. That brought to mind her new Iowa friend. She checked her email. There were two new ones.

Having next shift check on Timmons alibi. They should contact you. – Daniel Atkinson

The next one was sent just a few hours ago.

Watch commander Atkinson requested an expedited response to your query. Complete report to follow later. Club security footage shows Lonnie Timmons arriving Saturday 11:23 p.m. He left at closing at 2 a.m. There is no footage of him coming or going on Sunday night.

Hy-Vee Grocery has no credit card receipts for that Monday under his name. Their surveillance cameras were offline. Handed off contact info for on-duty cashiers to next shift. – Det. Kate Ventimiglia

Lonnie certainly was distinctive enough, with that mullet and those tacky half-assed tattoos that somebody might remember if he came through their checkout line. And the lack of credit card records didn't mean a damn thing – he could've easily paid cash. Sheila sighed. Sunday night looked good for a disproved alibi, but Monday was still an open question. She hated open questions.

She opened her only other new email, from Derek Orvan. The man really seemed to be enjoying the investigation. He'd volunteered to break into Clyde's cell phone – which sadly contained only bocce group phone numbers – and had actually written a full report, quite possibly for the first time ever. Maybe she should re-evaluate his potential for something more than patrol. He had done a good job talking to multiple co-workers of Clyde and taken a page from Sam's procedure, with actual quotes included in his report narrative. All the old men he'd talked to said the same thing. Clyde was quiet and usually kept to himself.

'He weren't stand-offish, just shy. Happy to be alone with his work. He didn't need the talking, like some of the guys do.' That was from Eric Hampton, who worked with Clyde for thirty of his forty years at the mill. He was happy just to do his job and go home. He would bring in vegetables from his garden, and his wife would send him with treats occasionally. 'He would bring 'em in so proud. They were damn good cakes. You could tell he loved her,' some guy named Ralph Anders said.

On the other hand, no one knew whether he was close to his son or not, because as the years went on, he talked about the boy less and less. There was no mention of him when Clyde started asking for a lot of time off. He had to ask people to cover his shifts, and word got out that his wife had cancer.

'It got to be too much for him real quick,' said Andrew Yasuda. 'I saw him go in to the office one day and he came out with a bunch of papers full of numbers. I asked him what was going on, and he said that he was going to have to retire early. That it wasn't going to be good, money-wise, but he had to take care of Nell. He was almost crying. It was the most words he ever said to me in a row, and I worked with him twelve years.'

It didn't seem appropriate to throw him a retirement party, so instead they took up a collection and bought him a bunch of garden supplies and a large balance gas card, so he could fill up plenty to get Nell to her chemo appointments. Within a year, they were going to her funeral, where they saw Lonnie for the first time. 'We'd all kinda forgotten he had a son,' Yasuda said. 'They both looked pretty devastated.'

After that, the lumber mill workers gradually lost touch. Clyde wasn't a big one for reaching out, and everyone else's lives moved on. Sheila could only imagine his lonely breakfasts at the diner. And the serendipitous Tuesday mornings when they started to meet one another. Even for a man who didn't mind being alone, meaningful contact with his contemporaries must have given him some happiness. Otherwise he wouldn't have kept going back. And he certainly wouldn't have leapt headlong into the bocce shenanigans if he wasn't enjoying himself. Clyde was finally starting to live again after Nell's death. And then . . .

Her phone rang in the quiet dark. It startled her so badly she knocked her mug over. She answered it and said hello to Sam as the last dregs of coffee soaked into her granny's handmade Thanksgiving tablecloth.

'Oh, good. I figured you'd be up.'

'Yes, I am,' she said. 'The question is, why are you up?'

'Getting started on things. Because I got to be done by five tonight. So what do you want me working on today?'

Sheila thought about where her day was headed and made a snap decision.

'Nothing. You take the day off. You weren't scheduled originally anyway, so just stick with that. I'll see you Monday.'

'Wait – what? What are you talking about? We've got an active homicide investigation.'

Yes, my sweet boy, but I also have a pending sick-out that you don't know about and that I don't want you pulled into. I just want to keep you out of it altogether, because I don't want you to have to choose sides . . . because I'm afraid that you might choose the side against me. But instead of that she said, 'Sammy, you've been working really hard. And you've done a great job. If I need you today, I'll call you in, I promise. I'm mostly just waiting on Des Moines and Lonnie's alibi.'

He grumbled some more and then hung up, but not before telling her to have a nice day. Yes, he surely was her sweet boy, she thought as she pressed her hand into the warm coffee stain. She needed to keep him that way and not have him sullied by the mud that was about to start slinging. Or by seeing how dirty she could fight.

TWENTY-FIVE

F in was asleep in one of Jerry's myriad guest bedrooms. Hank had made her leave her house last night for two reasons. First, it was always brutal to watch investigators go through your personal items, which started happening after a judge signed a search warrant for the whole Lancaster residence. And second, who knew if Lew would come back in the middle of the night? He sure as hell didn't trust the man, and he didn't trust Fin's safety in a place that Lew had ready access to.

He settled into Jerry's cushy leather sofa and started browsing the Mizzou football game day coverage as he finished his coffee. He was halfway through an analysis of the defensive line when Maggie called.

'Hi, babe. I figured you'd be up. Are you coordinating things?' she said.

He thought for a second. 'I wouldn't say that, exactly. It's more like I'm being a buffer between Fin and the local police.'

Wait, how did Maggie know what was going on? Then he heard a dish clatter on the other end of the line.

'What?' she said. Loudly. 'What the hell are you talking about?'

He rubbed at his stubbled jaw and looked out at the still dark morning. He took a deep breath and gave his wife the shortest synopsis he could.

'This has been going on for four days, and you're just now telling me?'

'Honey, it's not like that. It's just—'

She cut him off as everything clicked together in her mind. 'Wait – you knew before. Before you left. You knew something was going on. You and Fin. You were going to go up there and investigate, not relax. So that's why you were so OK with "taking a break".'

Her tone sent the air quotes zinging at him like spears. He winced.

'Has it helped Fin to have you there?' she asked.

'Oh, God, yes. We wouldn't have gotten this quick a police response or had good information to give them. And the . . .' he trailed off. He'd been about to say that Fin would be exposed to a possibly dangerous Lew if he hadn't moved her. Better to keep that bit to himself.

'Well, you're a sneaky bastard.' Now he could hear her fighting to keep from smiling. 'Do you think Fin is going to need to come down and stay with us again?'

They talked about the possibility. If it did happen, it would at least eliminate the problem of how car-less Hank would get home. If Fin stayed put, though, Hank would need a ride. Maggie, who was about to leave for a shift, said she would be working every day until Tuesday. She could drive up and get him then.

'That sounds good.' A childless, father-in-law-less, uninterrupted block of time with just his wife? It sounded like heaven. They never got that anymore. He smiled, and then paused. 'Wait a sec. What were you talking about? When you asked if I was coordinating things?'

'Oh, yeah. I was talking about the murder. Since you hadn't come back, I figured you were directing things from up there.'

Hank slowly straightened out of his sofa slouch. 'What murder?'

On the other end, the bustling background sounds of Maggie getting ready for work stopped.

'The body found out on Nighthawk. On Wednesday. You don't know?'

His nerve ends felt like they were sizzling.

'I just saw it in the *Daily Herald* this morning. I was surprised you hadn't mentioned it when we talked on Thursday – although now I'm understanding why.'

Hank still didn't say anything.

'Honey?' Maggie said softly. 'You OK?'

'I need to go now.'

'Hank? Hank. Everything's fine. It sounds like it's well in hand. I'm sure Sheila had a good reason to—'

Hank said goodbye and hung up before she could finish. Then he had to think for a minute to come up with the actual name of the newspaper, which he always thought of as the *Daily*

What's-It. The article led the paper's web page. He scanned it quickly and rose to his feet. He could see it all in his mind like a flow chart. The anonymous mailman had talked to his co-worker Tyrone Turley, who passed on the info about a welfare check to his wife. Sheila had then had somebody go out to make sure this Timmons guy was all right. Hank wondered who she sent. He hoped not Sammy. Either that, or he hoped the scene hadn't been too bad.

This all happened seventy-two hours ago. And Sheila had not told him. Sam had not told him. He took the stairs two at a time and threw his clothing back in his suitcase. He went back down to the kitchen, scrawled Jerry a note, took a set of keys that weren't his, and left through the garage.

At least he hadn't gotten all dressed in his uniform yet. He was still in sweats and a T-shirt when he called Sheila and got the smackdown. He couldn't believe she didn't want him to come in today. They always worked nonstop during a homicide investigation. He stopped with his hand halfway into the cereal cupboard as a thought occurred to him.

What if it had to do with overtime? Sam knew he was already in OT territory for the week, so today would just add even more to Sheila's balance sheet. But, come on. It was a murder. That took priority over everything. He sighed. Sometimes he thought he understood her pretty well. And then other times, it felt like he didn't understand her at all.

He pulled the Golden Grahams out of the cupboard, poured a bowl and started stabbing his spoon into it. So now what the heck was he supposed to do with himself all day? He'd been counting on a busy day at work to keep his mind off of tonight and how nervous he was. He ran through a dozen possibilities and two full bowls with milk before it occurred to him. The Chief's errand. He'd never reported back to Hank after looking at that storefront. He got out his phone and stared at it, but had the same problem he'd had yesterday. He couldn't write a text without feeling guilty. *Oh, by the way, sir – there's a murder going on. I must've just forgot to mention it when I talked to you before.* He shoved the phone away with a groan, but quickly pulled it back. He could do more. He could look into it further.

He could drive by there again. He could definitely run the plates of those cars that were parked out back of the building.

He quickly changed into jeans and a sweatshirt and went outside to scrape the frost off the Bronco's windshield. Not for the first time, he wished he'd been able to find a house to rent that had an enclosed garage. He hated having to do this every winter morning. The little place did have its good points, though. It had a washer and dryer, which a lot of rentals didn't include. And the shed out back had room for all his hunting gear, and his mountain bike. He loved that. It was so great not having to go back over to his parents' house every time he needed some of his stuff. A lot of the people he went to high school with weren't that lucky. Not only were their things still at home, *they* were still at home. And it'd been more than seven years since graduation. Granted, for some of them the problem was a lack of motivation rather than a lack of employment opportunities.

By the time he got everything cleared off, the sun was completely up. He made sure he had his notebook and his phone and headed out with the old Bronco's heater on high and a cloud of exhaust billowing from its dented tailpipe. Ten minutes later he was in an empty parking lot. This time he parked and got out. He peered in the windows but didn't see anything more than he had during his drive-by yesterday. He trudged around the building to the back, where the closed metal door looked the same, too. He paced for a minute or two, smacking his gloved hands together as he walked. Then he tried the door. It was locked. He was starting to turn away when he noticed scuff marks on the asphalt outside the door. He backed away and looked at them from different angles. Probably just boxes or something getting dragged into the store. See, they went toward one of the barely outlined parking spots up against the cinder block wall of the building. He took a few steps back toward his truck and then stopped to look again. The thing was, they seemed to be going away from the door, not toward it.

He shook his head in exasperation. They were dirty marks on blacktop. Behind an empty store. That was all. Hell, he didn't even know why the Chief wanted him to check out this location in the first place. What was he even supposed to be looking for? He wished he knew. It would occupy a lot more time if he had a genuine thing to investigate. He walked back to the Bronco, which had been joined by a Dodge pickup at the other end of the lot. He added that license number to his list and walked the length of the strip mall. Two spots from the far end, there was another empty storefront. This one still had the 'For Lease' sign in the window. He saw himself grin in the window reflection. Calling the phone number on the sign would give him more to do. He snapped a picture with his phone and hustled back to the Bronco. His ears were starting to freeze.

The inside of the sheriff's Branson substation wasn't much warmer than the parking lot had been. It was seldom used, with only two tiny offices and a barely functioning coffee pot. But it was much closer than department headquarters fourteen miles away in Forsyth. Sam kept his coat on as he booted up one of the old desktop computers. He ran the license plates and printed out all the information. Then he dialed the property management company. He knew it was a Saturday, but he figured he could at least leave a message.

The guy picked up immediately. Sam thanked him for answering on a weekend and explained why he was calling.

'Yeah,' the man sighed. 'I got this last lousy space to fill and two more across town, so I'm answering every call I get. It's not the high-flying nineties anymore, when this town could support umpteen outlet malls and people were banging down my door. Now even if I got tenants, they up and leave. I'm losing the one in the middle of that center next month. Oh, wait. Man, I can't let that get out while I'm trying to lease this last space.'

Sam swore that he wouldn't tell anyone that Nora's Quilts & Collectibles was closing. But he really did need to know who'd rented the one at the end but hadn't moved in yet. There was some paper shuffling and keyboard tapping. It was a limited liability company out of Columbia called Drawbridge Holdings, he said. They signed the lease five weeks ago. All done over email. They hadn't even wanted to see the space. Just made sure it had an enclosed storage room and back entrance. He was frankly a little surprised they hadn't moved in their merchandise and opened for business yet, since they'd been so hot to sign the lease.

Sam thought that was a little strange, too. Who had he given the keys to?

'Mailed them to a post office box up in Columbia,' said the lease man, whose name was Ray Gillespie. 'And you know . . . all of this was done over email, now that I think about it. Doing some of it that way isn't unusual, but to do the whole business and then have the keys mailed is . . . well, kind of odd, frankly.'

Sam thought so, too. Was this what the Chief was looking into? At least Mr Gillespie had been smart enough to make sure the deposit money and rent check cleared the bank before sending off the keys. He'd even upped the amount of the security fees from what he normally charged, just because he hadn't been able to speak with anybody directly. Which Sam thought was a pretty darn good idea.

'So, is something shady going on?' Mr Gillespie asked.

'That's a good question, sir. I don't know at this point, but if you could contact me immediately if they get in touch with you for any reason, that would be great.'

He agreed instantly and sounded almost excited as he hung up the phone. Sam loved people like that. They usually turned out to have wanted to grow up to be cops when they were kids, and they always turned out to be really helpful. He double-checked all the information and took a deep breath. Time to text Hank.

TWENTY-SIX

The paper was divided in half. Two columns. One had a long list of names. Some were written in pen – they'd already phoned in sick. The rest were in pencil, only because their shifts were later in the day and they hadn't yet called. Sheila was getting an average warning time of only ten minutes before a deputy's shift was supposed to start.

The second column had two names. Herself and Molly March. She had a couple of hopefuls, but she hadn't dared write down their names for fear of jinxing it. She flipped the notebook closed just as the office phone rang again. Another name went from pencil to pen. Then she programmed the phone so it would ring through to her cell and walked over to the jail. The sun was barely up and the shift was just changing. It would be the only time she'd get to be outside until God knew when.

'Well, good morning. *Ma'am*.' Bubba Berkins waddled out and didn't even try to hide his smirk. 'Why in heaven are you here on a Saturday?'

'Come to talk to that Timmons inmate. Why?'

A flash of disappointment crossed his face. He wanted to witness her anxiety over the sick-out. But there was no way she was going to let on that she knew anything was about to happen. She gave him a bland smile.

'You have a good day there, Bubba. You're back on tonight, right?'

'Well, yes, I am. Ma'am.'

He conjured up a little coughing fit and it was all Sheila could do not to roll her eyes. She wished him well and went inside. She'd bet money that he would call in sick less than five minutes before his next shift. She went through the motions of readying the interview room until she knew that everyone had left. Then she sent a quick text. Two minutes later, Earl Crumblit came in from the parking lot, where he'd been waiting. Earl was the civilian who worked the reception desk at the jail. He usually dealt with jail visitors and information requests. Not today.

'It's you and me until three o'clock,' she said. 'Lock the lobby doors and put up a sign that we're closed to visitors this weekend. Say it's a maintenance issue.'

'They're all actually sicking out, are they? Damn shame.'

'And you're OK with being here, even with that going on? There could be blowback for you.'

Earl snorted. 'I'm "just" a civilian. Most of them always make damn sure to let me know that I ain't in their league. So I don't owe them a thing. But Sheriff Worth, him and you have always treated me good. Like I'm somebody, too. So I'm happy to help.'

'Thank you.' She'd never meant it more. With the two of them, they just might keep things operational until Deputy

March came in at three o'clock. She went back in to the control station just as her phone rang with Ted Pimental's number. She held her breath and picked up.

Jerry's BMW ate up the miles to Branson. The phone rang through the Bluetooth stereo system halfway around Lake of the Ozarks.

'Hi, Jer. I'm sorry about the car. I'll bring it back when . . . well, I don't know when.'

'I don't care about the car. I want to know why there's an elderly woman making tea in my kitchen.'

Half a mile went by while Hank tried to process that one. Oh. Aunt Fin.

'I didn't leave that in my note?'

'Maybe. It's hard to tell.' Jerry was trying not to laugh. 'Little illegible, bro. What kind of fire got lit under your ass?'

'I just found out there's a . . .' He searched for words and came up empty. All he had was an enraged buzzing in his head. 'A work emergency. I need to get back to Branson.'

'Hmm . . . I'd think it was bullshit, except that your job actually does involve genuine emergencies. However, I'm pretty sure it *doesn't* involve leaving old ladies with your single roommate and cramping his style.'

'Oh, God, did you bring someone home last night?'

'Well, no. I was referring to wandering downstairs in only my boxers with a bottle of Tums in my hand.'

'That is more your style these days.'

'Don't be impertinent, or I'll call *my* police and tell them someone stole my car.'

'I said I was sorry.' Hank steered through traffic while explaining why Maggie's aunt was staying in Jerry's spare bedroom. 'You didn't scare her, did you?'

'Her? I'm the one who shrieked like a little girl. She, on the other hand, thanked me very nicely for my hospitality, gave me the once-over, said I looked too skinny, and offered to fix me some eggs.'

'Did you take her up on it?'

'I did not. Me and my closure-free underwear hightailed it back upstairs, whereupon I called you. You asshole.'

Fair enough.

'Can you keep her for a few days? Well, I mean, can you continue to house her? I don't want her going back home, but she has to stay in Columbia because the police are going to need to interview her again.'

'OK, then, I'll . . . wait, would they come here? To talk to her?'

'Maybe. I don't know.'

'Uh . . .' Silence descended on the phone line.

'Jerry . . . why would you be worried about that?'

'Um, no reason. I think. I should probably do a quick sweep beforehand, though.'

He was pretty sure Jerry was messing with him, but still . . .

'You didn't do that before I came?'

Jerry scoffed. 'You are easily outwitted, my friend. But I don't know these guys. They might be smart.'

Hank smothered a laugh. And then thought of something for the cheeky bastard.

'So since I have this car, I'm sure you could always use Fin's if you needed something bigger than the Acura. She parked in the driveway last night.'

'Oh, good. I might need to go to Home Depot.' He heard window blinds rattle. 'Oh, my God, a Buick?'

'Bye, Jer.'

The voicemail Sam left for Hank said he had information, but the Chief hadn't called back. In itself, that wasn't too big a deal, but he'd been hoping the Chief would give him something else to do. If he didn't have something to occupy himself, he would go crazy by the time tonight came around. Maybe he could sneak in some Timmons case work, if he could figure out a way for Sheila not to find out. He decided to canvass Nighthawk Lane again. It couldn't hurt. He was locking up the substation when Willy Hoch called.

'I just wanted to make sure you're on board, kid.'

Sam stopped, keys dangling from his hand. 'Huh? On board with what?'

'So you're going to play dumb, instead of manning up and admitting that you're with them?'

'Willy, I have no idea what you're talking about. Honest.'

'The sick-out. Right now. Every deputy is calling in. See what that bitch thinks of her no OT policy now.'

The keys slipped through his fingers and hit the concrete. That was why Sheila ordered him not to come in today. She'd known about the sick-out and wanted to keep him out of it.

'You better not be at work.'

Hoch's voice finally cut through the torrent of thoughts in Sam's head.

'Uh, no. I'm not on the schedule, actually,' he said slowly. 'So I'm not working today. Or tomorrow.'

'Good.' It came out as a grunt. Hoch had always been a dick. If it was someone else who'd called, he'd be tempted to ask some questions. But not with this guy. Hoch warned him not to answer any calls for overtime and hung up. Sam sagged against the wall of the substation.

Sheila had manipulated things so that he could avoid making a decision. Was he mad? Was he grateful? Was he with the rank and file or was he with the top brass? Could he keep walking the line between the two? There'd always been some tension there, ever since Hank took office and started using him for investigations more often. He saw the looks sometimes from other deputies. Not all of them, but definitely some. He'd always pushed it to the back of his mind, telling himself it wasn't something that would ever have to be dealt with. Now here it was.

He stood there, breath billowing around him in the freezing air. His fingers were going numb. His keys were still on the ground. He didn't know what to do.

Tyrone answered the door.

'Hi there, Hank. You're back in town? It's good to see you.'

Hank nodded as politely as he could. He liked Sheila's husband. Under normal circumstances, he'd love a cup of coffee and a nice chat. These were not normal circumstances. He asked to speak with Sheila.

'Oh, she's not here.'

Hank looked at her Toyota 4Runner in the driveway of the Turleys' ranch home.

'She brought a squad car home last night,' Tyrone said. 'I

think because she knew she'd be going in today. Said she had to get to the jail early.'

Had she arrested someone in connection with the homicide? The question must've been visible on his face, because Tyrone shook his head sympathetically.

'I know, man. It's just nuts. I can't believe they're doing it either.'

'Do you know—' Hank stopped himself. He had absolutely no right to interrogate this nice man. Especially when only Sheila could answer the one question that mattered. What the hell was she thinking, not telling him about the murder? 'Never mind. I'll find her. Thanks, Tyrone.'

Better that the conversation wasn't here, anyway. Tyrone didn't need to hear what Hank was planning to say to his chief deputy. He walked back out to Jerry's car and pointed it toward Forsyth and the main sheriff's department complex. The route would take him right by his own house. He thought about that. No one there was expecting him today. He would go home, certainly – but he didn't have to do it right this minute. He could get away with taking care of this mess first. But as he sped past the turnoff, he couldn't bear to turn his guilty gaze in its direction.

TWENTY-SEVEN

She'd forgotten how much she hated working the jail. The smells. The clanging noise. The visceral anger coming from so many cells. Resignation coming from the rest. All of it rolling off the inmates just as fiercely as the odors did.

She was almost four hours into her 'shift', which would last what – twenty-four hours? Would people report to work tomorrow, or would there be another sick day? She had no idea. She looked at the clock and nodded at Earl. The two of them had settled on a routine. Every half hour, he watched the monitors solo while Sheila did a swing through both the men's and the women's sections. It violated just about every procedure in the book, but she had no choice. She'd given him a deputy's coat to wear, so he looked slightly more legit than he did in his civilian employee button-down shirt. The last thing she needed was the population figuring out there was only one sworn officer in the whole building.

She decided to do the women first this time. It was a much quicker inspection on this side. There was only about one female inmate for every four men. She walked along the corridor. Most of the inmates were still asleep. She would be too, in this place. Thank God there was no one of either gender on suicide watch or with severe medical problems. She'd lucked out with that. She gave her nerves a good steeling and crossed over to the men's side. She was immediately met with cat calls and worse. She kept a bored look on her face and walked the circuit at the leisurely pace she'd settled on the first time she'd done it this morning.

Earl buzzed her back into the control room. Where Hank stood waiting. Arms crossed. Smoke coming out of his ears. Well, not in actuality, but in spirit, definitely. He must have seen the *Daily Herald* story.

'Why are you in here?' The words came out like cut glass.

She spread her arms wide. 'Do you see anybody else?'

He looked around and seemed to register for the first time that the man who'd let him in was Earl Crumblit, desk jockey. Earl stepped back under the heat of his glare. That wouldn't do. She raised her arm and was starting her reprimand finger-point when Hank seemed to give himself a mental shake.

'Earl. I'm sorry. I didn't realize that was you. A little too focused, I guess. Or you're conducting yourself exactly like a deputy and I didn't notice any difference.'

He gave Earl a smile that was pretty good – Sheila could tell it was forced, but Earl couldn't. He broke into a grin and stood tall, straightening his borrowed coat.

'Now that I'm here to help out, how about you go out and check the phone? Just in case there are any messages that are important. Don't bother with anything you think isn't, but maybe just give it a check, OK? Then come on back.'

Earl gave him a cheerful salute and hustled out toward the lobby. Hank turned slowly back to Sheila. She braced herself.

'I hear there was a homicide.'

'Yes, there was.'

'And you chose not to call me.'

'Yes, I did.'

'And why was that?'

His hands were in his pockets, probably so they wouldn't be balled into fists. She hooked her thumbs on to her duty belt, relaxed.

'You'd only been gone a day. And you took the time off in the first place to get your head right.'

He started to interrupt. She held up a hand. She'd decided this morning as she sat in her dark kitchen that when this conversation finally occurred, no words would be minced.

'No. That's why, and we both know it. And twenty-four hours is nowhere near enough time to accomplish that. You needed a break. By telling you about the murder, I would have been ensuring that you didn't take one. You would've come back immediately.'

To his credit, he didn't argue that point. He argued another one.

'I'm the damn sheriff. I need to be here. Regardless of the supposed necessity of my time off. *I need to be here.* There are public duties that are part of this kind of thing.'

'Duties that you hate.'

He glared at her. His hands were still in his pockets. He started to pace. He could only go three strides each way in the little room. He did that a few times and then slowly turned.

'You knew I would react this way, right? Which, let's be honest, isn't a great mood for me to be in, considering my "need for a break". So why risk it? Why risk more distress to me by keeping me out of a homicide case? You're always the one weighing the scales. Did it occur to you that *not* telling me might have a greater cost than telling me?'

Now he was standing stock still, staring at her.

He thought this was a very valid analysis. But Sheila just stood there, silent.

'Well?' he said.

She patted at her hair for the third time. He doubted she even realized she was doing it. It usually meant she was flustered, but other than that hand movement she looked calm as pie. It was not helping his temper.

'There is a command structure, you know.'

'Yes,' she said. 'There is. And when you are out of pocket, I'm in charge.'

He raked his hand through his hair. 'No. I wasn't that. I wasn't even halfway across the state.'

Now he got the eyebrow, arched above her brown eye like a sarcastic question mark. She was going to stick with that ridiculousness: he wasn't in command when the killing occurred and didn't have to be informed. He thought about insubordination. There was no going back if he uttered that word, though. His fingers dug into his palms as he jammed them back into the pockets of his jeans and tried to pace again.

'I know you don't think you were that bad,' she finally said. 'That you were going about things just like normal, and no one could tell that you were upset over the car crash.'

He stopped pacing.

'And that's not true,' she said. 'Everyone could see it. The line deputies, the civilian staff, everybody. And those kinds of people don't get worried, Hank. They get unsure. They get doubtful.'

'Doubtful? About what? I'm here, I'm fully present. If anything, doubt would be caused by me not being here.'

She shook her head and took a breath.

'No. It's the opposite. They saw the shape you were in. And the doubts were starting – about your ability to lead, your ability to handle tough situations. If I'd called you back for the murder, none of that would've changed. It would've been on even greater display. You'd have started . . . you'd have started to lose your authority.'

It was like ripping a Band-Aid off a still bloody wound. Who knew it would end up hurting worse when it was someone else's rather than her own? She felt behind her for the counter where the computer monitors sat and gripped the edge. Hard. Hank stood raw and exposed in front of her. She wanted to turn away and give him some privacy, but she hesitated – she didn't want him to think she was being dismissive. She was trying to protect his authority, not undermine it. Because as Hank went, so did she. And no one was more conscious of that than she was.

He straightened, to the full height she hadn't seen him bother with since the car crash, and started to speak.

'I think—'

The buzz knifed through them both, seizing Sheila's breath and making Hank slam into the counter as he whipped around toward the door. Earl waved through the window. Hank spun back toward her, knowing the room was soundproof. He seemed to have just remembered the oddness of a civilian in this area of the jail.

'What the hell is going on? Where is everybody? Are you the only one in here?'

'Yes. Which is why I need Earl. He's been a really big help, actually. We closed to visitors and he's been spelling me in here while I do walk-throughs.'

Oh, God, that was what Tyrone had been referring to. Not the murder, but the staffing.

'It's a sick-out, isn't it? Because of the new overtime. You. Should. Have. Called. Me.'

She allowed herself a you've-got-to-be-kidding-me, hands-on-hips glare for that one. 'Oh, yeah. Because that wouldn't be stressful at all for your mental health. *Hi there, Hank. Wanted to let you know that half your department's in open revolt. And the rest of them are just waiting to pick over the carcasses when it's all over. Wanna come back and watch it happen?*'

He raked his hand through his hair. Then, in a masterful avoidance tactic, he reached over and opened the door for Earl. A big smile and a hearty hello and the two men were off and running with Chiefs football opinions. Sheila stomped out. If anybody said so much as a word to her on her rounds down the cellblocks, she'd leave them hog-tied on an anthill.

TWENTY-EIGHT

The drive was aimless. It made Sam feel like he was doing something, taking some action, even though he really wasn't. He was still almost paralyzed. Usually decisions were easy. Do what was sensible, do what was right. But not this one.

He could side with the other deputies and keep them from making his life a living hell, or side with the bosses and keep his cushy gig helping them out. He sniffed, but just because the heater in the Bronco was turning the air and his sinuses bone dry. That was the only reason, he swore, as he sniffed again.

The sensible thing would be to side with the deputies. There wasn't much of an upside if he did – nobody was going to throw him a parade or anything – but the downside if he didn't would be enormous. Plus, these were the guys who taught him the ropes when he started the job, guys he went fishing with, guys who invited him to their kids' birthday parties.

But he knew the department was sinking financially. It had to cut costs somewhere. Sheila's overtime plan was definitely the best way to do it without having to lay off people. Why couldn't everybody see that?

He sighed and headed farther east. So there was the choice that was sensible for the department, and the one that was sensible for him personally. He scratched his ear. When he thought about it that way . . .

He was thinking about stopping for a soda at the Conoco by the Highway 76 junction when his cell rang. He saw that it was Ted Pimental. He pulled over on the grassy shoulder, took a deep breath, and answered it.

'Did you take a report a couple days ago about a stolen car?'

'Huh?'

Ted repeated the question. Sam struggled to switch his brain into the proper gear.

'The . . . what . . . you . . . you aren't calling about the sick-out?'

Ted snorted. 'No. I'm patrolling out by Stone County. Someone called in a suspicious vehicle out near Rozwell Road, south of the Hercules Glades Wilderness Area. It matches the description of the one stolen from those folks out off Highway Sixty-five. I thought since you took the report, you could check it out. I'm swamped over here.'

'I don't have a squad—' Sam cut himself off. It didn't matter that he wasn't in a department vehicle. 'You bet. I'll head over there now. And any other calls that come in you need covered, just lemme know, OK?'

Sam took a last look at the fallow field and pulled the Bronco into a sharp U-turn. The location was in the middle of nowhere, but so was he at the moment. He could be there in ten minutes. It would've taken Ted more than forty-five. He sped toward the mile marker. It'd be great to recover a stolen vehicle, even if it did belong to those insurance fraudsters.

Hank was starving, but that wasn't why he sent Earl out to pick up lunch for the three of them. He buzzed Sheila back into the control room and they stood across from each other, two foes in a dusty Old West town, ready to draw. Except she was the only one with a gun.

'Where's Earl?'

'I sent him to the Whipstitch for sandwiches.'

She nodded and stayed silent. He knew she would stay that way – she would not be the first to speak. She had nothing else to explain. She thought she'd done the right thing. He knew she hadn't. But a stalemate wouldn't do either of them any good as the whole place went up in flames around them. He softened his stance, leaning back against the counter. He was the boss; he should talk first.

'I'd expected that we would spend the day discussing the homicide and . . . your decisions. I hadn't expected the sick-out. So we obviously have a lot on our plate. We will revisit all this – but right now, what's the staffing like? How bad is it?'

She told him, and it was worse than the worst he'd conjured up as he waited for her to finish her rounds. Only Molly March was expected to report for jail duty today. And as for patrol, there were two men on the street – Ted Pimental and Derek Orvan. Hank felt like he'd been punched. Only two? And neither name was the one he'd expected. He nodded slowly.

'OK. Then that's what we work with. Are you all right here with Earl? I can get out and help with patrol.'

'I should be fine. Having another person on the streets would really help.'

He made no move to go. They were back to the gunslinger standoff in the dusty street.

'When would you like an update on the homicide investigation?' she asked.

Thank God. That was how it should be under normal circumstances – the commander gets briefed on important cases. Her bringing it up just like it was a normal briefing showed that she considered him fully back at work. And she was prepared. She gave him a run down in about five minutes. It didn't take any longer because they didn't have a whole lot of leads. The victim's son, who was apparently already a guest of their fine jail facility, looked good for it. But they hadn't been able to confirm that all of his alibi was no good. And then there were the bocce guys, who hadn't been completely cleared, either.

'I'm sorry . . . the what? Bocce?' He didn't think he'd heard her correctly.

That took even longer to explain. He still didn't feel like laughing, but he couldn't help himself.

'Hey,' Sheila said, 'for all we know, one of these yahoos is the killer. So you best keep a straight face.'

He tried to oblige, which was difficult until he considered how much he would have enjoyed taking this one from the beginning. A jolt of anger hit him because now here he was, nothing but a late-to-the-party rube who'd never catch up. He tried to refocus on what she was saying.

'I think it goes way back. The motive for this. The poor guy's wife died nine years ago, and that's when the relationship with the son really went off the rails. Which could just be further evidence that he's the killer. But . . . I don't know . . .'

She had his full attention now. 'Don't tell me what you think,' he said. 'Tell me what you feel.'

'There's something else there. I don't know what it is, but I don't think it's the son. Their crappy relationship was the same as it'd been for years. The only thing that changed recently in Clyde's life was that damn bocce group.' She shrugged. 'My head says Lonnie, my gut says bocce.'

'OK. At least we can be reasonably sure nobody's going to flee the area while we're dealing with this bullshit today.' He straightened from his lean against the counter. 'I'm going to check out a sidearm and grab a patrol car. Keep me updated?'

She moved away from the door, which she'd been standing in front of since re-entering the little room. As she did, she gave him a piercing appraisal that felt like an X-ray of his head.

He knew she was wondering if he was back on an even keel. He wondered if she'd figured out the answer. He sure hadn't.

The way Ted had phrased it, Sam expected the car to be sitting here abandoned. It wouldn't be unheard of out here in the middle-of-nowhere middle of the county. Instead, there were only tire tracks on the grass shoulder that looked like they'd turned in on a dirt track and then come out again. He walked along the road for about twenty yards in each direction and found nothing else. Then he started into the woods.

The cover wasn't too dense. Many of the trees had lost their leaves and their bony limbs didn't block the weak winter sun. His worn Scarpa boots kept traction on the slick floor of wet leaves. The slightly peculiar rhythm of navigating that surface came as naturally to him as walking across a carpeted floor. And with every stride, he felt himself relax. The outdoors always did that to him. He took a deep breath and then almost choked on the laugh that caught him unawares. He should have been doing this to help him make sense of the whole work controversy, not driving around like a damn gas-guzzling fool. He was an idiot.

He moved farther into the trees and the narrow dirt track that the car had come down. The tracks were ridiculously easy to follow. For all he knew, though, the car had every right to be here and it was a nosy caller who was in the wrong. He kept at it and got about a mile in. At that point, he sided with the caller. Nobody had business coming in this far. If he'd had something else to do, he might've turned back. Judging by the tracks, the car had obviously come out again. So it hadn't been abandoned out here or anything. But now he was curious. And he figured the more curious he got about something, the more illegal it probably was.

He finally got to where the car had stopped. Not very well, either. The tracks cut deep into the leaves and the tires had obviously spun. Sam outlined the world's worst three-point turn and walked over to where the driver had stopped in the middle of executing it. The car had been perpendicular to the road, with the hood facing the trees on one side of the track and the trunk facing the trees on the other. He walked to the trunk side because nothing was ever dumped out of a hood this far back in the woods. You loaded up a trunk and—

It had rolled a ways down the slight incline. It was wrapped in black plastic, with duct tape around the neck and ankles. Because it was clearly a body. Sam swore. Loudly enough to send a hawk into the air from its perch at the top of the nearest shortleaf pine. He swore again, then skirted the area until he was around at the downslope side of the body. He hadn't seen footprints. The asshole must've just given it a good shove and not bothered to walk out past the car.

Sam knelt down to get a closer look. The person was average-sized, or at least not out-of-the-ordinary tall or over-weight. Otherwise, he couldn't tell a damn thing. And he couldn't touch anything until crime scene got here. He had to walk back up the incline to get a strong enough signal to call Alice. Kurt had a well-known dislike of nature and the hiking that outdoor crime scenes usually required. Fortunately, his partner loved it. She said she'd be out in a jiffy. He watched the hawk circling in the gray sky for as long as he could justify, then took a deep breath and called Sheila. Circumstances – or the crime gods or whatever – had overridden her decision and, whether she liked it or not, he was going to end up spending his day working.

TWENTY-NINE

She wished she'd been able to present him with a solved case, or at least one that was a lot further along than the mess she'd just served up. Sure, Lonnie Timmons was a legitimate suspect, but that would turn to shit real fast if his grocery store alibi came through. At least Hank found the bocce gang amusing. That, more than anything, showed he was improving. The old Hank would've thought it was hilarious. Post-crash Hank would merely have shrugged at it. This version wasn't as good as the original, but it was a damn sight better than before he went up to Columbia. She wondered what he'd been doing up there. What did grown adults do in a college town? Revert, probably.

She picked at her Whipstitch fries and watched the guy in cell number eight gesture at the inmate across the aisle. He returned the middle finger and added a few more that would make her granny roll over in her grave. Her interest rose. Maybe things would get bad enough she could throw one of them in solitary. That would definitely make her feel better. She let it go on for another few minutes and then nodded to Earl.

'I'm going to do my rounds, starting with those jokers. I might not get to the women's side for a while – keep an eye on them, will you?'

Earl was still flush with his new responsibilities and swore he wouldn't take his eyes off the monitors. She patted him on the shoulder on her way out the door. The minute she stepped outside the control room, the yelling and swearing and clanging made her ears ring. The noise doubled when they saw her. Five minutes later, she felt her cell vibrate in her pocket. She was a little busy, however, and didn't look at it until she'd thrown the instigator in the one cell that had no view into the corridor. All the entertainment went with him, and everyone else settled down.

She decided to finish her lunch before rounding through the women's wing. She'd just finished off her soda when she remembered the phone call. Sammy. That child. She hit return.

'What are you doing? You're off duty. You don't need to be calling me.'

All she heard was breathing. Even and calm. Then some wind. He must be outside.

'Sammy?'

'I do, actually. Need to call you. I got a report that the stolen car I was investigating had been spotted so I came out to the spot. I didn't find the car, but I—'

'You are not supposed to be doing that. I gave you the day off,' she said.

'Just shush.'

Sheila almost dropped the phone. It was like she was talking to herself.

'What did you say?' she finally managed.

'You can scold me later. Right now I found a body.'

Now she did drop the phone. Earl spun around in alarm. She scooped it up.

'Where the hell are you? Are you alone? Is the scene secure? Do you need backup?'

'Unless you want to protect me from an upset hawk, no, I don't need backup. I've already called Alice. She's on her way out here.'

He listed off the location. Another damn backwoods killing.

'No, I don't think so. Not really,' he responded. 'It's pretty easily accessible, dirt track all the way in. It's definitely a body dump. It's all wrapped in black plastic.'

So there was an additional crime scene out there somewhere. She pinched the bridge of her nose, which was suddenly radiating pain back into her head. She couldn't leave this forsaken building. Pimental was patrolling the entire western half of the unincorporated county. Orvan was way out east. He might be the best choice. Then she remembered.

'I'm going to send you someone. Hank's back in town.'

'Really?' There was relief in his voice. She might have been offended under normal circumstances, but the way things stood at the moment, she had to agree with him.

'Yeah. I'll get him out there. Call me with an update, OK? Especially after you unwrap that plastic.'

Sam said he surely would and ended the call. She thought about contacting the coroner but decided that Hank could take care of that out at the scene. It'd make him feel like he was running the show. In fact, this whole thing might make up for missing the last murder. A brand new one, all to himself.

He hit the lights and hung a U in the middle of the block. People pulled over as he sped east toward the Wilderness. A body dump was bad. A body dump on a short-staffed day like this was horrible.

Having something to investigate again, however, was fantastic.

He tried to raise Sam on the radio, but got no response. When he pulled up to the coordinates Sheila gave him, he understood why. The Pup's Bronco was in roadside dirt. He must be off duty. Had he found the body while he was out hunting? Hank pulled up behind the Ford, got out, and started looking near the cars for the best way into the woods. He'd just started down what looked like a path when Sam hollered at him. The kid was standing on the other side of the road.

'It's this way, sir.' Sam gestured over his shoulder. 'The track is through here.'

Hank crossed the road. This side looked no different to him than the other one, but Sam seemed to think where he was pointing was as obvious as a six-lane freeway. They walked about twenty yards and then things cleared out enough that he could see the twin ruts where tires had worn into the soil.

'It's a pretty established track,' Sam was saying. 'You can tell it's been here a while. It certainly wasn't blazed by the killer or anything.'

'Any signs of other people using it recently?'

'Nah. It rained last week and the only thing since then is the dump car.' He continued walking briskly along the side of the track.

'Shouldn't we wait for Alice?' Hank said.

'She'll find it. You're the one I was worried about.'

And him stumbling off in the wrong direction had done nothing to prove Sam wrong. Hank sighed and walked faster. He only slipped on the leaves once before he caught up to the kid.

'You off duty today?'

Sam explained about his earlier vehicle theft case and the call from Pimental. By then they were at the spot at the top of the incline. Sam pointed downhill and Hank could just make out the black plastic. They both stood silently for a moment.

'Sheila told me not to come in, to take the day off.' Sam kept his gaze on the body. 'She didn't say . . . well, anyway. I don't know how, but I think she knew the sick-out was coming.'

'And you're out here anyway?' Hank needed to tread very carefully.

'There was nobody else available to respond. Plus, it was my stolen car case in the first place.'

'We can keep you off the books if—'

Sam didn't let him finish. 'I'm just worried about her. People are nasty. People are gonna be nasty to you, but she's gonna get a whole other level of shit.'

He finally looked Hank in the eye. Hank nodded slowly. 'OK.'
They heard footsteps behind them and turned to see Alice
jogging down the track, a duffel full of gear over each
shoulder.

'Kurt will drive the van in when he's done with the tire casts
out by the road.'

'Wait, you got him to come?' Sam asked.

'Made him come.' She grinned. 'First I buttered him up about
his casting skills, but then I told him he didn't have a choice.
He's getting fresh air whether he likes it or not.'

She set her bags on the ground and looked around. 'When's
everybody else getting here? Where's the grid search?'

'Yeah . . .' Hank said. 'About that. We don't really have the
personnel for that today. I'll need to get the volunteer search
and rescue folks out instead.'

Alice stared at him. She took in his uniform and Sam's lack
of one.

'They went and did it, didn't they? How many?'

'We've got two deputies on patrol. That's it. I can't pull them
off to come help.' He raked his hand through his hair. 'I appreciate you coming.'

She scoffed. 'I've got no truck with all that. Plus, we weren't
even invited to join. We're just the hired help. Our work schedules don't matter to them one whit.' She reached down for a
bag but stopped halfway. 'Did I screw up? By making Kurt
come? Did that hurt your budget? I didn't even think of that.'

'No.' Hank shook his head. 'Absolutely not. I need you both
here. Sometimes overtime is unavoidable.'

He scooped up one of the duffel bags and headed toward the
body before she could say anything else. He did catch the look
that passed between her and Sam as he turned away, even if he
wasn't sure what it meant. He blocked it out – he just wanted
to get to the body. He might not be able to navigate office
politics, but he knew his way around a crime scene. He tagged
scuff marks in the dirt so Alice could start taking photos, working
his way closer and closer to the body.

Then he stopped. He walked back up to where the car had
made its three-point turn and turned slowly, taking in every
direction.

'Who would know about this track?' he said.

'I was thinking about that,' Sam said. 'It's hard to see, but if you were looking for something to take you back here into the woods, you'd find it.'

Excellent. Sam was asking – and answering – these questions on his own. Hank felt a surge of energy he hadn't experienced in a long time. He swung his arms in the chilly air and pulled out his phone. Time to call the coroner and get this poor person up to the morgue for unwrapping.

THIRTY

'**N**o, man. I'm not kidding. A dead body. Seriously.'

Sam was walking back to the road to wait for the coroner. It seemed like a good opportunity to update Ted.

'Nah,' he said into the phone. 'It's all wrapped in plastic. So we definitely don't have an ID.' He wanted to remove the plastic right now and felt a little guilty about it. It wasn't a Christmas present, for God's sake.

'Oh, and the sheriff's back. He's out here right now.'

'Did he come back because of the body, or because of the sick-out?' Ted asked.

'Huh. I don't know, actually. It does look like he was intending to patrol – he's got a uniform on and everything,' Sam said, then paused. 'Could I ask you something?'

Ted said sure.

'Why aren't you doing the sick-out?'

There was silence on the line for so long that Sam thought maybe the connection had broken.

'I thought about it,' Ted finally said. 'And it just seemed to be whining. It's not a protest over working conditions. It's whining that you can't manipulate the system to take more overtime than is needed. Plus, my wife works for the county, and she's said over and over that there's no money. Turley isn't exaggerating.'

Sam noticed that he'd slowed almost to a stop. He picked up his pace. 'Thanks. I was just wondering.'

'And here's the other thing,' Ted said. 'I was out for a long time. That rehab on my leg sucked. Everybody came by at the beginning, when I was in the hospital. And there were a few who kept with it, like you and Bill and Derek. But that was it. Except – you know who kept coming the whole time? The sheriff. He'd come to the house. Even drove me to physical therapy a few times I didn't have a ride. His wife would come and check on me at home so I wouldn't have to go all the way in for an appointment.'

There was silence for a moment.

'So if I've got to pick a side – and that's what it seems like it's come to – I'm going with the side that I feel good about.'

Sam hadn't known all that. It gave him a lot to think about as he hung up the phone. He kicked at the dirt some as he walked along the path, muttering to himself. He was well into a list of everything that was currently stressing him out when he rounded a curve and realized they hadn't blocked off the road yet. He strung up crime scene tape just as the coroner's van arrived. Once the body was brought out of the woods and loaded, Hank turned to him.

'Will you go up and watch the autopsy – see if there's any ID once they've got it unwrapped?' Hank asked.

Sam glanced at his watch. As he looked back up, he saw Hank's face fall.

'No, no,' Sam said quickly. 'It's just . . . I have something to do tonight. As long as I can get back down here by six thirty, I can do it. It's no problem.'

Hank looked relieved. It dawned on Sam that his boss thought he was hesitant because of the sick-out. After all, he was out here in civilian clothes. He'd obviously not expected to be working. So Hank wouldn't know what his intent was. Hell, he hadn't known what his intent was.

'It's no problem,' he repeated, with more certainty. 'As long as you don't mind me being on duty in my jeans, I'll head there right now and report back as soon as I know anything.'

Hank nodded. It looked like he was having trouble getting

any words out. He clapped Sam on the shoulder and turned quickly away.

Hank was back in the control room at two thirty, a half hour before shift change.

'Why're you back? This is when it actually gets a little better. Deputy March comes on duty at three,' Sheila said. 'That'll double my staffing levels. So I don't need you here.'

He ignored her and handed over the coffee he'd picked up for her at the Whipstitch. She took several sips before she spoke again.

'Do you have an ID on the body dump yet?'

'No. Sam and Kurt should be calling any minute, and at least be able to tell us what they saw when it got unwrapped.' He hated that he'd been forced to ask Sam to watch the autopsy. But he couldn't leave the county. Not with the damn sick-out going on. He looked at his watch. The deputies who were 'sick' should be calling in soon. And there was one in particular he wanted to talk with.

Sheila allowed herself to sink into one of the two chairs in the room. Exhaustion was carving lines around her eyes and mouth. She drank her coffee in silence, which was the final proof of her fatigue right there – she'd given up telling him to leave. Hank scanned the monitors and was about to ask where Earl was when the phone rang. Sheila started to rise but he waved her back and answered.

'Yes. I see. All right, that's fine. But deputy . . . I fully expect you to feel better in time for your next shift, do you understand?'

He listened for a moment and hung up. Sheila hoisted her empty cup and sent it sailing into the trash can across the room.

'That means Tucker's the only one on the incoming shift who still needs to call in,' she said.

Hank nodded. That was why he was here. He'd be taking that call and making clear that this whole overtime crackdown was his decision. And that whatever plot Tucker was busy conniving, he'd be up against Hank and the full weight of the sheriff's elected office. It must have been plain on his face, because Sheila rolled her eyes.

'I can handle him.'

'Oh, I know. You absolutely can. But I've left you hanging on this whole thing, and that stops right now. We both decided this was the road we were taking, and so far you're the only one who's had shit shoveled at you. So now it's my turn.'

'Well, when you put it that way . . .' She stood up to buzz in the young female deputy, who saw Hank and snapped to attention. That got him another Sheila eye roll. He sent the kid to walk the female wing just as the clock hit three. The two of them looked at each other. Tucker hadn't called. And he sure as hell wasn't here. They grinned at each other.

'Excellent,' Hank said. He was about to say more when his cell started buzzing. He answered it and put Sam on speaker.

'So, it's some dude. No wallet or ID on the body.'

'Dammit,' Sheila said. 'If it's another one of those bocce players, my head is going to spontaneously combust.'

Sam snorted with laughter. 'No. I've seen all the bocce guys. This guy is not one of them. Plus, he's nowhere near that old – probably just in his late twenties or early thirties. Skinny-to-medium build, wearing what look like pretty standard Walmart-type clothes. Kurt's bagging all of it, then he'll take fingerprints.'

'Cause of death?' Hank asked.

'Probably blunt trauma to the head. He was a little decomposed.' Now Sam sounded queasy. 'But not so much that Dr Whitaker couldn't see those wounds. He was definitely bashed on the head. It's just whether that killed him. I left before the doc got to the lungs and stuff so I could come out and call you. I hope that's OK.'

Sheila was nodding emphatically. 'It's fine,' she whispered, holding up two fingers. 'Two bodies in four days. The kid doesn't need to see all that after the week he's had.'

Hank assured him that was fine. 'Can you stay up there until Whitaker's done? Just in the lobby. If somebody's still in the building waiting, there's a better chance we'll get a preliminary report tonight. If you go, he'll cut out and we won't get anything for days.'

Silence.

'How long you think that'll take?' Sam finally said.

Hank and Sheila traded puzzled looks.

'You'll get paid,' Hank assured him. It was unlike Sammy
to balk at, well, anything. He was always up for whatever got
thrown at him. But it was also unlike normal circumstances
around here, so he supposed he couldn't fault the kid.

'That's not . . . oh geez . . . that's not it. I didn't mean . . .'
Sam sighed. 'I have a date. At six thirty.'

Now they both looked like proud parents. Then Sheila
smacked her hands together so suddenly Hank jumped.

'The coffee girl,' she said gleefully. 'It's the coffee girl, isn't it?'

'She's. A. Barista.'

'So it is her?'

'Yes. Her name is Brenna.'

Hank couldn't help himself. 'When do we get to meet her?'

'Oh, my God. Stop.'

Now they were laughing. Sheila clapped a hand over her
mouth and Hank cleared his throat to keep from chortling
straight into the phone.

'So I'm asking,' Sam said, his voice climbing a little higher
with every word, 'when I'll be done here. I don't want to be
late.'

Sheila jabbed a finger at Hank, then pantomimed driving a
car.

'OK, how about this,' Hank said. 'If you don't have what
we need by five fifteen, I'll come up and relieve you. That
should leave you enough time to get back here and shower
before you meet her. Where are you taking her?'

'Great. I'll check in at five fifteen or sooner.' The phone
clicked off.

'He hung up on me.' Hank stared at his phone.

''Cause you're being nosy.'

'Oh, and you're not?'

'Nope,' she said. 'I don't have to be nosy. Because I knew
it already.'

'You did not.'

'I did so. He's been sucking down those expensive Donorae
lattes like they're water. And that coffee girl was a witness in
our last homicide. She lived downstairs from the victim. Sammy
interviewed her during his canvass.'

'Then why did you seem to have an epiphany just now? If you knew before this? Hmm?'

'Oh, that was just me delighting in being proven right, because I—'

Her cell buzzed and stopped the patently ridiculous claims coming out of her mouth. Hank jabbed a finger at her and pantomimed answering a phone. She rolled her eyes.

'It's just a text. Your Marcel Marceau isn't needed.'

She pulled it up and said it was Sam with a photo of the dead man's face.

'Well, it's not as much decomp as it could've been, I guess,' she said. 'I wonder if he's a meth user – kinda has that skinny look to him.'

'I wonder how fast we can expedite a tox screen and . . .' Hank trailed off. He took her phone without asking.

'What?' she said.

He stared at the badly lit snapshot. The metal autopsy table was visible behind the man's head. His hair was more matted than he usually wore it. And there was certainly no volatile flicker in his eyes.

'What the hell is wrong?' Sheila said.

'His name's Vic Melnicoe.'

'Are you kidding me? You know him?'

Hank handed the phone back and sagged against the counter. He felt like he'd just had an iron anvil dropped on him.

'I think I need to tell you what I was doing up in Columbia.'

THIRTY-ONE

Sheila was pissed off. He brings murder back to town with him – and takes away resources from her homicide in the process. She'd been quite pleased with herself, getting him to laugh as they talked about Sam's date. Now this. Him freelancing a missing person investigation in a different county. It was obviously helping to pull him out of his funk, but God damn. That man. Knowing her luck, they'd find the missing woman dead in their jurisdiction, too.

She'd left him in the control room trying to get a hold of some Columbia detective. What she really wanted to do was take a walk in the fresh air, but since she was trapped in the damn jail, she did rounds instead. Her expression was so thunderous that no one even spoke as she walked by. She was ten feet past Lonnie Timmons's cell when it occurred to her that there were two other deputies here at the moment. She spun on her heel, yanked the asshat out of his cell, and marched him down to the interview room.

'What you want now?' He slouched in the chair and rattled his chain like an ill-mannered dog.

She dropped her notepad on the table. It landed with a smack, and Lonnie started to shift uncomfortably.

'I already told you. I didn't kill my dad.'

She sat down and folded her hands together. 'Yeah, I remember you saying that. But you didn't say why exactly the two of you didn't like each other.'

'He was an asshole. He wouldn't ever help me out. He said I was a loser.'

She did not disagree with the elder Timmons.

'You did say that,' she said. 'And I gave it some thought after we talked the first time. You hating him for that reason – that makes perfect sense to me. But for him to hate *you* for that reason? That's what doesn't make sense.'

She could imagine that the whining would irritate the living daylights out of a parent, or disappoint him or sadden him or whatever. But provoke hate? She couldn't see it. Especially considering that – by all accounts – Clyde was an otherwise decent guy. Good co-worker, loved his wife.

'So what happened to make your dad feel that strongly against you?' She leaned forward, putting her elbows on the table. 'Why did he go from being a hard ass to being an asshole?'

'Who told you that?'

'You did.'

'Oh.'

Sheila didn't blame Clyde for wanting to stay away from his son. She certainly wished she could. 'Did it have something to do with your mother? It happened around the same time she died, right?'

Lonnie picked at a fingernail.

'Your dad wasn't a jerk to other people once she died,' Sheila said. 'So why did he start being such a jerk to you? Did you say something about your mom? Were you mean to her when she was sick? Did you not come see her or something?'

'What? Wait, no way. Where the hell did you hear that? I was there all the time. Well, a lot of the time, anyway. Christ, I was the one who was there when she died. Not him. So really, I should be getting thanked, not getting accused.'

That was an interesting word choice. *Blamed* would seem to be a better description. Unless . . . She mentally searched through Sam's reports from his interviews with Nell's friends. Someone had said . . . dear God.

'Your dad told people he thought she'd been taken too soon,' she said slowly. Was that not a platitude? Had he been speaking literally? She leaned forward. 'What did you do?'

He froze, then started shaking his head. 'Nothing. I didn't do nothing.'

Her hand came down with a smack on the tabletop. 'Bullshit. Why would a perfectly ordinary person like your dad accuse you of something? You, who were with your mom when she died?'

'My God, is Dad talking to you from the grave? No, I didn't kill my mom, no matter what that old bastard thought. I didn't even know he thought that anyway. Not until that day at the house with—'

The words came out of him before self-preservation had a chance to kick in. Once it did, he shut up, which thank God gave Sheila a second of silence to corral the previously unrelated facts now spinning through her head.

'Unless you start explaining why he believed that and how all this shit started, I got no choice but to think you killed him,' she said. 'Which means you probably killed your mother, too. Which is two murder charges.'

Lonnie started to cry. It seemed to surprise him even more than it surprised Sheila, who was flat out astonished. He dragged his hand across his face, smearing tears and snot as he tried to suppress his reaction.

'Man, I didn't kill her. I don't know why my dad thought that. It explained a lot, though. He changed after she died. He just wouldn't have anything to do with me. But I was hard up this time. I owe people. I needed a loan.'

Clyde wouldn't take his calls, so Lonnie was forced to come down to Branson. He went to the house and asked for money.

'He lost his shit, man. Totally lost it. Started yelling at me about how dare I come in the house where Mom died. I said, "What does that have to do with anything?" and he's shouting about how I killed her somehow. That he would've had more time with her. I was like, "What the fuck?"'

'Had your dad ever accused you of this before?'

Lonnie shook his head. His dad had never said the words outright, but after that day, a lot of the comments that Clyde made over the years about Nell going way too soon suddenly made sense.

'Then what happened?'

He shrugged. 'I left.'

She leaned back and gave him her rock-hard disbelief look. He wiped his nose and then examined the sleeve of his jail scrubs.

'You didn't yell back? That seems unlike you.'

He scowled. 'You know everything then, don't you? So why ask? I want to go back to my cell.'

'You did more than yell, actually. You busted some furniture. You got violent. You got mad enough to kill.'

'So I threw a table. It doesn't mean I killed him. I left town and I only came back when you . . .' – he stabbed his finger at her with a shaking hand – 'you called me. You. I wouldn't be here except for you.'

She calmly pulled a sheet of paper from the middle of her notepad and slid it across the table. It was a copy of the parking ticket Pimental had tracked down that showed Lonnie's stolen car in Branson just before the murder. His white-boy complexion went from pasty to ashen.

'Well?' she said.

He sagged down in his hard plastic chair. She hoped this would puncture his last reservoir of hot air.

'I was living out of the car. I thought I'd try again with Dad in a week or so. Because I had no place else to go.'

'What would happen if you went back to Des Moines?'

'I'd rather not get my legs broke, OK?'

'Who do you owe the money to?'

'Oh, hell no. I ain't saying. That . . . no . . . that's it. I'm done. I want to go back to my cell.'

Sheila plucked the ticket from his hand and walked out of the room in a much better mood than when she walked in. He was still sniffling as the door closed behind her. She was a little ways down the corridor when the next door opened and Hank walked out of the observation room.

'You made a grown man cry. That was a beautiful thing to watch.'

She patted at her hair. 'Shouldn't you be helping Deputy March in the control room?'

'Nah. She's darn sharp. She can handle it. Plus, Earl's back.'

'Good,' she said. 'I need to run over to the office and get my case file.'

Hank turned toward her. 'Do you believe him?'

'If he was going to put on an act, I think he'd choose blasé. Or bored. Not weepy. But maybe I'm not giving him enough credit. Maybe he is a devious genius, and that whole thing was first-rate theater.' She slowed her brisk walk. 'There is one thing that I do absolutely know is true. Clyde Timmons believed that his wife was the victim of a mercy killing. I don't know if she really was or not, but he thought so. And somehow, that ended up being his death sentence.'

He'd talked to Ghassan three times in the past hour, so when his cell rang again he didn't even look at it.

'Yeah.'

'Why is Aunt Fin staying with Jerry Heinrich?' his wife said. 'Have you taken leave of your senses?'

'Um . . . how'd you hear that?'

'She called me. She said she couldn't get a hold of you and wanted to know if you made it back safely.'

Hank cringed.

'Where have you made it back to, *dear*?'

'Here in town. At the office, actually. It's that murder you called me about this morning. I was going to call you . . .'

'What a relief that I'm not getting added to your list of abandoned family members.'

When Maggie went sarcastic, it was a blowtorch that left behind only scorched earth and his charred skeleton.

'Honey,' he said, 'I'm really sorry. I should've called. I just . . .'

'Yeah, yeah. I knew when I called you this morning that you'd probably break land-speed records getting down here. That's not my point. My point is why the hell isn't Aunt Fin at her own house?'

He didn't have the half hour necessary to properly explain the rest of the story he'd abbreviated during their phone call earlier that morning. Sam was on the office line, and Ghassan was leaving a voicemail on his cell right now.

'Lew might be having some . . . financial difficulties. It was easier for Fin to stay somewhere else.'

'Well, I told her to come straight down here.'

'You what? No, that's not . . . don't do that.' He thought of Lew's employee lying in the local morgue. The danger had migrated to Branson County. Aunt Fin was safer where she was.

'Why not?' Maggie said. 'You can't just go dumping people on random strangers.'

There was dumping people, and then there was *dumping* people. He was a little occupied with the second kind at the moment.

'Honey. Calm down. She's fine. Jerry's fine. He's certainly not a random stranger.'

'He is to her!'

'Your aunt could handle a horde of invading Mongols if she needed to. She's not going to be flustered by an extroverted forty-year-old. She should stay where she is.'

But Maggie had already hung up. Hank set his phone on the desk and dropped his head in his hands. If she was mad now, she'd go volcanic when she heard the whole story of what Lew was suspected of doing. The only hope was that it would be directed at Lew and not him. He promised himself that he'd tell her everything tonight.

The office phone beeped. Sammy was still on hold. He grabbed it and apologized. 'The fingerprints Kurt sent me match Melnicoe in the state database,' he said. 'He's got priors in St Louis for theft and assault.'

'So what was he involved with in Columbia?' Sam asked.

Hank sighed. 'He worked for Maggie's uncle. The Columbia police are searching for the old man right now. Turns out there's been some fraud at his company. And he's also a suspect in the disappearance of his secretary, who's probably dead somewhere just like Melnicoe.'

'Damn.' Sam drew out the word. 'That's insane. Is Columbia going to help? Melnicoe definitely died of blunt force trauma. A pipe or something similar cracked his skull pretty good. Whoever it was whacked his neck and shoulder, too. I think those were the first hits and then the one to the head finished him off.'

Hank was glad the Pup was reporting in such a detached way. He hoped that meant the kid wasn't too traumatized after seeing his first autopsy. He heard road noise on the other end of the line and looked at his watch. It was just after five o'clock. Sam would be able to keep his date. At least something was going right today. He hung up and picked up his cell to listen to Ghassan's voicemail.

We found a cache of papers under Hardy's mattress. We're going through them now. I'm skeptical that you missed those on your visit to her condo.

Hank shifted guiltily in his chair.

I'd care a lot more under normal circumstances, but right now I've got the damn feds asking about the bogus inventory and a chief financial officer who's staring at me wide-eyed like he doesn't know anything about it. He's throwing Lancaster under the bus, which is easy to do since the bastard is still missing. I want you to get going on the – wait, what? You found what?

There was shouting in the background and then the message cut off. Hank hit redial so quickly the phone didn't register it. He jabbed it again, swearing as the call took forever to go through.

'Hang on,' Ghassan said. There was some muffled conversation about evidence. Whatever they'd found, they'd found a lot of it.

'Blood. Tons of blood. In her bathroom.'

Hank sat there, not able to process Ghassan's words. There hadn't been blood anywhere. He and Fin had searched the whole condo. They sure as hell checked the bathrooms. He was starting to speak when it hit him. Luminol.

'Oh, shit.'

'Yeah. Downstairs bathroom is clean. The one off the upstairs master bedroom lit up like goddam Las Vegas. She had to have been killed in the bathtub.'

Hank sagged against his desk. He'd hoped – so hoped – he could find her alive. He hadn't been fast enough. And Fin. Dear God, this was going to destroy her. He sucked in a wet breath that finally caused Ghassan to stop talking.

'Sorry . . . I . . . just the bathroom?' he managed to say. 'Anywhere else?'

'There are drops down the upstairs hallway. The techs are doing the stairs now. Hopefully we can figure out whether they took her out the front or the back.'

Yeah, because that really mattered at this point. Hank hung up and turned to stare out the window. Instead of brittle tree branches and parking lot asphalt, all he could see was a tastefully feminine bathroom, decorated in subtle silver and purple and covered in glowing blue splatters.

THIRTY-TWO

He'd originally offered to pick her up, but she told him she'd just meet him at the restaurant. Now he was grateful – not having to drive to her apartment gave him just enough extra time to take the quickest shower ever and shave before racing over the lake to Hollister at twice the speed limit. He tucked in his shirt as he jogged across the road from the row of parking to the Downing Street Pour House. He made it only two minutes later than he wanted, which was still five minutes before the time they'd set. He'd definitely wanted to get there first.

He took a shaky breath and waited. She came in exactly on time. Her dark blonde hair curled around her shoulders and her green eyes lit up when she saw him. He felt a little light-headed. It was probably because he hadn't eaten since this morning. He said hello and prayed he didn't sound as awkward as he felt. He stepped aside so she could go first as they were shown to their table, resisting the desire to touch her back with his hand. They settled in and the hostess set down the menus, shooting him a sympathetic wink as she turned to leave. Dear God. Did he really look that nervous?

'So,' he said after they ordered drinks, 'have you had any luck finding a house to rent?'

He knew from their conversations at the coffee shop that she was searching for a better place to live than the apartment where she was now.

'No. But the next best thing. The old bat who lived upstairs moved out.'

Sam busted out laughing. He'd made the acquaintance of the judgmental Bitty Jean – unfortunately – and he could totally see why Brenna was happy she was gone.

'I would've thought she'd never leave,' he said.

'Me, either. I guess she broke her hip or her ankle or something. I certainly wasn't going to ask her for specifics. Anyway, she couldn't climb the stairs anymore, so she had to move in with her sister. You should've heard her complain about it. The whole building threw a party the night she left.' She was talking and laughing at the same time. When she got to that part, she suddenly blushed. 'I wanted to invite you, but . . . I, um, I didn't know what to say.'

She trailed off and gave a bashful shrug. He just sat there. Stunned. He hadn't been sure. Even when she said she'd go out with him. But now the nerves jangling around his insides like wind chimes in a storm fell quiet. He felt a smile spread across his face.

'And then you asked me out,' she said. She was still the most beautiful shade of pink. 'Just that next Monday. So . . .'

He just wanted to sit there and look at her but he needed to say something. He lifted up his pint glass.

'So we'll have our own celebration. No more old bat. Here's to peaceful living.'

They clinked drinks as she laughed. They ordered their entrées and then she smiled.

'So how's your day been going?'

This was what Hank had missed. Her white boards. Jerry's dining room wall just wasn't the same. He stood in front of the one in the conference room and examined the meticulous timeline that laid out what looked like the entire life of Clyde Timmons. He smiled. Whoever killed that man had no idea what was coming for him. Sheila was an unstoppable force.

His phone squawked with the new ring tone he'd assigned to Ghassan. He wanted to make sure he didn't miss a single call from the detective.

'Are you done searching the woods for Hardy?'

Hank couldn't bring himself to tell Ghassan that he didn't have the personnel to do it. He'd practically begged the Missouri Conservation Department for a few sworn law enforcement agents to augment the volunteers searching around the dump site. It was better than begging his own men, at least.

'They just called it off for the night,' he said. 'It's almost pitch black out there. They'll be back in the morning.'

Ghassan grunted unhappily. Hank had a feeling the guy had no idea how dark it really got out in the middle of an Ozark forest.

'We think,' Ghassan said, 'that Melnicoe might have been down in your area because of a Branson strip mall location. We came across a lease agreement in Hardy's stolen papers.'

Shit. He'd completely forgotten. He hung up as Ghassan was reading off the street address. He almost dialed Sam but stopped himself just in time. Instead he dug a scrap of paper out of his wallet as he ran for his squad car. A half hour later he barreled into the nearly empty parking lot of the nearly empty strip mall. Lew's leased space was at the end. Was it going to be another store with a shadow inventory that funneled money who knew where? He got out and tried the door. It was locked, the lights were off, and he couldn't see a damn thing when he peered through the front window.

He stepped back and took in the whole strip. It was like it wanted to be part of the bigger complex next door, but hadn't quite made the cut. The ladies' clothing store had closed for the day. So had the quilt shop. He headed for the still open shoe store and yanked open the door, sending the bell tinkling. The teenage employee, half-heartedly adjusting shoeboxes on the shelves, actually groaned.

'We close in ten minutes. Clearance items are in the back.' He turned to point and saw the uniformed Hank. 'Oh. You're probably not here to buy shoes.'

Hank said that he wasn't and asked about the empty store at the end. The kid, who was wearing a black T-shirt, baggy jeans, too many necklaces, and a baseball hat with a brim so flat it looked like it'd been ironed, shrugged.

'I ain't seen anybody down there. But I'm stuck in here all day, so I wouldn't really know.' He didn't seem any more interested in Hank's question than he was in the shoes.

'I need you to keep an eye out for me. It's important.' He handed over a business card.

Flatbill might as well have said *Why should I help the cops?* out loud, the look on his face was so blatant.

'It's a big case,' Hank said, leaning conspiratorially on the counter and trying to think of a crime that would turn even a teenager into a dutiful citizen. 'Possible elder abuse. We think he's in a lot of danger. He's quite old, and his relatives are really worried.'

The clerk considered that, then perked up.

'I don't know if people been going in and out, but I did see something this morning.' He took in Hank's encouraging look and kept going. 'This guy, like, drove around back and then out to the parking lot again. Got out and walked around, but none of the stores were open yet.' The kid thought a minute. 'I'd say he was pretty suspicious.'

It was an observation. Whether it was based on genuine reconsidered hindsight or on watching too many TV crime shows was unclear. But it was better than nothing. Hell, it could have been Lew. Or Marco. Hank asked what the man looked like.

Pretty tall with short brown hair. Flatbill couldn't tell how old he was, but he seemed pretty stressed. He saw something and then lit out of here like his pants were on fire. That, Hank thought, was the surest sign the person was involved in this mess, even though it wasn't the pomade-slicked, silver-haired Lew. He asked if Flatbill had gotten a good look at the vehicle.

'Yeah. It was this beat-up old red Bronco. Looked like it might've had hunting gear in the back.'

Hank's hand balled into a fist. He thanked the kid and walked outside. Now he had no choice. He pulled out his phone and hit the button to interrupt a date.

Sheila was seriously considering putting Earl through the academy despite his advanced age. He was doing a bang-up job in here. And Molly March was the find of the century. She'd just answered the employment posting when the job at Billy Bob's Dairyland restaurant fell through. But she was a natural. She could intuitively sense who the troublemakers were and was capable of handling multiple crises at once. Her only deficits were a lack of confidence and her current focus on Sheila's spread-out paperwork instead of the jail inmates.

'So these are your murder suspects?' She made no attempt to hide the excitement in her voice.

Sheila shuffled things around. She had separate sheets for them all. Every person associated with the bocce bandits, to use Hank's melodramatic term. She pointed at the men and told March about their Tuesday breakfasts at the diner. Then she explained about the bocce raids and held up the other four papers.

'You think one of the wives had something to do with it?' March asked. 'They didn't play bocce, too, did they?'

'No. But I do think they're involved. One of them, at least. Because the men had been getting together for the past five years. If one of them wanted to kill Clyde, it's likely he would've done it already. Something changed recently that triggered the murder, and the only thing in his life that was different was the bocce. And everybody's wives knew about at least some of it. So I think we need to look at all of them.'

Adam Moreno and his wife were in Texas visiting a new

grandbaby at the time of the killing. So they were out. That left Dick and Roberta Maher, Ned Hodges, Ward and Belinda Ullyott, and bachelor Owen Lafranco. Sheila had stared at this information repeatedly, but now she looked at it through the lens of her conversation with Lonnie. What if he didn't kill his mother, but Clyde was right and someone had helped her along to her heavenly reward? Who would've been in a position to do that, and then panic when Clyde figured it out all these years later?

She put Lafranco at the bottom of the pile. He worked construction and would have been unlikely to cross paths with Nell. Hodges was a schoolteacher – maybe he'd taught Lonnie at some point and gotten to know the boy's mother. Sheila made a note. Ward Ullyott had been an attorney and his wife an accountant. Not much there one way or the other. She looked at Sam's notes about his interview with the Mahers. Dick was a retired pharmaceutical rep and his wife had been a nurse. Well now. Either one of them might have had the expertise to assist Nell Timmons.

She flipped through the rest of her file. There was a notation that Sam had talked to some of Nell's work friends yesterday, but there was no report attached. She scowled. That wasn't like him. She reached for her cell and then stopped. She'd ordered him to take today off. If she hadn't done that, she was quite sure she'd have the report in her hands right now. This damn OT mess. She looked at the clock. Sammy and his coffee girl were probably just finishing their entrées. She wondered if she had enough self-discipline to give them time for dessert before she called him.

THIRTY-THREE

She grew up a little bit north of here in Republic. She was the middle of three children, with a brother on each side. That made Sam a little nervous. He had a feeling they were very protective of their sister. He knew she was soft-spoken from all the conversations they'd had as she worked the counter at Donorae's. What he hadn't known was how funny she was. She told some hilarious stories about the coffee shop and customers coming in off the Strip. She was also really interested in him. He talked about being close to his grandfather and Branson Valley winning the district championship in football when he was a senior. So far, he'd successfully avoided talking too much about work. He did tell her about the fraudster couple trying to fool their insurance company by pretending more stuff got stolen than really did. Otherwise, he had to go back to the rash of shoplifting at the Easy Come & Go convenience stores over the summer to find something entertaining. Things hadn't been too funny lately.

His phone went off as he finished his pasta dish. It buzzed softly in the pocket of his slacks. He cursed himself for not turning it all the way off. At least he'd silenced the ringer. And thank goodness the restaurant was noisy enough that Brenna didn't hear. It buzzed again five minutes later. And then again. He didn't care if it was another dead body, he wasn't going to answer it. They decided against dessert and Sam asked for the check. Brenna excused herself and headed to the restroom. The second she was out of sight, he yanked out his phone. Hank. Two calls and a text.

What did you find out when you checked the strip mall address?

Oh, shit. He completely forgot to bring that up when he'd talked to Hank earlier. Although he had texted this morning and Hank hadn't responded.

Store empty. Leased to Columbia holding company. Keys mailed to PO box. Two cars outside yesterday. Ran plates. Don't have names with me now.

He saw Brenna coming across the dining room. He quickly dropped his napkin over the phone. Just as she sat down it buzzed again, rattling against the wood table. He was going to kill Hank. Or drag him here and force him to explain to Brenna why he was interrupting. That would be more painful actually, so that was the better choice. He uncovered the phone.

'It's my boss. He's asking a question about a case. I'm sorry.'

She smiled. 'That's OK. It's kind of exciting. What's the case about?'

At least they were done eating. He tried to choose his words carefully. 'I checked out a location for him earlier today. He decided he needs the report on it earlier than he thought.'

'Why is it so urgent?' She sounded genuinely curious, not annoyed.

'Well, turns out it might be linked to, um . . . a deceased person we found way out in the woods, that dense stretch south of One Sixty and Hercules Glades.'

Those beautiful green eyes got huge. Then he got a slow smile. 'There's a lot you don't mention when we talk at the coffee shop, isn't there?'

He nodded just as his cell went off again, this time with a call. He felt his ears go red and then the rest of his head. But Brenna just laughed and leaned forward eagerly. He kept his eyes on her, the only way he could think of to stay calm, as he answered.

'I said I don't have the names with me right now.'

'What?' Sheila said.

'Oh. I thought you were Hank.'

'He's bothering you during your date?'

'You are, too.'

'At least I waited until you were done with dinner.'

'You get no points for that.'

Guilty silence. Finally she said she needed his notes from the interviews with Nell Timmons's co-workers to see if they supported her theory that it was the Mahers who helped kill her.

'Assisted suicide? What?'

'Lonnie says his dad thought he helped Nell die when the cancer got too bad. I completely believe that Clyde thought his son had done that. It's just whether Nell really was helped along, and whether Clyde could suddenly prove it. If so, somebody would have quite the motive to silence him.'

It wasn't bad as theories went, but Sam didn't see why it couldn't wait until tomorrow. He told Sheila the notes were in his car and he'd get them to her later in the evening. He said goodbye before she could ask for anything else. Brenna looked disappointed.

'Sometimes it's exciting,' he said, 'but mostly it's boring. I'd much rather go to our movie. Shall we?'

This time he'd make sure to turn his phone all the way off.

I left my car unlocked. At the IMAX. Info is in the glove box.

Hank read the text and whooped. He'd been about to start checking every restaurant in town. He turned the squad car toward the theater. Sam's Bronco was parked in one of the middle rows. A hint of perfume floated out when Hank opened the door. He smiled and hoped the date was going well. Even with the interruptions.

The sheaf of papers was wedged in tightly. He wondered how two car registrations produced that much information until he saw that the top sheets were notes from an interview with someone named Mary Johnson. And a Jeanette Pistoresi. It looked like Sheila's case. At the bottom were two printouts, a Chevy Traverse registered to William Kern of Hollister and a Toyota Avalon registered to . . .

Lewis Lancaster of Columbia.

Lew's car had been in Branson yesterday, and Hank hadn't known. He wanted to vomit. Sam had conscientiously included copies of the driver's licenses. He could see the gleam off Lew's pompadour even in the black-and-white printout. Had the old man been in the car? Or was he dead somewhere, just like his employee? Where was the car now? He slammed Sammy's door and reached for his radio to put out a BOLO for Lew and his Avalon. There'd been one issued up in Columbia, of course, but no one down here would've paid much attention to it. Now the manhunt for Uncle Lew was going to go statewide.

He climbed into his cruiser and rested his head on the steering wheel. His duty belt dug into his middle and his vest into his sides. And now his phone was ringing.

'You need to find Sammy. He's got the notes I need in his car.'

'I have them right here.'

'What? He told you about it?'

'No. He told me about mine. What I needed. Yours were there, too.'

'Well, send them to me.'

'Fine. Don't suppose you'd be interested to know that Maggie's uncle is probably in the area and might be a killer?'

'Jesus. Really? How'd he go from being the employer of the body dump to a murderer?'

'There's a massive fraud going on. I was hoping it was the CFO and not Lew, but with Lew being down here, I got no other conclusion to draw.'

'And the secretary's still missing, isn't she?'

'Yep.'

'Well, I don't envy you that conversation with your father-in-law.'

'You want to be there for it? I could probably use some protection.'

She scoffed. 'So you'll send those notes?'

'I get your theory and all, and I'll do it as soon as I hang up, but what's the hurry? These bocce guys are older folks. They're not going anywhere.'

Silence.

'OK, that was stupid,' he said. 'Old people run away. Obviously. You think you need to move on this tonight?'

'I wouldn't be so worried if I could station a deputy outside the Maher house to make sure they don't flee. But I got no personnel. There's only so much I can ask of Earl,' Sheila said. 'I'd like to at least read through it and see if there's follow-up that needs doing. I know Sam didn't do anything, because I made him take the day off.'

Hank snorted. 'That ended up working out well.'

'Yeah, just like everything else lately. I'll be waiting.'

The line went dead. Hank shifted so his gun would stop jabbing him in the side, and started snapping photos of Sam's chicken scratch notes. Thank God the information for his case was on computer printouts.

Sheila put Earl to work deciphering Sam's handwriting.

Bea Kircher was the one co-worker Sammy hadn't been able to track down. He'd left himself a note at the bottom of the paper to check with the company on Monday. Hell, he might have pushed through and found the woman today if Sheila hadn't ordered him not to work. This lady might be the one who could finally give her some concrete link to the Mahers that she could use to confront the couple. As of right now, all she had was a vague theory and a lot of supposition. Which wasn't great ammo for a confrontation.

She looked over Earl's shoulder as he transcribed. There was a scrawl in the margin with a 'manager Alex Chung' and what looked like a business phone number. It was no good. She ran the man through the driver's license database. She was guessing he lived locally – which could be a completely erroneous assumption, but she had to start somewhere. And luckily southern Missouri did not have a whole lot of Chungs. There was only one Alexander. She took down the address and plugged it into a reverse directory to find his landline phone number. If he didn't have one of those, she'd move on to the databases that had access to cell phone numbers.

But this guy was old-fashioned. He had a landline and picked up on the second ring. Molly mimed applause and Earl pumped his fist. She swatted them away and told Chung why she was calling.

'No, sir, I assure you, it has nothing to do with your company business at all. Yes, sir. I realize it's the weekend. Is there any way you can access that information from home? You could? Yes, I'd be happy to wait.'

Her expression didn't reflect the sentiment of those last words. But she had no choice but to listen to what sounded like an NCIS rerun as Chung set down the landline and stomped off. She flipped through Earl's translation again. Sam's interviews with the other two women had been pretty thorough, but this Kircher woman seemed to have worked most closely with Nell Timmons at White Tail Manufacturing.

There was a rattling noise and Chung came back on the line. 'A Kircher did work for us. Retired five years ago. There's a notation about a name change.'

'What does that mean?'

'It means she changed her name.'

Sheila was not enjoying her time with Mr Chung.

'Well, does it mean she got divorced? Remarried?' Became a nun? Joined the CIA?

'I have no idea.'

'What's her new name?'

'That's not in this database. That would only be in payroll. They mail the old company's pension checks that we're forced to keep paying out. I don't have access to it here at home. You'll have to wait until Monday.'

Alex Chung was very lucky he wasn't in the same room with her right now. She spent ten minutes trying to convince him. It didn't work.

'I'm going back to my TV show now, lady.' And then he hung up.

'He didn't . . .' Molly whispered as Sheila put down the phone.

'He did. And he and I will be having a conversation about it Monday morning when I show up at his office.'

'Can't you make him do it right now?' Earl said.

'Not without a search warrant, which no judge is going to grant at this time of night unless it's an emergency. And really, the records aren't in danger of getting destroyed. So the Mrs Kircher-slash-Whoever avenue of investigation will have to wait.'

She grabbed the interview notes again and dialed Jeanette Pistoresi's number. The woman was very nice but had never heard of Dick or Roberta Maher. There'd been a Bobbi who worked in shipping years ago, but she didn't think Nell knew her. Sheila added that name to her Monday morning South Sun Manufacture Inc list. Then she called Mary Johnson.

'I've been thinking about Nell ever since that young man called yesterday. I don't know that I have too much more to add, but I did remember that Clyde loved to garden. Is that helpful?'

Sheila stifled a groan and told her that could be very useful.

'Oh, and for a time Nell did a baking circle with some ladies. It wasn't through church because she didn't attend, so maybe the community center? I don't recall any names but I do know I laughed when she told me that it was always the nurse who brought the unhealthiest treats.'

Sheila shot up out of her dejected slouch.

'Ma'am,' she said, 'that is more helpful than you could ever know.'

THIRTY-FOUR

'You want to bust down the door of a business at this time of night? You've tried just asking, and they're refusing to let you in?'

The judge stood on his porch in a velour jogging suit and slippers, squinting at Hank's slap-dash application for a search warrant.

'The store proprietor is currently wanted for fraud by authorities in Columbia and we want him because he's linked to that body we found today.'

'A body? The one on Nighthawk Lane?'

'No, sir. A different one. In the woods south of Hercules Glades Wilderness.'

Judge Sedstone's white caterpillar eyebrows hiked up toward his hairline. 'You sure do seem to bring them out of the woodwork, my boy. We haven't had so many killings since the late sixties, early seventies, when—'

'We should be able to get the property manager to let us into the unit,' Hank cut in. 'It's part of a strip mall off Gretna Road.'

Sedstone adjusted his glasses. 'Are you worried evidence will be destroyed if you don't get in there tonight?'

'Yes, sir. The suspect's car was spotted by the shop's back door this morning. And we don't know what's in that back room. So yes, sir, we're definitely worried about that.'

He had a feeling the judge was thinking of financial documents or shadow inventory lists. He was thinking of a bloody pipe or the lifeless body of Tina Hardy. He tried not to fidget as Sedstone ruminated. He'd learned in the almost full year he'd been here that the judge took his own good time. Trying to hurry him along only made it worse. Finally, the caterpillars relaxed and he took a pen out of his pocket. Hank swallowed a sigh of relief, took the signed document, and hustled off the porch before the judge came up with any more questions. He slid into the driver's seat and punched the property manager's phone number as he was pulling out past Mrs Sedstone's bare rosebushes. The guy seemed genuinely excited to meet him at a deserted strip mall on a freezing cold Saturday night. Hank started to consider deputizing him.

He was just getting out of the squad car by the store's back door when Ray Gillespie pulled up in a five-year-old Lexus. He was younger than Hank expected, maybe early thirties, but with thinning hair and lines around his eyes a little too deep for someone that age. He looked like he just came from work – navy blazer and brown tasseled loafers that showed way too much argyle sock. He broke into a grin and shook Hank's hand enthusiastically. He was happy to help in any way he could. Pleasure to be of service. Hank extracted his hand and asked for the keys. He handed Argyle the warrant and told him to wait by the Lexus. The lock opened easily, lit by the cruiser's deliberately aimed high beams. He drew his gun and pulled the door open. The light bounced off metal shelving and disappeared into the dark corners.

He quickly moved to the other side of the doorjamb and looked at the room from that angle. It was small, about ten-by-twelve, and the shelves lined the two interior walls. A sink and counter were on the long exterior wall. The other exterior wall, where he was standing in the doorway, was bare. There was nowhere to hide. He stepped inside, the leasing agent on his heels. He glared until the guy stepped back over the threshold, then checked that the front of the store was empty, too. When he came back, he turned on the overhead light. Argyle gasped.

Blood darkened the floor just to the left of the door. Only one streak, a rusty brown just about the color of Argyle's loafers. Their owner got very pale. Hank ignored him. It looked like someone had tried to scrub the stain but given up after a few swipes. It smeared exactly where a body would've slid as it was dragged through the door to a waiting car. Say, a 2002 Honda Civic. He wanted to know right now whether the stain really was blood and whether it belonged to Tina Hardy. Or Vic Melnicoe. But with the state crime lab backlog, he'd be lucky to get DNA results back by next Easter. He sure as hell wasn't getting them by Thanksgiving. He was pulling out his phone to call Alice Randall when Argyle recovered his composure.

'Why would there be a toothbrush?'

Hank turned. The leasing agent pointed. A travel toothbrush stood inside a plastic cup on the edge of the sink. A small mirror leaned against the wall and a towel lay on the counter. Hank walked over and stared at the toiletries. This was turning into a DNA jackpot. He called Alice.

Sheila pounded on the door again. There was some swearing and it finally swung open. Roberta Maher practically spat in her face.

'Do you know what time it is?'

'Yes, ma'am, and I frankly don't care. I'm conducting a homicide investigation, and you're going to answer some questions. Did you know Nell Timmons?'

'Who? Is that someone to do with Clyde? Was that his wife? Was she murdered, too? Because if not, I don't give a shit. Get off my porch.'

Her husband materialized at her side, patting her arm and trying to coax her back into the house. Both women waved him off.

'Have you ever participated in a baking club or cooking group or any kind of community activity like that?'

'No. I had a career. I didn't have time for that crap. What the hell does this have to do with anything?'

'Let's talk about that career. You worked as a nurse and had the knowledge to help someone end their life,' Sheila said. 'Did you help Nell Timmons end hers?'

Roberta gaped at her. 'I never met the woman. I didn't even really know Clyde.' She turned to her husband, who was clutching a highball and looking shell-shocked. 'Tell her I'm telling the truth.'

Dick Maher blinked several times before he seemed to come back to himself. Nell was already dead when he met Clyde five years ago, he said, so nobody had the chance to know her. Hell, even the wives still living had only ever met one another once, when Ward got remarried. And Clyde hadn't even been there. He'd been home with a bad case of pneumonia.

'All the men met me plenty,' Roberta snapped. 'You brought all those old goats over here when you started playing bocce. I was subjected to them four times.'

'How charitable of you to keep track, Mrs Maher,' Sheila said. 'I'm sure with your excellent memory you can tell me whether you and Clyde had any conversations on those occasions?'

She glared at Sheila. 'I'm done with this. If you're bent on harassing the wives, why don't you go menace the other ones? Mine wasn't the only backyard those idiots destroyed.'

She took a step back and swung the door shut in Sheila's face. Sheila's jaw dropped. No one had ever dared do that to her before. Certainly not when she was fully uniformed and armed. She raised her hand to do to the door what she'd like to do to the woman's backside – and stopped. The bocce boys had gone to another house. She stomped back to her cruiser and pulled the initial interview notes out of the file she brought with her. In the middle of Orvan's scribbles, she found it. Ward Ullyott had the group over, but they determined his yard was too rocky to use. It was after that they started sneaking on to the proper courts around town.

Sheila looked back at the Mahers' front door. She didn't have any probable cause to bring that woman in for questioning, much as she wanted to. Come Monday, she would be checking every baking club membership roster for the past two decades and showing Nurse Maher's photo to everyone she could think of. If that woman was lying and she really had known Nell Timmons, Sheila was going to find out. And hopefully arrest her in a public place. That would be enjoyable.

But until then, she could check in with the Ullyotts. Maybe Roberta Maher said something about a personal connection the one time she met Belinda Ullyott. Maybe Clyde said something about Roberta to his good buddy Ward. And maybe she was just grasping at straws late on a Saturday night, Sheila thought as she started the car.

Ward invited her in and offered her a cup of tea. She declined and asked about Roberta's interactions with Clyde the times they played bocce at the Maher house.

'Oh, I don't know that they ever even exchanged words,' he

said. 'We all just tried to keep away from her. That's why I said we could try my yard. I have a nice wife.'

He smiled. Sheila tried not to – professional objectivity and all.

'Is she here? I'd like to ask her about any conversations she's had with Mrs Maher.'

'She's asleep. I'm sorry.'

Sheila tried to tamp down her impatience. 'I really need to ask her these questions. I'm trying to find out if Mrs Maher knew Clyde's wife before she passed on.'

'But that was so long ago. None of us knew each other then.'

Sheila raised an eyebrow.

'Oh. You think one of us did know them? Before?'

She nodded and watched him carefully. He looked more confused than anything. Befuddled, almost. She wondered how intact his mental faculties still were.

'I need you to get your wife, sir. I'd like to talk with her, and then I won't have to bother you two again.'

That was almost certainly not true, but truth wasn't going to get Mrs Ullyott out of bed. Reassurance was. Ward nodded and shuffled toward the hallway. Sheila wanted to tell him to hurry up. She took a deep breath and forced herself to relax. She felt like she was running on a hamster wheel, and that pent-up frustration wasn't something she needed to take out on Ward Ullyott. She looked around the room again – the wingback chairs where she, Sam, and Derek had sat two days ago, the flowery curtains, the mantel knick-knacks, the awards that spoke to a lifetime of work.

Two days ago, she'd thought it was a lifetime together. Now that she knew this was a second marriage she stepped closer, curious about what they'd done separately. An attorneys' bar association award, a thirty-year anniversary medallion from some law firm, an old Cadillac key in a velvet-lined shadow box. An American Institute of Professional Bookkeepers certificate, a retirement plaque from a company that had just bought into the area a few years ago, a sprig of pressed Ozark bluestar flowers in a crystal frame.

Sheila stared at the collection of achievements until it blurred in front of her eyes. Then she whipped out her phone and made a call. She hung up without saying thank you and turned to greet Mrs Ullyott as she came through the kitchen.

'Hello, Bea.'

THIRTY-FIVE

Alice was working her way around the storeroom. She'd just knelt down and was closing the door between the three of them and the main retail space when headlights flashed briefly through the front windows. She started to open the door back up but Hank blocked her movement.

'Hit the lights.'

Argyle obeyed instantly and the room went pitch black. There was no reason for anyone to be here at this time of night. Hank slowly opened the door and slid between the rows of bare shelving, his eyes on the section of parking lot he could see through the glass. The car, a sedan, was still cruising the lot – now with its lights off. Hank crept closer. It turned to make another pass and Hank saw the Toyota Avalon logo on the back. He spun and burst into the back room at a full run. Shouting for both Alice and Argyle to stay there, he threw himself behind the wheel of his cruiser and reversed with a screech of tire rubber and a string of profanity.

He rounded the strip mall building doing twice the speed he should have. Lew was at the far end of the parking lot. Hank saw the brake lights flash and then the old bastard floored it. He cut left and bolted for the nearest exit. The Avalon caught the curb and bounced in a way Toyota never intended as he bottomed out before regaining control and fleeing north. Hank hit the emergency lights and then decided Aunt Fin deserved the full package and flipped on the siren, too. He easily caught up with Lew, but the octogenarian refused to pull over. Hank radioed Branson city PD for backup. He'd rather get Lew with a nice, easy roadblock than have to conduct a solo stop by forcing him off the road. That'd probably give the guy a heart attack, and Maggie was mad enough as it was.

Hank relayed his position as Lew sped down Gretna Road where it turned into Shepherd of the Hills Expressway. The few cars on the road got out of the way, thank God. Branson PD was making a calculated guess as to his path and starting to set up, but before Lew reached them he turned left, barely slowing before he gunned it again, this time into a neighborhood. Hank's stomach started to twist. Lew turned right, then left, then swerved down a long, straight street, taking out two of the neighbor's geraniums before coming to a stop cockeyed on the lawn. He pushed himself up out of the driver's seat and rushed to the door.

Hank pulled up and angled the squad car so he blocked in the Avalon. He shut off the siren, which he knew was too little, too late. Maribel's face popped up in a bedroom window seconds later. But hell, if that hadn't done it, Lew's frantic pounding on the front door sure would have. Hank got out of the car and was starting to come around it and walk up to the house when the door swung open.

'Uncle Lew?'

Maggie stood there in her flannel pajamas, alternating blue and red as the cruiser's light bar flashed over her. The surprise on her face melted into confusion and then slack-jawed astonishment as she saw her husband zeroing in from behind. Every step closer made Hank hate him more. Making him do this in front of their family. He reached for his handcuffs.

'Lewis Lancaster, you're under arrest for financial fraud, and for the murder of Tina Hardy.'

Maggie staggered back. She bumped into Duncan, who materialized behind her at just that moment. She pointed, but couldn't get any words out. Dunc didn't have that problem.

'What the bloody hell?'

'It's not Beatrice. It's Belinda, isn't it?'

Mrs Ullyott's face had gone a very pinched pale. 'Of course my name's Belinda,' she finally managed. 'You knew that.'

'I did. What I didn't realize was that people shortened that to "B". The initial, maybe? Or "B-e-e"? But not "B-e-a". That was our mistake. Just like we didn't realize that your former name was Kircher.'

Belinda just stood there. Ward's brow furrowed in confusion.

'That's not a secret.'

'You're right, Mr Ullyott, it's not. What your wife did want to keep secret, though, was that she knew Nell Timmons.' She turned to Belinda and pointed. 'You lied to me.'

The last sentence came with all the condemnation Sheila could summon. Belinda shrank back like some no-account violet. Sheila advanced.

'You worked for White Tail Manufacturing.'

Belinda went no farther. She stopped in the space at the edge of the kitchen where the tile met the carpet. She put her hands in the pockets of her robe, but not before Sheila saw them tremble.

'I retired from South Sun Manufacture Incorporated.'

'Yes, I see that.' Sheila gestured toward the plaque on the mantel. 'But nine years ago, South Sun was White Tail. Where you worked with Nell Timmons. Why didn't you mention that?'

'You weren't asking after Nell. You were here about Clyde.'

Sheila hated hair-splitting on a normal day. After the day she'd had today, she wasn't even going to acknowledge it. She took a step forward.

'You were Nell's best friend at work. So supportive when she got sick.'

Another step.

'Tell me about what she was like then, after the cancer diagnosis.'

Belinda stammered and clenched her fists. Sheila could see them through the robe pockets.

'She . . . she was in chemo for a while, and she had to stop working. It made her feel horrible. She lost so much weight. I'd take her over the food that folks made for her, but she couldn't keep any of it down. And the chemo didn't even help. The cancer spread anyway. It got in her bones. That was when they said there was nothing else they could do.'

The woman started to tear up.

'How often did you go see her?'

'As often as I could.'

She wasn't going to give Belinda more opportunity for
grieving sniffles. She switched subjects. 'When was the last
time you saw Clyde?'

'It must've been at her memorial service.'

'Really?'

One step closer.

'Oh . . . yes. I saw him here, of course. When Ward had
them all over to try to play bocce in the backyard.'

Step.

'And?'

Belinda was matching Sheila's advance with a sideways
shuffle that put the protruding kitchen bar counter between
them. 'And what?'

'Then when did you next see Clyde?'

'That was it. Only that time.'

Ward let out some confused mutterings. Neither woman paid
him any attention.

'When you would go visit Nell at her home, what did you
think about how she was being cared for?'

Belinda blinked rapidly at the shift.

'Clyde wasn't . . . he wasn't doing it properly. She was in
too much pain.'

'Did Nell say anything to you about it?'

'No. That wasn't her way.'

'Was Clyde there when you would visit?'

'Not usually. He'd have to leave, run errands. Take a breather,
that sort of thing.'

Step.

'So you were there with just Nell? No Clyde?'

She stiffened. 'What are you getting at?'

Step.

'What'd you and Clyde talk about that day everyone came
over here to play bocce?'

The woman looked like her head was starting to spin. Her
hands came out and she clutched the countertop.

'What? I don't . . . you mean a month or so ago? Nothing.
Just a hello.'

Sheila's next step took her to the opposite side of the counter
from where Belinda stood. She laid her hands on the cool granite

surface. '"Just a hello" for the woman who'd helped nurse his dying wife? The woman he hadn't seen in years?'

Belinda nodded. Sheila spun to her left, startling Ward so badly he bumped the sideboard and sent a glass off the side. She asked her question before it even hit the carpeted floor.

'Did you know they knew each other?'

Ward, his face almost as gray as his hair except for two red splotches on his cheeks, shook his head.

'Did she tell you after that bocce get-together that she realized who Clyde was?'

Ward gave her another mute no.

'Were the two of them ever by themselves?'

Now she got a nod. Clyde had gone inside to use the restroom. When he came out, he hadn't said much of anything the whole rest of the time.

'But I don't know if they even talked,' Ward said in a tone made up of one part hope that he was helping, and two parts fear that he wasn't.

'Doesn't matter.' Sheila whipped back toward Belinda. 'I don't care if you two had a conversation or if he just saw you and recognized you. I don't care what brought it together for him, I only care that he figured out you killed his wife.'

The glass Ward had picked up slipped from his fingers and hit the floor again, sounding like it didn't survive the second fall. Belinda didn't move.

'I'd like you to leave my house now.'

'No.'

That produced a flinch. Ward started to stammer. Without taking her eyes from his wife's face, Sheila gave him a palm-out stop signal and he immediately fell silent. Then she went out on a very thin limb.

'We found the bocce balls. The bag has your DNA on it.'

If the woman had somehow destroyed them, the lie wouldn't hold. If she knew it was highly unlikely DNA would be left on a bag, the lie wouldn't hold. Sheila pressed her hands against the cool granite and prayed.

'Of course it has my DNA,' Belinda said, her voice suddenly high and scratchy. 'It's my husband's equipment. Of course I've

touched it. You'd know that if your deputy had asked me before
he took it in for evidence.'

It was a good response – an innocent-sounding response – but
Belinda's careful word choice showed she knew exactly what
Sheila really meant.

'Not your husband's bag, Mrs Ullyott. I'm talking about the
equipment belonging to Clyde Timmons. The set you used to
beat him to death.'

The two women stared at each other, separated by only a
countertop and two killings. Sheila heard Ward's breath hitch
and glassware clink as again he staggered against the sideboard.
Belinda glanced over at him.

'I went to talk to him. She's been gone nine years. What was
the point of him saying something now? It wouldn't have
changed anything.'

Sheila thought about a bad mullet rattling the chains around
his ankles. 'Oh, yes it would have,' she said. 'It would've
brought his son back to him.'

THIRTY-SIX

Everyone was talking at once. At each other, over each
other, against each other. What are you thinking, Hank?
Who's Tina Hardy? Why would you bring this here to
our doorstep? Where's your judgment gone, boy? Take the damn
cuffs off, it's all a mistake. Get the kids away from the door.

That last one was Hank, trying to make himself heard over
the din as his precious children pushed their way to the front,
staring fearfully up at their handcuffed Uncle Lewie. Suddenly
a voice cut through all of it.

'Leave the handcuffs on.'

Aunt Fin appeared behind her brother, her expression hard
and her hands clasped. The little crowd parted and she walked
the few steps to her husband.

'Where is she?'

'Where's who? Tina? I don't know. That's what I've been

trying to figure out. Why is he . . .' Lew tried to turn and look at Hank. 'Why are you saying I killed her?'

Hank grabbed his shoulder and forced him back around toward Fin. He was more than happy to let her start the interrogation.

'Because she's been missing for weeks,' Fin said. 'And you've lied from the beginning. She wasn't on vacation, she didn't have a sick mother, and she wasn't keeping you updated. She's dead.'

'Like hell she is,' Lew yelled. 'She took my . . . she took off. I was, uh, worried. So I was looking for her.'

Hank heard someone call from within the house and the kids disappeared inside. He and Fin looked at each other. Hank started to speak, but Fin beat him to it.

'We know everything. The fraud, the false inventory. The police are at the business right now. And Tina's condo. They're searching that, too.'

Lew let out something between a groan and a moan. 'The office or the stores?'

'That's all you care about, isn't it?' she snapped. 'Just the business. You broke the law for it. You killed for it when Tina found out about it.'

'Why do you keep saying that?' Lew was still yelling. 'I didn't kill anybody. I'm the victim in this.'

'So why,' Hank said, his grip still tight on the old man's shoulder, 'were you at the strip mall? Why did you run?'

'I was running *to* you. I didn't know it was you in that police car. I thought if I could get to you here at the house, you could help me explain things to the other cops.'

Maggie stepped forward. 'You thought you'd lead a police chase to my home, where my children are, where they are supposed to be safe and sound?' She kept advancing and Hank made no move to let Lew back up. 'How dare you?' She was in his face now, stepping on his shiny loafers. He started to cry.

'I didn't know what to do. I couldn't go home. That would pull you in, Finella. And Marco would find out.'

'Both of those things have already happened,' Hank said. 'So now, you and I are going to take a ride to my jail and I'm going to tell the Columbia police that I have you in custody.'

'Oh, hell, no,' said the one person with veto power. Maggie

jabbed a finger at Lew's blazered torso. 'We're standing right here until you tell us what you did with Tina's body.'

Hank, still so furious that his grip was making Lew wince, felt a bolt of pride cut through his anger. No one went from zero to sixty faster than his emergency room doctor wife. She'd gone from knowing practically nothing about Tina's disappearance to controlling the situation within minutes. Lew tried to shift away from her but she wouldn't let him.

'We're waiting,' she said.

They waited a full minute. Lew couldn't pull himself together. Hank started to worry that the old man would suffer a permanent mark-down right on the front step. Maggie seemed to realize the same thing – she put her fingers on his neck to take a pulse and then took a step back, telling him to take some slow breaths. Hank turned him and looked him straight in the eye for the first time that night.

'I'm going to ask you one question at a time. You're going to answer. Got it?'

Lew nodded.

'Why were you at the strip mall in the first place?'

'I thought she might be there.' He didn't specify whether he expected her alive or dead.

'And what were you planning to do if you found her?'

'Ask her where the money is.'

Alive, then. Fin's breath came out in a hiss. Duncan started to mutter.

'How many times have you been inside that particular store?' Hank said.

'None. I don't have the keys.'

Argyle had said he mailed them to a Columbia PO box.

'I never got them,' Lew said.

'Why'd you even need a store down here?' Dunc said. 'You planning on defrauding people in Branson, too?'

Lew's shoulders curled inward. That wasn't how it worked. No customers got taken advantage of, he said. They were just going to say the store was full of stock and had good sales. That's what they'd done with the store in Kingdom City, and to a lesser extent the other three stores in the chain. Those figures were passed on to potential investors.

'I needed to raise money. That was the only way I could keep things going. No one is buying anymore. They want to find things online and they want them too cheap even for me. I can't cover my costs.'

'What did you do with all that investor money?' Hank asked.

'Is that who you stole from?' Dunc said.

'I was going to pay it back.' Lew was pleading now – for them to understand, for his old life back, for anything that would stop the hell encircling him right now. 'But I needed it to pay the other vendors, and the employees.'

The other vendors. Two pieces of information shifted in Hank's mind and clicked together. 'You created a vendor. You made one up. That "miracle vendor" that Marco told me about, whose merchandise sold like hotcakes – that was all fake.'

Everyone but Lew stared at him in confusion. He'd have to pull off a verbal flow chart. The Castle 'bought' nonexistent merchandise from Discount Express Trading, Hank explained. That payment, made with investor money, went into an account controlled by Lew. He was the one who made up the whole Discount Express company in the first place. Then, because none of the other stores were really bringing in money, Lew used what he collected as Discount Express to pay real bills – like genuine vendor invoices and employee wages. That money was slipped into the everyday account that the Business School kid used to write the actual checks.

'That's why you refused to sell online,' Maggie said. 'You'd have to tell the world what you were claiming your stock was. And what if people bought it and you didn't have it?'

Lew nodded. Dunc threw up his hands and kicked at the front doorjamb.

'Did Marco know?' Hank, already a good six inches taller, purposefully loomed closer. He wanted the whole truth with his next two questions. 'Did he?'

Lew shook his head. 'No. He's a . . . a good man, and I couldn't've built the business without him. But he's got no head for numbers.'

The old man looked too beaten to be lying, too tired to try and pin it on Cortello. He started to sag into Hank. We're not done yet, old man, he thought as he took hold of Lew's other arm as well. 'Where's Vic Melnicoe?'

Lew started to protest, then swayed forward a little. Maggie swatted away Hank's hands and took his pulse again. 'He needs to sit down. He might even need an ambulance.'

'We are not calling an ambulance,' Hank said through clenched teeth. 'He's riding right where he belongs. The back of my squad car.'

He took Lew's elbow and walked him across his parking lot of a lawn. Over the sobbing, he heard Duncan kick the doorjamb again and swear. 'Goddam it, I wish he had been having an affair.'

THIRTY-SEVEN

S am held open the passenger door. He was going to give Brenna a ride back to her car at the restaurant. The glove box was ajar – the Chief must've come by for the case notes. He wondered if Hank had grabbed the Timmons notes as well. He could check once he got Brenna safely on her way. He gently closed the door and walked around to the driver's side. Ten minutes of driving through empty streets and they pulled up next to her little red hatchback. They chatted a little more about the movie and then she said she should really be going. She had the busy pre-church Sunday shift at the coffee shop in the morning.

He got out and as he walked around the car to her door, he tried to talk himself into asking her out again right then. He helped her out and took a deep breath. And then an old blue Honda stopped at the new traffic light they'd put in right near the parking lot. Close enough for Sam to see the license plate.

'What?' Brenna stepped back at the look on his face. 'What just happened?'

'That car . . . body dump . . . I got to go. I'm sorry. I'm so sorry.' He grabbed her hands. 'Can I call you? I really had a good time. I'd love to take you out again.'

He let go of her before he had an answer. His eyes were on

the Civic. The light was about to turn green. 'Please, I need you to get in your car and lock the doors. That's a . . . a wanted person. In that car. I have to go. And you have to be safe. I want you to be safe.' She got all flustered as he bundled her into the driver's seat of her car. He laid his palm on the window glass and then ran for his Bronco, leaving a little piece of his heart behind.

The Civic was halfway down the street. He accelerated until he was about four car-lengths behind. He spent a quarter mile happy with the anonymity of his personal car before it sank in that he had no way of pulling over the Civic. No police cruiser, no uniform, no gun. And no radio. He worked his cell phone out of the pocket of his dress slacks and punched the Chief's number. It went to voicemail immediately. He tried twice more and then dialed Sheila. The same thing happened. What the hell? He needed some help here.

The Honda went through the intersection with Highway 76 and then turned left on Green Mountain Drive. Sam made the turn one-handed as he scrolled through his contacts to find the Branson PD number. When all this was over, he was definitely – finally – going to get around to turning on the voice-activated commands. He looked around and swore – they were now the only two cars on the road. And he couldn't find the PD's damn internal patrol number. He dropped a little farther back and used the only option left to him. He called 9-1-1.

'Wait – say again? You want a Branson County sheriff deputy?'

'No, ma'am. I *am* a Branson County sheriff deputy. I need a Branson police patrol to respond to my location. And I need you to patch me through to them, because I have to explain what I need.'

'Just state your emergency, sir.'

The Civic was slowing down and then speeding up. Sam had a feeling the driver was testing to see if the Bronco really was tailing it. Green Mountain had a lot of development as it looped south of the Strip, but it also had stretches of empty woods. Which they were fast approaching.

'I am stating my emergency. I need to speak with the patrol officer nearest to the Jim Stafford Theatre. I'm on Green Mountain about a quarter mile south.'

'We can't send an officer till we know the nature of your emergency. Sir.'

The Civic was slowing way down, giving Sam no choice but to pass, or to stay put and confirm that he was in pursuit. He dropped the phone on the passenger seat without disconnecting and sped up to go around. He had a sinking feeling that the driver would turn off the road once they were back in a populated area and be lost in the tangle of side streets. He yelled out the car's license number and suggested that the 9-1-1 operator look up the BOLO. Was that emergency enough?

'Sir, that car is wanted in connection with a homicide in the Branson County sheriff's jurisdiction.'

Sam's heart was louder in his ears than the idiot emergency operator's voice as he pulled alongside the Civic. It slowed even more and the Bronco sailed ahead. He said one more thing and then pulled at the wheel in a way he'd only ever done during practice maneuvers. His beloved Bronco jerked to the right as he slammed on the brakes. He heard tires scream as the guy hit the Honda's brakes. Sam braced himself and watched the smaller car careen toward him at a speed that would do a stunt driver proud. The car lost control just as Sam saw the driver's face for the first time.

The Civic glanced off the rear passenger side of his Bronco and shot into the oncoming traffic lane. He hadn't figured on it not having anti-lock brakes. He pulled around in a clockwise circle until he was behind the car again as the driver fought to keep it from going off the road completely. It shot up over the curb and on to the grass shoulder. Noxious smoke rolled out from the wheels and most of the tire rubber had been left in skid marks on the pavement.

He could faintly hear the tinny yelling of the operator as he stumbled out of the Bronco. He approached from the side just as he would during a traffic stop, shouting for the driver to put hands on the steering wheel and wishing like hell he had his gun. He moved at a slow sidestep and continued to issue orders, even though he could now see that the airbag had exploded. The driver sagged against its deflating bulk. He crouched down, grabbed the door handle, and yanked.

'Put your hands where I can see them, or I will shoot.'

Shaking hands came forward and rested on the airbag. Sam lunged forward and grabbed both wrists. He used his body as a weight to pin the half-conscious driver back in the seat and reached down to undo the seatbelt. Then he hauled her ass out of the car and forced her facedown on to the roadway. He used his belt to lash her wrists together behind her back as she moaned and groaned.

'I don't know who you are,' he said, 'but you're under arrest for the murder of Vic Melnicoe.'

THIRTY-EIGHT

I t was a different lifetime, twenty-five years ago. She had just gotten divorced and needed to support herself. After a good amount of time at a women's shelter up in Springfield, she finally found work at White Tail Manufacturing because she had a knack for bookkeeping. That was when she met Nell. They hit it off immediately. Best friends for sixteen years, until Nell passed on.

Sheila crossed her arms and frowned. Belinda stared back with no expression.

'Did you give her pills?'

'No.'

'Use a pillow?'

That made her flinch. 'No. I held her hand.'

'Was she on an IV?'

A pause. 'Yes.'

'You put something in it?'

Silence.

Sheila moved on. 'What happened after that night when Clyde and the other bocce players came over here?'

Belinda half-raised a weary hand toward her husband. Clyde had recognized her right off, of course. He was stunned that all this time he hadn't known that Ward had married his wife's best friend. Why, he asked her, hadn't she said something – to him or even to Ward? She tried to brush it off, but Clyde persisted. He was genuinely puzzled, kept talking about how he'd hadn't seen her since the memorial service and before that, the morning that Nell had died.

And that was it. Nell had died in the afternoon, Sheila knew from the death certificate. Lonnie had been there. Clyde had gotten home minutes too late.

'You did what you did, and you left. And then Lonnie came to see his mom. And that's who Clyde put the blame on, all these years.'

'He looked at me, here in my kitchen, and he . . . supposed things,' Belinda said. 'I could tell. He was thinking – why would I keep Nell a secret from Ward when I knew he and Ward were friends? Clyde stared at me and then he walked out. I thought and thought about it, and then I went to see him.'

'Belinda, for God's sake, stop talking.' Ward was still pressed against the sideboard, shards from his dropped glass around him on the floor. 'We'll get you a lawyer. Please.'

'Oh, honey. You were my reward, for all the stuff before. My horrible ex and the threats and the hitting and the poverty. I couldn't let this – I couldn't let *us* – get screwed up. I just went to talk to him. To make sure everything was all right.'

But it hadn't been. Clyde was raging, in his quiet way. Nell hadn't been ready to go, he told Belinda. It wasn't her time. Belinda pointed out that at the end, the poor woman was just a collection of bones knit together by nothing but pain.

Clyde kept saying, 'No, no, no,' over and over as Belinda kept talking. He walked away from her, into the kitchen and then down the hall, muttering about calling the police. He wouldn't listen to her. She followed him, and he turned and exploded.

'He was yelling and crying and saying all these horrible things. Half of it I didn't even understand. Things about Lonnie and him. And he started to come back at me. I was there in the hallway and I had to back up to get away. I ended up in a little area by the back door with the laundry, and I was frightened. I grabbed for anything. I put my hands on something heavy, and I swung at him.'

Ward whined something about self-defense and begged her again to stop talking.

'Why didn't you just go out the door?' Sheila said. 'Or swing once, and then run away? You followed him down the hallway into his bedroom. Why?'

Belinda lifted her hands off the counter and then limply dropped them back down.

'He kept calling me a murderer. Saying what a horrible person I was. Telling me I'd as good as killed their son, too. I swung again. By that time he was in the bedroom. I swung again and then I left.'

'You didn't "swing",' Sheila said, leaning forward over the counter. 'You beat him to death. And then you took the murder bag of balls and you wiped your prints off the doorknobs and you locked up the house and you fled. You did all of these things, yes?'

They stared at each other a good long minute. Belinda finally broke the connection and turned her head toward the window. Sheila took out her handcuffs and thought about the cell phone they'd found on Clyde's nightstand. It must have been what he was looking for as he walked through his house for what turned out to be the last time. Now she made a manacled Belinda take what would almost certainly be her last walk through her home. She guided the woman out of the kitchen and across the living room toward the front door, the shattered glass crunching underneath their feet.

'Son, you run this lady off the road? You best step away now.'

'Hell, no, I didn't. I don't know who she is, but she's driving a car last seen at the site of a homicide body dump. I'm placing her under arrest.'

The Branson PD officer had his hand on his gun. Sam couldn't really blame him, seeing as he looked like some random dude who'd dragged a lady out of her car and was holding her wrists together as she lay facedown on the pavement. He rattled off his badge number and pointed out that he'd called 9-1-1 asking for backup, and that there was a BOLO out for the car. The officer radioed to verify the BOLO, but no one could confirm whether someone named Samuel Karnes worked for the sheriff's department. Sam listed every city officer he knew who could

vouch for him – none were on duty. That resulted in both him
and the woman sitting handcuffed on the side of the road while
Officer P. Romero tried to get a hold of someone at the sheriff's
office in Forsyth office. Finally, he got patched through to
somewhere.

'Yeah, I got somebody here says he's Deputy Samuel Karnes.
His DL confirms his ID, but he's got no badge.'

'Is he driving a Ford Bronco, faded red?'

'Yeah, he is. That mean he's legit?'

'Yes, he's legit. Can I talk to him?'

The officer still looked super skeptical. He walked over and
instead of uncuffing Sam, stuck the radio mic in his face. 'Talk,'
he ordered.

'Hi, sir,' Sam said.

'Sammy, are you all right?' Hank's voice crackled over
the radio. 'I'm a little busy here and—'

'Sir, I found the blue Civic. From the body dump. I have the
driver in custody. I haven't searched the car because I'm still
handcuffed and—'

There was some commotion on the other end of the radio,
then Hank said, 'Officer!' with such authority that all three
people on the side of the road reflexively straightened.

'Yes sir, Sheriff?' Romero said.

'I need you to uncuff my deputy. And I'd appreciate any help
you could give him. This suspect could have vital information
about a homicide and a missing person.'

Romero responded as Sam tried to keep an I-told-you-so look
off his face. He couldn't wait to search the car. He'd need Kurt
or Alice for the trunk – he was positive that was how the unlucky
Vic Melnicoe was transported out to the woods. He was thinking
through the calls he'd need to make once his hands were free
when the woman scrambled to her feet and started running. She
went down the sloping shoulder of the road and into the trees,
her hands still locked behind her with Romero's spare set of
cuffs.

Sam yelled and heaved himself upright at the same time.
Romero swore and lumbered forward. Sam didn't wait – the
officer probably weighed the same as him and the woman
combined. He crashed forward off balance and barely kept his

footing as he tried to gain ground. What the hell was she thinking? This was close to several populated areas. It wasn't like she was going to be able to get away. She was just making it harder on both of them. A bare branch lashed his cheek as he tore through the trees. He hoped the same was happening to her as she bulldozed forward about ten yards ahead.

He cursed his dress shoes as he slipped and slid on the slick leaves. At least she seemed to be doing the same in her Ugg boots. Their pale color was about all he could see of her in the dark. He focused on them and dug in, finally gaining some ground. She heard him coming and tried to cut to the side. It made her stumble and try to right herself just in time to avoid a sapling. Sam angled toward her and launched himself with a grunt and a prayer. With his wrists locked behind him, he crashed forward like a falling tree and hit her full on. She shrieked and came tumbling down. He landed on top of her, crushing the breath out of both of them.

The woods went silent. Sam didn't move – he couldn't exactly haul her to her feet and he certainly didn't trust her to stay put. Slowly, their lungs started to work again as Romero blundered toward them with a flashlight. He could hear sirens in the distance as the older officer uncuffed him. He rolled off his escapee and lurched to his feet. Romero handed him the flashlight and trained his gun on the woman. Sam took a grateful step away and took stock. He'd demolished the sapling and most of the skin on his chin. And he wasn't quite sure how his shoulders would ever work properly again.

He waved the light to guide the arriving Branson city officers. They hauled the mystery woman to her feet and marched her out of the woods. Romero looked down at the cuffs that had just been around Sam's wrists and turned red. He started to speak, but Sam waved him quiet. Then he found the dress shoe that had come off during his leap and limped his way toward the pulsating emergency lights on the road.

THIRTY-NINE

Hank switched Lew's handcuffs to the front and put him in the back of his cruiser. But he couldn't leave. Not yet. He had three adults clustered on the front step who would not be put off in their demands for an explanation.

And now there was Sammy, somehow finding the car in the Melnicoe homicide and getting himself taken into custody by city police. He hadn't heard anything from the Pup after ordering the Branson officer to release him. He'd call once he sorted his own family out as best he could, he thought as he trudged back up the lawn to the house. Maggie, Dunc, and Fin had stopped talking. Which was more worrisome than the cacophony before.

He looked around at three sets of blue McCleary eyes, and held his hands out to his sides in a gesture he knew was both placative and beseeching. 'I'm sorry. I have to take him in. I have to arrest him. There's no getting out of this for him. His only hope is a little bit of leniency if he tells us where Tina's body is.'

'He said he didn't kill her,' Maggie said. 'He admitted to the other stuff. He would've admitted to that, too, if he did it.'

'Murder's a damn sight different than fraud,' Hank said. 'He's not going to admit he killed her, especially if we don't have a body.'

'That's a problem, isn't it?' Fin said. Hank nodded. She looked at him and gently moved Dunc to the side so she could come down the steps. She straightened her tweed skirt and walked across the grass to the squad car. Hank started to say something, but thought better of it and went to crack the back window so she could talk to her husband.

'You need to tell them where Tina's body is,' she said. 'She has a family. They need to know, they need to bury her. You can't make this right. You can't take it back. But at least do this. Tell them. Please.'

Lew started talking, saying the same things he had on the

front porch. Hank's cell buzzed in his pocket and he took a few steps back and pulled it out. Sammy.

Suspect ran but back in custody now. No ID. BPD transporting her to our jail. Will take prints there.

And then a photo of a scraped face, broken glasses, angry eyes. Oh, God.

'Fin . . . Fin. Stop. Come here.' He gestured her closer as he texted Sam a question. Just to confirm what he was seeing. He got a one-word response. *Yes.* He put his arm around Fin and steered her toward the house. He leaned closer and spoke softly as he showed her the picture on his phone.

She stopped dead. 'I didn't believe him.'

She said it so quietly, Hank wasn't sure he'd heard anything at all. She turned to the side and his arm fell away from her shoulder. She looked back at her husband and then sank to her knees in the wet grass and started to cry.

'I need you to come to my house right now.'

Sheila, just leaving Branson with a confessed murderer in the backseat, was about to refuse. But there was something in his voice. She turned the car around. When she pulled up, his squad car was parked on the lawn, its spotlight washing everything with cold white light. He and Maggie were crouched in the grass with an older woman in between them. It looked like they were trying to coax her to her feet. Sheila parked, cracked the windows to give Belinda Ullyott some air, and approached just as the woman tried to rise. She looked terrible, her face a devastated mess of both guilt and grief. What the hell was going on?

Hank saw her and nodded. He and Maggie managed to get the woman up just as the father-in-law came out carrying a blanket. Hank stepped back and Maggie and her dad helped the woman into the house, the blanket shawled around her trembling shoulders.

'I need you to transport a prisoner for me. I can't leave.' He pointed at the little group as it disappeared inside.

'I already got a prisoner,' Sheila said. 'I made an arrest in the Timmons case.'

Hank pivoted toward her car and bent so he could see inside. 'An old woman?'

'She confessed.' Sheila paused. 'Well, we had a chat, and then she confessed. I was on my way to book her when you called.'

Hank straightened and raked both hands through his hair. 'I had no idea. That's . . . that's fantastic. I . . .' He trailed off and looked at the house and then at his car, where Sheila finally noticed someone sitting hunched in the back. She walked closer and peered in. He looked almost as ravaged as the old woman did. She turned back to Hank and raised an eyebrow.

'Is that the body dump employer fraud guy? Are you arresting him for murder, too?'

'No. Because it turns out the secretary isn't dead.'

She gaped at him. 'Say again?'

'Sammy just arrested her – in the car seen at the body dump site.'

'So all of this is Columbia-based,' she said, giving the old man a more careful look. 'And we have to mop it up.'

Hank glanced at Lew and then up at the house. 'That's an understatement.'

Sheila wouldn't want to be him right now. Though he seemed to be . . . OK. Not great, but not terrible. He caught her scrutinizing look.

'I've had a few more days to get used to the possibility of a criminal in the family than they have.' He contemplated his relatives for a minute. 'Except Fin. It turns out that what Lew did wasn't as bad as she thought . . . which, it turns out, is worse.'

Sheila had no idea what he was talking about. But now was not the time to ask for an explanation. 'All right. How we going to play this? I don't want either of these geriatrics expiring because they've . . .'

She stopped as Maggie came outside. She walked across the lawn and gave Sheila a wan smile. Then she ordered her husband to leave. Hank started to protest, and she laid a hand on his chest.

'No – you need to go. You find out what the hell is going on with that secretary woman. She's caused immeasurable grief here, and I want to know why. And maybe it'll help Aunt Fin. So go.'

She kissed him fiercely on the mouth and went back in the house. A muffled sob came from Hank's backseat. Hank stifled a groan. Sheila thought a minute and pulled out her keys.

'Want to switch cars?' She didn't care if the old man wept the whole way to the jail. And he knew it as he saw her approach. He shrank back as she opened the driver's door. Good. You don't make an auntie cry – that was one of the cardinal rules of life. Especially one from Hank's precious family.

No one was responding to Sam's request to open up the outer sally port door. He waited in awkward silence as Romero tapped on the steering wheel impatiently. Usually there was no delay, regardless of which agency was bringing in a prisoner. Usually the jail had a full staff, though. Why it didn't on this particular day wasn't something he wanted to get into with a Branson city officer. He tried again. Was there anybody in the building at all? Romero was starting to scowl.

Finally, the metal door rolled up and Romero nosed the car inside. They waited until the door shut behind them to get out. Romero opened the back door.

'Welcome to the well-oiled machine that is the county jail,' he drawled as he took the woman's arm and guided her out of the car. Her hands were still cuffed behind her. Her glasses were broken and hanging crooked on her face and she was covered in mud and leaves, a sight that was enormously satisfying to Sam. He'd tried to brush the same mess off himself before he got in Romero's car but hadn't been very successful. And that was the least of his problems. His chin was scraped and felt like it was embedded with tree bark. He had a slash on his right cheek that was starting to hurt like hell, two wrenched shoulders, and wrists rubbed raw where the cuffs had cut into him.

He looked at her wrists. They weren't as bad, probably because the Branson officer had tightened the middle-aged woman's more gently than he had the twenty-something man's when he cuffed them on the road. His plan, once Romero left, was to put her in an interview room still sporting dirty clothes and unwashed cuts. Keep her uncomfortable. She could change into clean jail scrubs later. He took her arm and walked her toward the door into the facility. No one was there to buzz them in. He swore to himself and Romero grumbled something about not wanting to be stuck here all night. He was saying something even less polite when the outer door rolled up again.

Both men spun toward it in astonishment. It was totally against procedure. The whole point of the structure was to ensure a completely secure transfer into the building. The door shouldn't have gone up unless the prisoner was inside the locked building. Instead, a sheriff cruiser pulled two feet into the garage and stomped the brakes just in time to avoid rear-ending the city squad car. The tire screech echoed off the walls and the concrete floor. It hadn't even died down before Sheila was talking over it.

'What the hell is this?' She got out of her car. 'Are you insane? Get her inside.'

'I'm trying,' Sam said, his fingers tightening on the woman's arm. 'No one's answering the buzzer.'

All the starch went out of Sheila. Her shoulders sagged forward. 'Shit,' she muttered. 'Molly. It's just her. And Earl. I need . . .'

She was pulling out her phone when a wail let loose from the back of her cruiser. It bounced around the garage, its emotion rattling the rafters. The old man in Sheila's backseat pressed up against the metal grill separating the seats.

'Tina! Is that you? Where the hell have you been? Are you OK? Where's the money?'

Sam turned on the woman. 'Is that your name? Tina?'

She tried to move away, but he still had her arm.

'No way. Not after what you put me through tonight.' He marched her over to Sheila's car. The old man's yelling got louder. 'Sir, you can identify this woman?'

'Her name is Tina Hardy. She's his secretary,' Sheila said.

How would Sheila know that, he wondered. Why were there suddenly people he didn't know anything about involved in his case? He had tons more questions, but she interrupted his thoughts.

'What the hell happened to your face?'

Sam shot a pointed glare at his prisoner and her similar scrapes. Sheila started to say something but stopped when the woman shifted her position, trying to avoid looking at the old man as he sobbed about her ruining everything. She tried to shield her face with her hair, but as the old man went on, she began to stiffen.

'You started it,' she burst out, turning toward Sheila's car as much as she could with Sam still gripping her arm. 'You're the one who ran your business into the ground. You're the one who stole from investors to keep it going. You're the one who hid the money where a semi-computer-literate five-year-old could've found it.'

The old man sagged against the locked car door and it became harder to hear him through the open driver's window. 'Not my business. I'm talking about my wife. My marriage. You ruined it. She thinks I killed you.'

'That was what everyone was supposed to think, wasn't it?'

FORTY

Hank walked into view. He'd heard Lew's lamenting and Tina's response as he tried to recover from the shock of squad cars sticking out of his sally port like it was the line at a Hardee's drive-thru. He'd parked off to the side, fastened Belinda Ullyott's handcuffs to his car's metal grate – he'd had bad luck before with manacled backseat prisoners – and got there just in time for one of the main topics he wanted to talk about with Ms Risen from the Dead.

'When did you decide to dump your own blood in the bathtub?'

Everyone else recoiled, but Tina smiled slightly.

'Oh, you found that? Was I officially a murder victim?'

There was a mix of incredulity and thrill in her voice that Hank saw Sammy squelch with a squeeze of his hand on her bicep. Hank looked at her and felt cold – an icy anger that was close to freezing into no feeling at all, which he knew would be far worse. He'd been desperate to save this woman, then anguished that she was probably dead. Instead, she'd been busy traumatizing his family and committing murder in his county. He stared at her and thought about that. She returned his gaze, probably unaware that he was Lew's relative. That his uniform sleeve was still soaked with Fin's tears. He wasn't going to dignify her question with a response.

'The blood?' he repeated.

'I did it just before I left,' she said. 'I'd put the papers under the mattress and was thinking it wasn't . . . definitive enough. It didn't necessarily say that I'd been taken. So I cut myself in a few spots and smeared it all around. It didn't take that much, really. I was kind of surprised. Then I cleaned it up. You guys would still see it with your lights, but I was pretty sure you wouldn't know how much had really been there.'

'And your purse?' Hank said.

She gave a little smile. 'If you're asking, that means you found it. I snuck into their backyard the night I left town.'

Hank glanced at Lew through the car window just as the old man realized what she'd done. His face went slack and then flushed red. 'You tried to frame me? My God, what did I ever do to you?'

Sheila moved forward like she was going to get back in the car and remove Lew from this whole bizarre confluence. Hank caught her eye and she stopped. He was hesitant to disrupt the dynamic when both suspects were talking so freely. Plus, Fin would never get the opportunity to yell at Tina Hardy like this – he might as well let Lew do it.

'You steal my money – which I needed for the original investors, the ones who were getting suspicious. And to pay the store leases and the payroll and my mortgage. And then you not only fake your death, you set me up for it? How dare you? I gave you a job.'

'You'd already run that place into the ground,' she said.

Lew yelled a denial, then slumped against the seatback.

'When did you figure that out?' Hank asked her.

She'd known since she randomly stopped in at the Kingdom City store in early summer and seen the empty shelves. She'd just prepped a big investor pitch for Lew, she said, and there was no way the reality matched what he was saying in that prospectus. That prompted her to dig into the files on his personal laptop when he left it unattended at the office. That's where the emails and most of the documents under the mattress came from. 'They weren't hard to find. No security at all. He uses his wife's birthday as his password.'

That set off a fresh tirade from Lew. She shut him up when she started talking about the investor they landed in October. Some decent-sized venture capital firm wanting to plump up their 'heartland' portfolio. Five million dollars. Then three million of it went straight back out to the Discount Express vendor, for items she knew weren't at the stores or the warehouses. She poked around some more and found a banking app hidden on Lew's laptop. Once she broke in with the same wife-birthday password, she saw that the deposit was exactly the same amount. So she emptied the entire account.

'That kind of thing would leave digital fingerprints all over the place,' Sam said.

'Yeah, I know,' she said. 'But what was he going to do, call the police? *Excuse me, my embezzled money has been stolen, can you help?* No way. Plus, he didn't necessarily know at first who did it. Just that it'd been done.'

'But Vic Melnicoe figured it out.'

Sammy looked like he hadn't intended to say that out loud. Tina started to nod, but everyone swung back to Lew, who was pressed against the window again.

'That's what Vic's been telling you?' he shouted. 'That he figured out what I've been doing? Hogwash. He was part of it. I paid him to help with the inventory records. It made it more solid if it came from the store that way, instead of being changed at the office. When you took that money from my Express account, I couldn't pay him. I owed him for months' worth of work.' Lew slumped back on to the seat. 'What a way for him to get back at me.'

Hank looked at Sam, who looked at Sheila, whose look clearly said *This isn't my case – you two break your own bad news.* Hank bent to get a better view of his uncle-in-law and swore at himself. Lew's face was splotchy and worryingly swollen. Even with his hands cuffed in front of him, it still had to be agony for a set of eighty-one-year-old shoulders. He opened the car door and unlocked the cuffs. Once free, the old man practically collapsed on the seat. Hank reached out and took his pulse. Steady, thank God. He straightened and turned to Tina, who was once again trying to avoid Lew's gaze.

'Did Vic come down here to Branson searching for you?' Hank asked. She nodded.

'Why'd you pick here?' he said.

'I had the keys to the new store that the agent mailed. So I knew I could get in, stay there while I got sorted out. I heard you could get a good fake ID here. But when I got down here, that . . . didn't turn out to be the case. I'd left mine in the purse I buried in Lew's flowerbed, and I couldn't get a fake one, so I . . . I was just stuck. My car broke down. I walked around off the highway until I found one I could steal. Then that Vic asshole shows up. Demanding money. I said he already made enough from Lew. He told me I'd taken it all. And he wanted it back, plus more.'

Lew stopped rubbing his wrists and struggled to climb out of the car. Hank took his elbow and helped him.

'He knew where you were and he didn't tell me?' Lew said. He looked around. 'Well, where is he?'

They all stayed quiet. Hank looked pointedly at Tina. Time to see if keeping them together out here would pay off. 'Answer him.'

FORTY-ONE

She clearly hadn't been expecting such a direct order. Hank could see her frantically think through different responses as she shifted from foot to foot. Finally, she decided on one.

'Not till I get a deal. *If* I did something to him, you'll never know what it was or where he is – unless I get a deal with the prosecutor.'

Hank couldn't keep the smile from creeping across his face. He started to speak and then saw the same smugness on Sam's face. His scratched, scraped, bruised face. Hank wasn't the only one who'd been injured by this woman. He nodded at his deputy. *Take it from here.*

'You bashed him over the head and dumped him out east,' Sam said. Her face drained of color and then flushed a deep red. 'But you didn't take him far enough out. Waste of a good trip to the woods, if you ask me. So now he's in the Springfield morgue. Where he's giving us all kinds of evidence.'

She looked from Sam to Hank and back, the import of that hitting like a meteor impact.

'We've even got blood in the back room of the empty store. So we don't need to talk to you anymore,' Hank said. Having her say that Melnicoe had come to her demanding money should be good enough to establish motive in court. And she admitted to having the store keys – if the blood there came back as Melnicoe's, the case was almost airtight. 'You can go get nice and comfortable in a jail cell. Because you're going to be there a long time.'

Sheila stepped forward and tapped out a text on her phone. The door into the jail building began to swing open. Both Tina and Lew jerked back. If that simple thing scares them, Hank thought, wait until they get to the state penitentiary. Sam stepped forward, but Tina refused to move. He took hold of her other arm as well and, clearly fed up, pushed her inside. The door was pulled shut by Earl, manning a post that was definitely not his authorized reception desk work station. Hank turned to Sheila but she already had a hand up to stop him. 'Just don't,' she said.

Then a voice Hank had never heard before boomed through the large space.

'So now is someone going to let me the hell out of here?'

A very large man in a City of Branson police uniform was sitting in the squad car that had brought in Tina Hardy. He must be the one who'd called with questions about Sam's deputy credentials. Hank hadn't even noticed he was there. He bit back a groan. An outside agency had just witnessed a highly unorthodox interrogation, a potential escape, and several half-ass prisoner transfers. Fantastic.

'Do we have anybody who can open that?' Hank asked, pointing to the other garage door opposite the already open one.

Once it was raised, the Branson officer could just pull straight out without having to reverse. Sheila texted, and a minute later it rolled up. Technically that wasn't supposed to happen while the first door was still open, but what the hell. The guy had already seen half a dozen procedures violated in as many minutes. Hank's thank you was overpowered by an eye roll and an engine roar as the officer drove away.

'We're just going to pretend that none of this ever happened,' Sheila said, waving a hand that encompassed both the sally port delays and the ongoing jail staffing mess.

'And pray that guy does the same thing,' Hank said as Branson PD disappeared from view.

Sheila muttered in agreement as she stomped over to the door and was buzzed inside. Hank turned back to Lew, who was leaning heavily against the back fender. Hank took his left arm to guide him toward the door, but Lew laid his right hand on Hank's coat and stopped him.

'She really killed him?' When Hank nodded, his head slumped forward on to Hank's chest as well. 'God, he was just a kid looking to make some extra money. All he did was generate false sales reports.'

And get greedy, Hank thought. Although yes, as blame went, he deserved a lot less of it than the other players in this. He certainly didn't deserve to die.

'Did you tell Vic to come down here, Lew?'

'Oh, heavens, no. Why would I do that? I needed him where he was. Plus, I owed him money. You think he would have followed my orders if they went beyond what his duties were? No way.'

Hank looked at his uncle-in-law. 'And I think he would have. If you told him that was the only way to get the money. How did Vic even know that Tina was in Branson? How did he know to come here?'

Lew pushed away from Hank, who reflexively rested his hand on the Glock in his holster.

'I swear to you, I didn't know Tina was down here. I knew the keys to the Branson store had never arrived. Vic knew, too. Because he was supposed to be the one to come down here and set it up, but he couldn't do that until we got the keys and the paperwork. We did get the papers, but not the keys. I didn't know she had them.'

Either Vic figured out on his own when Tina disappeared that she probably stole the keys, or Lew was lying. 'When did you know that Tina was the one who stole from you?'

The third day she didn't come to work, Lew said. The first day she called in. The second day she didn't, and he just pulled an excuse out of his hat. And started getting suspicious. When she didn't show the third day, he checked the Discount Express account and saw the theft. He was so stunned he fled the office, falling on his way out and scraping himself up on the pavement. He needed time to figure out what to do without anyone getting suspicious, so the next day he invented Tina's sick mother.

'And when Fin came to stay with us? She left you for weeks. Didn't you think she was suspicious?'

'I prayed that she wasn't. When you brought her back, I was so relieved. I missed her so much. And then in the middle of the night Thursday I saw her going through my study. I thought she'd found something down here when she was staying with you. Maybe Tina'd contacted her. Maybe . . . I don't know. I got scared. So instead of going to work the next morning, I drove down here.'

Hank wanted to throttle him. 'Why not just close the business if you couldn't raise the money?'

'Because it was everything. My whole life. I knew I could turn it around. If Tina hadn't stolen all that, I would've been able to.' He looked up at Hank, his face only inches away. 'It was only a . . . a temporary kind of borrowing.'

'No. It wasn't. It was a crime. From the beginning. It was a rock you threw in a pond, Lew, and the ripples came out in every direction. That's how it always happens. Things you don't expect. And consequences that are going to hit all sorts of people.' He touched his tear-dampened sleeve. 'Your employees will have to testify in a federal investigation. Your niece will have a felon for an uncle. And your wife . . .'

He let Lew contemplate that last sentence for a moment, then led him into the building, the steel door clanging shut behind them.

FORTY-TWO

This seemed like the hundredth time Sheila had walked the cellblocks since she'd entered the jail yesterday morning. Now it was past midnight, the lights were dim – and by some small miracle that she certainly deserved at this point in her day, the inmates were quiet. So too, unfortunately, was the control room. The graveyard shift hadn't shown up for work. It was just her and Molly. She'd coaxed Earl into going home about an hour ago and practically shoved Hank out the door when he tried to stay.

She turned and walked back up the other side of the corridor and came to a slow stop as she saw that she wasn't the only one still awake. Lonnie Timmons sat on his bed with his elbows on his knees, rubbing at a cut on his hand. He looked up at her, but otherwise had no reaction at all. She'd planned to tell him in the morning, but what the hell.

'We arrested someone for your father's murder.'

'Really.' Emotionless.

'It was a woman named Bee. She was a friend of your mother's.'

Now an eyebrow went up. 'What the hell's my mom got to do with it?'

It would mean divulging her theory of the crime, but she owed him some kind of explanation at least. Or maybe Clyde was the one who owed him. Bee Ullyott definitely owed him.

'We think this lady helped your mom along, on the day she died. Put something in her IV bag. And then . . .'

She stopped. Lonnie's mouth had dropped open. As she stood there, his eyes filled with tears. 'I'll be. The old bastard was right. She didn't die of natural causes. You can prove it?'

Sheila shook her head. 'But sometime recently, your dad ran into this woman for the first time in years and started to figure it out. So she killed him to keep him from reporting it to the police.'

ACKNOWLEDGMENTS

Once again, I was incredibly fortunate to have help bringing this novel to life. My first readers – Carol Adler, Paige Kneeland, Mike Brown, and Sarah Pollock – always have feedback, opinions, and advice that is invaluable. I couldn't do it without them. Thank you so much. Another debt of gratitude goes to Luis Enrique Meneses Jr. for his generous help with Spanish translations, as well as Meredith, whose initial guidance in this area got me started in the right direction. I also want to thank Brian Hall, who is always so giving of his time when a friend needs assistance.

Carl Smith and Kate Lyall Grant and the rest of the Severn House Publishers team are great to work with and have provided the Hank Worth series with wonderful care and support. And my agent, Jim McCarthy, has helped me navigate this business for a long time and knows just when I need that extra dose of encouragement.

And lastly, my family is the reason I'm able to reach this finish line every time. You are always first in my heart.